Wolf's Howl

A MAVEN & REEVE MYSTERY

First American Edition 2022
Kane Miller, A Division of EDC Publishing

First published by Penguin Random House Australia Pty Ltd.
This edition published by arrangement with
Penguin Random House Australia Pty Ltd.
The Wolf's Howl © A. L. Tait, 2021
The moral right of the author has been asserted.

For information contact:
Kane Miller, A Division of EDC Publishing
5402 S 122nd E Ave
Tulsa, OK 74146
www.kanemiller.com
www.myubam.com

Library of Congress Control Number: 2021944886

Printed and bound in the United States of America
1 2022
ISBN: 978-1-68464-438-4

the WOLF'S Howl

A MAVEN & REEVE MYSTERY

A. L. TAIT

Kane Miller

A DIVISION OF EDC PUBLISHING

CHAPTER ONE

F or a squire of noted charm and alleged cleverness, Reeve of Norwood is displaying neither of those traits today. As he rides past my window yet again, waving and grinning, flaunting his freedom and independence, it is all I can do not to stick out my tongue and cross my eyes at him.

But, of course, I do not. Ladies must be demure. And there are five other ladies squashed into this hot, airless carriage, three of whom are tittering at Reeve's antics, one of whom is staring out the other window at her new husband, Sir Garrick Sharp, and one . . . one who sits opposite me and watches my every move from beneath dark, heavy lashes.

Anice reminds me of the sleek, ginger cat that prowls

the kitchens of Rennart Castle, watching and waiting for the tiny field mice who scamper in and risk all for a skerrick of flour. Few of them ever taste it, scooped up in seconds by sharp claws and carried off by the cat to be toyed with until they die.

If anyone knew that I was comparing the Airl of Buckthorn's daughter to a sadistic cat, my place as companion to Lady Cassandra, Anice's own cousin, would be in jeopardy. But, as yet, only jesters and charlatans lay claim to reading minds, and so my secrets are safe.

A fortunate thing for many.

To avoid looking at Anice, however, I must look out the window, which means I must watch Reeve, prancing about on Airl Buckthorn's enormous black destrier, his stubbly blond hair gleaming in the golden afternoon sunlight. Envy crashes through me and, in an effort to keep a blank expression on my face, I summon up my mother's voice in my mind:

"Maven, young ladies do not ride astride their horses."

"Maven, young ladies are safe inside the confines of a carriage."

"Maven, young ladies are not allowed to have fun."

She would never have said the last, of course, not even at the height of her reign as haughty Lady Sybyll of Aramoor. But she thought it then and I have no doubt that even now, as plain Sybyll, genteel companion to Lady Fenlon, she thinks it still.

Thinking of my mother has had the required effect, though, and I have no desire to crack even the hint of a smile at Reeve's antics.

Reeve, however, is determined to provoke a reaction from me, knowing better than anyone how utterly and horribly confined I feel, stuffed inside this airless carriage with Lady Cassandra, Anice and three of Anice's interchangeable friends. Besieged and beset by a thousand whispered exchanges and giggles, I am all but buried under yards of silk and satin skirts in the colors of the rainbow.

My serviceable brown dress disappears into the carriage's burnished leather upholstery, and I have a splitting headache, my nostrils assaulted by the aggressive wafts of lavender, rose and gardenia Anice's coterie seems to bathe in every morning.

The only thing that has kept me sane over the long hours of travel to Harding Manor are occasional sympathetic looks from my Lady Cassandra, but they are few and far between – she is far too enamored with her view of Sir Garrick to pay much attention to anyone else in the carriage.

That said, I am half grateful that Cassandra is distracted; Anice's calculating gaze misses nothing, and I don't want to inadvertently reveal too much. It suits me to be overlooked and for my friendship with Anice's cousin to remain hidden beneath my role as Cassandra's servant.

And so the hours roll on, every sway and creak of the carriage taking us further from Rennart Castle toward Harding Manor, where we will rest for tonight – and leave Anice and her friends behind when we head much further north on the morrow.

I allow myself a tiny smile at the thought.

"I hope you have brought your warmest kirtle with you, cousin, I believe there is no such thing as a nice day in Glawn," Anice says, drawing Cassandra's attention from the window. "I am glad to be going no further than Harding."

"Thank you for your concern, cousin," Cassandra says, with a polite smile. "Indeed, I am well stocked with layers of warmth. I even have several pairs of fine Talleben gloves."

"Talleben gloves?" Anice says, her shock evident. "Sir Garrick must like you a great deal to have paid for those."

Cassandra's gaze slides to the carriage window once more. "It seems he does. Maven will show you."

I stand, bracing my feet so that I can rock back and forth in the moving carriage without falling into Anice's lap, and retrieve the small trunk above my head. Fishing out two pairs of impossibly light and warm knitted gloves, one pair in black, one in a blue that reminds me of spring, I hand them to Cassandra. She passes one glove to each of the other girls, who immediately *ooh* and *aah*, even Anice, over the intricate patterns knitted into each glove.

As I drop back into my seat, the trunk on my lap, I am reminded of a late night in my father's solar, me on one side of the desk, he leaning in from the other as he told me, in hushed tones, stories from the last Kingdom Wars. For a moment, I can hear again the note of admiration in my father's voice as he explained the different ways in which the rebels had sent coded messages to each other. One way was to use different patterns of knitting, adding rows to scarves that had crisscrossed the kingdom wrapped around the throats of innocent-looking women and children, right under the noses of the other side.

Looking at Cassandra's gloves, I wonder whether my father, or anyone else for that matter, even remembers that story. Not that it would be of any use to me – knitting is not a skill I've ever acquired.

Perhaps because he knew I had not the patience to learn handicrafts, my father had also shown me how a book code works, and we had used it to send messages to each other, before . . .

A sudden wave of homesickness washes over me and I swallow it down, surprised by the pain even after five years. Every time I think I am finished with the horror of my father's betrayal and my mother's rejection, a tiny reminder shows up to needle me once more.

To stave it off, I focus on remembering the book code, a simple but effective way in which to hide a message. All it took was two people, one book and a lot of patience. The person sending the message nominated the book and then a page number. The message was created by choosing the words one needed from that page. Every word was given a number and the chosen numbers listed in order to create the message.

Simple, but such fun when you're ten years old and exchanging secret messages with the person you love best in the whole world . . .

A sudden jolt pricks my reverie with a bang, and Anice and her friends all shriek as one. Ignoring them, I focus on Reeve, who is no longer looking so carefree. His huge horse has spooked at the sound of the carriage wheel hitting a deep pothole, and the sight of Reeve fighting to bring the skittish beast under control widens my tiny smile into a full-fledged grin.

The grin lasts only until another jolt rocks the carriage and I hear the coachman swear in a most ungenteel fashion that carries over the ear-piercing scraping sound rising from beneath my feet. As the carriage shudders to a halt, thundering hooves rocket past, and the coachman swears again as the four horses hauling us all stamp and neigh.

"We're going to die!" Anice's friend Honora looks as though she's about to swoon.

"Why would we die now?" Cassandra asks, her voice low and calm as though dealing with a panicked hound. "We're at a stop."

"It must be a bandit!" Honora quavers, big blue eyes full of tears, as she twists a blond ringlet around and around her finger. I can't look away as the fingertip turns pink from the pressure, and I wonder if it's possible it might fall off with enough time.

"It's not a bandit," Cassandra says, reaching over to pat the girl's other hand. "Sir Garrick is talking to the coachman, just over there — he'd hardly be doing that if we were under attack."

"He might," Anice's sly voice inserts, "if he's in on the holdup."

I daren't look at Cassandra, knowing that I am the lowliest person in this carriage, but I can feel her stiffen beside me.

"Cousin, you jest," Cassandra says with a tight smile, but I can see her nails digging into her palms as she forces herself to remain calm. Anice is the daughter of the Airl of Buckthorn, and Cassandra merely the fourth daughter of the Airl's brother-in-law and married to a knight in his service.

7

It will not help Cassandra to get on the bad side of Anice.

And, from what I have witnessed, there are few good sides to Anice.

We all turn to Anice to see where the exchange will go next.

One beat, then two go by, before Anice tosses one long, coppery braid over her shoulder and takes Honora's hand.

"Indeed, I jest," Anice says with a brittle giggle. "How could anyone imagine that the Knight Protector of Rennart Castle would ever consort with bandits?"

But as she says this, her eyes find mine and her gaze holds just a fraction too long.

Fortunately, a light rap on the carriage door breaks the polite deadlock, and the door swings open to reveal Sir Garrick.

"My ladies," he says, bowing to us all, though in reality his attention is fixed on Cassandra, who blushes a fetching shade of rose pink. "It seems the carriage wheel has been damaged and is unfit for further travel. I must ask you to alight now."

"Ladies, give Maven the gloves and then we'll get out," says Cassandra. Anice and her friends reluctantly peel off the gloves and I fold them back into the trunk, buckling it up.

I gather my skirts, preparing to step down from the

8

carriage, but Anice sticks out one delicate foot, almost tripping me over.

"I will not alight and ruin my new shoes," she says, showing Sir Garrick the pale-pink kid slipper, laced up her ankle with a velvet ribbon a shade or two darker.

A tiny wrinkle appears between Sir Garrick's dark brows, but he is not Airl Buckthorn's Knight Protector for nothing.

"My lady's slipper is quite lovely," he says, and I can almost see his mind whirring behind his polite expression. "But the coachman will be unable to fix the carriage unless we unpack it."

Anice straightens, staring down her fine nose at Sir Garrick. "I am not baggage to be unpacked." She sniffs, placing her hands just so in her lap with haughty precision. "I am the Airl of Buckthorn's only daughter and I will not be discarded on the side of a dusty road at the pleasure of a mere coachman."

I want to roll my eyes as she spits out the last word, thinking that baggage is exactly what she is. But, over the past week, Anice has taken it upon herself to ensure that I know my place in the hierarchy at Rennart Castle.

My quiet, lowly place.

Reeve still cannot understand Anice's malevolence toward me.

"But you saved her from a disastrous marriage — and asked nothing in return," he repeats, bewildered, almost daily. "She should be grateful!"

Repeating does not make a thing so, as I have explained to him over and over. Anice is embarrassed and I am a constant reminder of that weak, silly moment when she almost found herself betrothed to the opportunistic never-will-be-a-knight Brantley.

She wants me gone.

But to get me gone, she has to get past Cassandra, and I am secure in my lady's affection.

"How long must we wait for the wheel?" Cassandra intervenes now.

"An hour or two, perhaps more," Sir Garrick answers, appearing to brace himself for Anice's response.

"Then I'll not move," Anice hisses. "My complexion will be quite ruined by all that sunshine."

I study her face, which, it has to be said, is lovely. Even at sixteen, her pale skin is not marred by a single freckle, though her copper hair marks her as one prone to the kiss of the sun.

Cassandra sighs. "It does seem a long time to stand about in the dust," she says to Sir Garrick, reaching over me to place a hand on his arm. "Is there no other way?"

As Sir Garrick considers her request, weighing up the pros and cons of insisting that the ladies alight, a windswept Reeve rides up behind him, his horse blowing hard.

"It's not far to Harding Manor from here," Reeve says. "No more than twenty minutes' ride without the carriage. Could we not each take a lady up on our horses? They'll arrive in time for a late luncheon and we can send help to fix the wheel?"

Reeve's sensible suggestion is greeted with shrieks from Honora and her friends. "We could never do that!" Honora breathes, while the other two — I do wish I had been properly introduced so that I could remember their names — giggle. "Imagine what people would say."

But Anice looks at Reeve, and then at me, before responding. "I would rather a few minutes on horseback than hours standing in the sun," she says, before pausing theatrically. "But, Sir Garrick, there are only five horses, and six of us."

Sir Garrick is so surprised by her acquiescence to Reeve's suggestion that he says nothing, so Anice speaks again.

"So, you would take my cousin Cassandra, your beloved, I would need to ride with Reeve, your trusted squire. And Honora, Faith and Thora would have to arrive at the same time as me, to ensure I am properly chaperoned and looking my best for Mama."

So I am to be dumped on the side of the road with the ancient coachman, to wait who knows how long for help. Cassandra can hardly protest — after all, which of the delicate flowers that surround Anice would she sacrifice to include me?

Would I even want her to do so?

"I am happy to stay behind, Sir Garrick," I say, keeping my voice even to avoid revealing my thoughts to Anice. "Give me a moment or two to fix my Lady Cassandra's hair for riding, and then I will join you all later once the carriage is mended."

"Oh, don't worry about that," says Anice, moving to alight from the carriage, all her concern for her kid slippers apparently forgotten in her rush to get up on that horse with Reeve and gloat. "Mama has any number of maids capable of fixing my cousin's hair once we arrive."

I suck in a deep breath at the slight.

"Maven will do it," says Cassandra, her hand once again on my arm to calm me. "She has many gifts, hair being just one of them."

Anice wrinkles her nose, but I am mollified by the words. My position as Cassandra's companion has been a savior to me, and I treasure our special bond. I have told Reeve on more than one occasion that I am careful never to forget my place, knowing that I remain a servant, and to most people one maid is interchangeable with another.

But the truth is that there are times, when it is just Cassandra and I, that I can imagine us to be friends.

Anice, I fear, knows it, and takes every opportunity to remind me that while I was once Lady Maven of Aramoor, those days are gone — and companions can be replaced while cousins are for life.

I follow the tittering girls through the door, and turn to help Cassandra. But Sir Garrick is one step ahead of me, as he places both hands around her tiny waist and lightly swings her to the ground.

"Come, my love," he says, "let's get you settled."

Cassandra turns to me. "Will you braid my hair, Maven? I think that's the most sensible option."

"Wait a moment," says Sir Garrick, as I move toward her. He disappears to the back of the carriage and returns lugging a heavy trunk.

"Here," he says, dropping it in the dust. "Sit here, my love — it will be easier."

Cassandra sits and I bury my hands in her luxuriant dark hair, removing the hairpins before fighting to braid the thick tresses and bring some semblance of control. Within minutes, she looks neat and tidy, and I slip the hairpins into the pocket of my skirt as I move to stand in front of her.

"You'll be all right, won't you?" Cassandra whispers, as I make a show of choosing the perfect curls to pull from the braid to frame her face. "You won't be too far behind and I think the coachman is to be trusted."

I hide a smile at her worried expression. "I'll be fine,

my lady," I whisper back. "To be honest, I will enjoy the break from our company."

Cassandra grimaces. "At least we have company only for one night," she says. "I think Anice will be less . . . Anice when she is in the presence of her mother. And we move on to Glawn Castle tomorrow without her."

I bite my lip and my tongue, unwilling to share my thoughts on her cousin. Although Cassandra is not a fan of the girl either, they are still kin. As for the mission that takes us to Glawn Castle . . . neither of us should be even mentioning that out here in the open.

"I look forward to seeing Lady Rhoswen again," I say instead, gently pinching Cassandra's cheeks to bring a little color into them, before brushing nonexistent dust from her shoulder. "It has been many years."

I have but one clear memory of the good lady — I was only nine or ten the last time I saw her — at the wedding of a distant relative.

But I remember that my mother was half in awe of Lady Rhoswen, half disparaging.

"She chooses to live entirely apart from her husband," I overheard my mother tell my older sisters in the carriage on the way home. "Scandalous."

I sometimes wonder now if, given half a chance, my mother would not have made the same choice regarding living arrangements, particularly knowing how things would turn out for our family. Had my mother had her own residence, would we all still have a place to live, rather than be scattered across Cartreff?

My father lives above the farrier's workshop in the small village he once owned as part of our estate, Aramoor. The same estate has been lost to gaming debts, my powerful father reduced to poverty, my mother and sisters compelled into dependent lives as companions to women they once considered equals.

And I was bartered to Cassandra's father, which turned out better than Cassandra or I expected.

"There you are, spick-and-span," I say to her now, trying to ignore Anice's shrieks and giggles as Sir Garrick boosts her up onto Reeve's horse, to sit side-saddle before him. A sensible person would, of course, have jumped up behind Reeve – riding astride to make it easier for both horse and rider.

But girls and women in Cartreff do not ride astride, hampered as they are by full skirts and decorum.

"I am going to have to sit across Garrick's lap," Cassandra mutters, watching the scene.

"It will not be for long and you will not mind," I tease. She has been married only a week, but I know how remarkably her attitude has changed toward Sir Garrick, the man she once thought to flee.

Cassandra blushes. "I would still rather ride myself."

I nod, knowing her words to be true. "But then Anice will know you can ride astride and she will never let it go."

"You're right," Cassandra sighs, and I take her hand and pull her to her feet.

"Come, my lady, Sir Garrick awaits, and Reeve and Anice are already leaving."

"I am sorry it must be this way, Maven," Cassandra says, clasping my forearm for a moment. "I know this is not what you want."

She is not speaking only of this moment on the road. Her plans to flee Sir Garrick before their wedding had included me.

Had those plans not gone awry, had the dazzling Fire Star ruby not disappeared, had Cassandra not fallen in love with the man she was supposed to hate ... had all of those things not happened only a week ago, we would probably be across the water in Talleben right now.

Free to live our lives any way we choose.

There is so much I could say, and so little point to saying any of it, so I give her the reassurance she needs.

"It's fine, my lady, I am fine. You made the right choice for both of us."

With a last searching look, Cassandra turns away to where Sir Garrick awaits her with a smile that lights up his otherwise dark and brooding features. I do not watch as they ride off together, following in the hoofprints of Reeve, Anice and the others at a steady pace.

Part of me thinks I should be relishing this opportunity. If I wanted to, this would be my chance to make a run for Talleben. I could simply disappear right now. Pick up my skirts and run. Somewhere nearby there will be a village, and in that village there will be a member of the Beech Circle and . . .

And I am fifteen years old, and I have no money and no plan.

Even Myra, wyld woman and a member of the Beech Circle near Rennart Castle, told me to stay with Cassandra and Sir Garrick for now, reminding me how difficult it is for a woman to make her own way in the world.

With Cassandra, and the Fire Star, I would have had a chance. But as it is . . .

"Just a year or two," Myra had whispered to me. "And then . . ."

Then I will be gone.

But that is a secret I keep to myself for now.

Thinking of Myra, however, reminds me that others also have secrets. When I visited her cottage in the woods after the wedding, Reeve insisted on escorting me. He thinks I did not see Myra slip him a tiny pewter tincture bottle, but I do not miss much.

If I gambled – which I do not – I would bet that bottle is now hidden beneath his tunic, hanging off the simple chain I sometimes glimpse when he bends forward to serve Sir Garrick at table.

I will not ask Reeve about it, though it bothers me. If I am allowed to have my secrets, so is he.

A loud curse interrupts my thoughts and, with one last lingering glance at the line of trees beyond the road, I follow the sound to the back of the carriage, where the coachman is wrestling with the broken wheel.

"Now, good sir," I say, "what can I do to help?"

He pauses, turning his wrinkled face to mine, a twinkle in the deep-set mud-brown eyes. "Know much about carriage wheels, do you, miss?"

I pretend to consider the question, before squatting down on the road beside him, gathering my hem in an effort to keep it out of the dirt. "Not a thing," I say. "But I'm willing to learn, particularly if it gets me to my next meal sooner."

The truth is that, as a bored little girl, when my father was away from home and my mother wanted me to focus on embroidery or harpsichord practice, I often snuck away to watch Kevon the wheelwright in Aramoor ply his craft. In the same way that I watched the blacksmith, the farrier, the candlemaker, the bowyer and the baker. And if I wasn't there, I was in the kitchens, soaking up the warmth of companionship as much as the heat from the always burning fire under the always bubbling pots.

Before my father's downfall to gambling and debt, Aramoor was a thriving fiefdom, and I hid from my mother's attentions as often as I could.

Fortunately, the craftsmen of Aramoor never seemed to mind me sitting in the shadows of their workshops, and the cook never turned a lonely little girl away from her long kitchen table.

The coachman stares at me now, then grunts, poking the center of the wheel. "They'll send someone for you before we get this fixed, I reckon. The outer pin is broken and the bushing is cracked. We'll need a replacement."

He sits back on his heels before pushing himself up, knees popping and cracking as he stands.

"Sorry, miss, but there's nothing to do but wait," he says, cheerfully, taking himself off to lie in a patch of soft green grass.

I wait until his eyes are closed before leaning in to examine the wheel hub. As much as I am not eager to spend any more time with Anice than I must, I also have no desire to sit here for hours waiting to be rescued.

I'm not generally one for waiting.

I peer at the wheel hub, noting that the iron tube that allows the wheel to rotate is cracked as the coachman said, but, from what I can see, it does not seem to be broken through. This must be the bushing.

The bigger problem seems to be that there is nothing

to hold the wheel onto the axle, meaning that, if we go any further, it will simply fall off.

So how did Kevon affix the wheels?

I lean in for a closer look, noticing that there are two tiny holes across the end of the axle. This must be where the missing pin was supposed to be.

But surely if we could replace that, we might be able to slowly make our way to Harding Manor?

Standing up, I dust my skirts off before approaching the dozing coachman. I need to ask some pointed questions without looking like I know what I'm talking about.

Nobody likes a girl who asks questions, least of all a man who asks none.

"Good sir," I begin, clenching my fists into my pockets with the effort of keeping my voice light and friendly. "I wonder if there might be a way for us to repair the carriage ourselves?"

He opens one eye. "Why would we want to do that? The only thing waiting for us both at Harding Manor is more work. Take the break while you can."

I stand for another moment, swallowing my impatience at being dismissed, but, knowing that words will serve no purpose here, go back to examine the wheel.

On one level, the coachman is right – there is no reason at all for me to fret about having to wait for help to come. A sensible servant would be relishing the enforced time to do absolutely nothing but enjoy the peace and quiet.

But I was raised a lady and I cannot help railing against Anice's treatment of me, leaving me by the roadside to be collected like an unwanted parcel. Particularly when I know how much it will be pleasing her to think she has bested me by riding off with Reeve.

I scan the road beneath the wheel but there is no sign of the pin. Standing, I wipe my hands on my skirt, thankful as ever that the heavy wool is the perfect brown to hide the dirt, and feel a long, thin shape in my pocket.

Drawing out the pins I'd withdrawn from Cassandra's hair, I study them. Fashioned from sturdy brass, they are about the length of my little finger and decorated with a curling scroll at one end.

Squatting down beside the wheel again, I lay the length of one pin against the wheel hub. It's a little bit long but . . .

I glance over my shoulder. The problem of how to fix the wheel may be solved, but the real problem is lying behind me, snoring under his hat.

In an ideal world, I would slot the hairpin into the end of the bushing and tell the coachman we can be on our way. But this is Cartreff, and girls like me are not supposed to know how to do anything beyond fix hair, sew a fine seam and fetch and carry.

If I present the man with a repaired wheel, he's as likely to accuse me of witchcraft as thank me for my endeavors.

As a sigh rises up from my boots, I slide Cassandra's hairpin into my own fawn-brown hair and turn back toward the coachman, ready for a performance. I will play the curious and admiring maiden, leading him to come up with the solution for fixing the wheel with my hairpin, without him recognizing my input.

All the while longing for a day or a place where such a performance was not necessary.

"Good sir," I begin . . .

CHAPTER TWO

"I'm going to give that coachman a bonus," said Sir Garrick to Lady Cassandra, as they sat at Harding Manor's high table awaiting the first course of the evening meal. "Imagine using your hairpin to fix the wheel! Ingenious!"

Reeve concentrated on pouring wine into Lady Cassandra's silver goblet, mindful of not spilling the deep-red liquid on her cream-colored gown. He had his own thoughts about whose ingenious solution that hairpin had been, but Reeve knew that Maven would not thank him for drawing attention to her.

"Very clever indeed," was all Lady Cassandra said, but Reeve noted that her eyes searched the shadows of the back wall of the manor's hall, and he knew it was

Maven that she sought.

"'Twas lucky indeed that Maven had put the pin in her own hair for safekeeping," said Sir Garrick, taking a sip of his wine. "Otherwise the coachman might never have thought of it."

Reeve smirked inwardly, knowing that luck had played no part in the placement of that hairpin, and Lady Cassandra's droll "indeed" told Reeve that she agreed with him.

"But enough of the carriage wheel, husband," Lady Cassandra continued. "My thoughts are with Lady Rhoswen."

Reeve stepped back behind Sir Garrick's chair at her words, feeling a frown wrinkle his forehead. Their arrival at Harding Manor that afternoon had not gone at all as he'd expected.

Beyond the fact that he'd arrived at the gates with Lady Anice perched across his saddle, his ears throbbing from the number of insults she'd thrown his way about his horse management skills, Lady Rhoswen had not been on hand to greet the party as they'd clattered through the manor's gates and up the long drive.

Instead, Marsden, Steward of the Household, had informed Sir Garrick, Lady Cassandra and Lady Anice that her ladyship was "under the weather" and would join them later.

Anice had barely seemed to notice her mother's

absence, happy enough to hug her friends as they dismounted, squealing as though they'd all been through a great adventure. But, worried, Reeve had rushed to the kitchen, where he knew he would find out the truth of Lady Rhoswen's illness.

To Reeve's dismay, even the kitchen staff had been tight-lipped, saying only that her ladyship was resting.

"She'll be fine," Sir Garrick said now, mopping up a puddle of thick gravy with a crust of bread. "The Steward said she would see us later."

Lady Cassandra shook her head. "She did not make the trip to Rennart Castle for our wedding, Garrick, which means she's been unwell for a week or more."

"Surely Lady Rhoswen would have sent word to the Airl if it was serious," Sir Garrick said, pushing his trencher away and sounding fed up with the subject. "She has never been backward in coming forward, as you know, but he has said nothing."

Cassandra turned toward her husband, one hand on his arm. "She is . . . forthright, it is true, but she is also a loyal wife. She would not add to his troubles when she knows he is . . . busy."

Reeve caught the long look between them and knew they thought of the Airl's current delicate negotiations regarding the management of the young King Bren. But they would not speak of it here.

"If Lady Rhoswen does not appear later, you can

escort Anice to see her," Sir Garrick decided, placing his own hand over Cassandra's. "That should show us the truth of the matter."

Lady Cassandra sighed. "Yes, I'll do that. After all, my dear cousin looks bereft at the absence of her beloved parent."

Reeve bit his lip to suppress a grin, consciously not looking at the other end of the long high table, where Anice sat with her friends, each more elaborately gowned than the next, hooting with laughter.

The grin disappeared when they all looked at him as Anice whispered something, before dissolving into giggles again.

Cheeks burning, Reeve leaned forward, as though checking that Sir Garrick's goblet was full, allowing him to ignore the girls. Anice's suggestion that she ride with him that day had taken him by surprise, and he'd had to work hard to maintain outward composure, particularly under the force of Maven's mocking stare.

Even thinking about it now, Reeve could feel his anger at Maven's censure rising. He'd had several long conversations with her over the past week or so about the lack of power of girls in Cartreff, and his eyes had been opened – but Maven never considered that Reeve might share some of the same problems.

If Lady Anice wanted to ride sidesaddle with Reeve, Reeve had little choice but to agree to it. Especially if he wanted to stay at Rennart Castle as Sir Garrick's squire for the four years it would take him to earn the right to become a knight.

And Maven knew how desperately Reeve wanted to become a knight.

If Reeve did not succeed, he would be sent home to his father, the Baron of Norwood, who would waste no time in placing Reeve upon a ship bound for whereabouts unknown, never to return.

As the second son of a minor noble, Reeve had very few options. He could not inherit the barony and all the funds inherent — they went to his brother Larien, as they would one day go to Larien's son.

Reeve had to make his own way in the world — or so his father had told him over and over. And Reeve's current position at Rennart Castle was his best chance of success.

Had he not teamed up with Maven only one week ago to perform the impossible — finding a missing jewel and unmasking a killer all in the space of three days — just to keep his toehold in Airl Buckthorn's household?

Couldn't Maven see that bowing to the whims of the Airl's daughter was a small price to pay?

"Reeve," said Sir Garrick now, looking up and over his shoulder with a frown, "my lady has dropped her napkin and requires a fresh one."

Reeve's cheeks burned again at being found derelict

in his duty. "My apologies, sire," he said to Sir Garrick with a tiny bow, "I will return with one in a moment."

Picking up the napkin from beneath Lady Cassandra's chair, Reeve strode toward the door of the hall in search of new linen, glad that Lady Rhoswen had not been at the table to see him so rebuked.

Then again, had she been there, the whole occasion would have felt very different. With a pang, Reeve realized how much he missed his lady's presence. He had been with her as a page from the age of seven, and she had taught him so much, in many ways more of a mother to him than his own.

Which is why Reeve was so worried about her — only dire circumstances would keep her from her hostessing duties.

"I really don't see why you would have me disturb my mother this night when she has made it clear that she is unwell."

I stand silently behind Anice and Cassandra outside the heavy wooden doors to Lady Rhoswen's bedchamber.

"My friends have not been to this house before, and you have made me abandon them when we had plans to set up for dancing," Anice continues, her prettiness marred by the ugly twist of her lips.

Cassandra exhales and straightens, and I can see her fighting the impulse to snap at her cousin. "Is your mother not worth five minutes of your time?" she manages in a reasonable tone.

"It's never five minutes," Anice spits. "How can she fit a one-hour lecture about my failings into a five-minute window? No, I'm not staying. She'll have heard about . . . you know . . . and I don't want to talk about it."

You know. That's one way to put the incident that had nearly seen Anice disastrously betrothed to Brantley.

Cassandra opens her mouth to speak, but Anice has already turned on her heel, stalking past me with a furious glare before disappearing down the hallway in a rustle of skirts, those pink slippers, apparently undamaged by the horse ride to Harding Manor, slapping on the stone floors.

"That went well," Cassandra murmurs, turning to me with a raised brow.

"We cannot drag her back," I respond. "And it was not Lady Anice who Lady Rhoswen asked to see. It was you."

"Yes," Cassandra says, turning back to the door and rapping on it sharply. "That's what worries me – and why I invited Anice to come along."

I say nothing. There is no point reiterating my earlier point that if Lady Rhoswen had wanted to speak to her daughter, she would have sent Anice an urgent message as well.

"Anyway," Cassandra goes on, as the dark wooden door to the bedchamber begins to creak open, "at least we will be able to speak freely about recent events without Anice's presence."

"My lady awaits you." The maid curtseys to Cassandra, her gray curls bobbing under the frilly white cap worn by Lady Rhoswen's servants. As I follow Cassandra through the door, I run my hands down my own plain dress, glad that Cassandra has no such preferences for my own attire.

As Reeve pointed out the first day I met him, as a companion, I do not have to don the garb of a servant and could wear clothing that would not mark me as such.

But, as I told him, my place in this world is not what it once was, and it will do me no good to forget that.

Besides, I prefer my plain dresses, cut wide in the skirt to allow me to ride a horse like a boy, and with secret pockets, which would never work in a more fashionable cut.

"Ah, Cassandra, my dear, you're here." The croaky voice draws my eyes to the huge four-poster bed, bedecked in swathes of ice-blue and cream damask and froths of delicate lace. The chamber is large, with wood panels stretching to the high ceilings, and a floor of intricately decorated tiles of dark blue and cream. A huge fire burns brightly in the grate to my right, and the room is hot and stuffy, despite the cool tones of the decor.

But it is the enormous tapestry above the bed that stops me in my tracks. Depicting a beech tree with a tiny red bird high in its leafless branches, it is so beautiful – and so dangerous – that I cannot stop my gasp.

"But who is that?" Lady Rhoswen croaks at the sound.

"My aunt," says Cassandra, ignoring the question and moving to sit beside Lady Rhoswen. "You are unwell."

"Never mind that for the moment, who have you brought into my chambers? Come here where I can see you, girl." Lady Rhoswen's blue eyes have not left my face.

"This is Maven," says Cassandra as I move toward the bed. "She recognizes the beech."

It is all she needs to say to let the good lady know that we are both members of the Beech Circle, a secret network of girls and women who work together to support each other to do and be . . . more. The Kingdom of Cartreff is not kind to girls who think, nor to girls who chafe in the constraints that our society imposes.

"I see," Lady Rhoswen says, but her frown smooths out.

"You wanted to see me," says Cassandra, prompting her aunt.

"I did." Lady Rhoswen's sharp eyes meet mine, and I can see that once she would have been beautiful. Tonight, she just looks gray and tired.

"I need you to take Anice with you," Lady Rhoswen continues. "Tybalt tells me that you go on to Glawn, and it is my dearest wish that she accompanies you there."

Tybalt, I deduce, must be Airl Buckthorn's first name, but I stiffen at the request — as does Cassandra. More time with Anice is not something either of us would choose.

"My lady," Cassandra begins, "would not my cousin be of use to you here? Some company as you recover?"

"There is no guarantee I will recover," Lady Rhoswen announces baldly, her thin fingers clenching the top of the counterpane. "In fact, on the contrary, it seems more likely that I will not."

Cassandra gasps, reaching out to grasp the older woman's hand. "No, that cannot be true."

Lady Rhoswen's eyes shine with tears, but her voice does not waver. "Some things cannot be argued against," she says, squeezing Cassandra's trembling hand. "No matter how much we would wish it were not so. But we have no time to discuss it now. I need you to take charge of Anice."

Lady Rhoswen pauses, seeming to try to catch her

breath before continuing. "I heard about that business."

Cassandra winces but does not try to dissemble. "We did not want to worry you."

Lady Rhoswen's lips twist into a little smirk. "More likely Tybalt did not want to feel my wrath," she says. "But no mind. I know. I cannot have her at Rennart Castle unsupervised. Someone needs to take charge of that girl, Cassandra, and who better than you? I know no one else headstrong enough to withstand and guide her."

As much as my stomach is sinking, I cannot help but agree. Cassandra's reputation for pushing the boundaries of polite society as far as they can go – and beyond – was well established before I went to live with her. The youngest of four daughters, she was angry with the world long before her mother died when she was young.

It is not easy to be amiable when you know your only role in life is to be married off in the best possible deal your father can make – and that's the best possible deal for him, not for you.

Sometimes I wonder what my own father would have done, had he a choice. When I was ten, he was secretly teaching me about the moon and the stars, the tactics of battle, the ancient lore of herbs and trees, the polite strategy of politics.

Would he have put all that aside to betroth me for

advantage? My mother thought not, and it was just one reason she railed against our lessons when she discovered the truth.

That and the fact that Mother knew that even teaching me to read was enough of a crime to have both my father and I killed – let alone the rest of it.

Cassandra, chewing her lip, has still not responded to Lady Rhoswen's request as I shake my head to clear it of these thoughts, knowing they are of no use. Putting aside my own wishes, no one of any note would stoop so low as to marry me now anyway.

"Cassandra? Surely you would not deny the wish of your dying aunt?" Lady Rhoswen may be weak, but her tone still commands and it seems to jolt Cassandra from her shocked state.

"I – well, that is to say . . ." As I watch, Cassandra seems to finalize an internal debate before reaching forward across the counterpane and once again taking her aunt's hand in her own. "It would give me no greater pleasure than to spend time with your daughter, but we will not return to Rennart Castle for some weeks. Would you not prefer that she spend time here with you?"

Lady Rhoswen licks her dry lips before responding.

"I do not wish Anice to see me like this and there is no one here with sufficient . . . strength to keep her in line if I cannot. And it has been some time since I have been able to keep her in line, even at full strength.

34

But I cannot send her back to Rennart without ... supervision. No, she must stay with you. It will do her good to see more of Cartreff, and Glawn will be ... refreshing."

I almost snicker at her last word. I've never been to Glawn but everyone in Cartreff has heard tales of its open, waterlogged spaces, roaring winds and stunted trees.

Not a natural habitat for pink kid slippers.

Cassandra manages a chuckle, though her expression is troubled. "Yes, I hear Glawn is at its loveliest at this time of year – we should be right on time to experience the Wolf's Howl in all its glory."

I cannot contain my frown at her words. The Wolf's Howl is notorious across all of Cartreff as the fiercest and most bone-chilling of winds, rising without warning to roar across the desolate marshland. It is named after the last wolf in the kingdom, which roamed upon the wild moors many years ago before disappearing forever, leaving only its unsettling cry behind. Or so legend has it.

Most people avoid going to Glawn at this time of year lest they encounter the fury of the Howl.

But we are not most people.

"Indeed," says Lady Rhoswen, managing a tiny smile. "Some might say it is a strange time indeed to be paying a visit to Airl Riding, but I know that Sir Garrick has his reasons – and I know who is behind the whole venture."

The two women share a look heavy with meaning and, for a moment, the only sound in the room is Lady Rhoswen's labored breathing.

"You must look after him," she finally continues, and at first it is not clear which "him" she means. "He is in deep, and I heard — the same way I heard about Anice and, no, I will not tell you how — that Airl Broadfield has taken his thoughts to King Bren. One wrong move by any of you and Tybalt will not survive it. Broadfield will make sure of that."

There is a heavy silence, and I can see that Cassandra has no placatory words this time, for there are none. Airl Buckthorn is sending us, as a first move in a dangerous game, to sound out Airl Riding of Glawn about his loyalty — or not — to the King, looking to build an alliance of airls strong enough to "convince" King Bren that he needs an older, wiser adviser to help steer Cartreff out of unrest.

There are few moves to make in this that are not wrong, and if Airl Buckthorn feels the King's wrath — and the hangman's noose — then so shall we all.

"But that is by the by," Lady Rhoswen continues, as though we are not discussing treason and execution. "Take Anice with you and keep her safe."

Lady Rhoswen slumps back on her white embroidered pillows, her eyes closed, before speaking again.

"If nothing else, if I know her – and I do – she will give you a reason to leave in a hurry should you need to do so."

Cassandra's brow wrinkles in a delicate frown, and I know she is considering the words, as I am. We know little of the Glawn community beyond what Airl Buckthorn has told Sir Garrick. "Dashed long way from anywhere, keep themselves to themselves, but tough enough when called upon."

It does not sound like a place in which the Airl's spoiled daughter will flourish, and Lady Rhoswen is right – having Anice to blame would provide us with a logical and diplomatic ticket out if our welcome at Glawn is not what we'd hoped and Sir Garrick decides a hasty retreat is in order.

No airl could deny a young woman who wants to go home in a hurry, providing the perfect excuse for Sir Garrick and Lady Cassandra to walk away without Sir Garrick – and thereby Airl Buckthorn – losing face.

And Cassandra will not need to be sacrificed as the "difficult" wife.

The more I turn the idea over in my head, the more I admire Lady Rhoswen's forethought.

"And the other three?" Cassandra enquires after a short pause, not looking at me. "Anice has three friends with her."

Lady Rhoswen sighs as I hold my breath. Anice on

her own for several weeks will be unbearable. Anice with Honora, Faith and Thora around her is the stuff of which nightmares are made.

"Send them back to Rennart," Lady Rhoswen says, finally, and I allow myself to breathe again. "They can wait for her there."

"Very well," Cassandra says, rising from her position on the bed.

"Wait," says Lady Rhoswen, eyes still closed. "The Beech Circle in Glawn is small but growing. Look for the laundress. She'll know exactly what you need to make Sir Garrick's . . . visit a success. Wear your locket. Give her my name if you need to."

"Your name?" Cassandra says, her raised eyebrows speaking volumes. That a humble laundress should be on first-name basis with the wife of one of the most powerful men in the kingdom is one thing. That Lady Rhoswen has allowed herself to become so openly tied to the Beech Circle in this way is quite another.

I remember Reeve's shock when he first discovered his beloved Lady Rhoswen was part of our secret network — but, even then, Myra had not mentioned her by name.

Mind you, poor old Reeve had received shock after shock that day, and over the days that followed, so that particular shock may not even have been the greatest one . . .

"And give my regards to the cook," says Lady Rhoswen now. "I have fond memories of her chicken soup. A family recipe, I believe. I asked for it, but she would not give it up. Would you believe she is one of five sisters? All cooks in great houses across Cartreff."

"Part of the Beech Circle?" Cassandra asks, surprised.

But Lady Rhoswen shakes her head, a slight movement from side to side that seems to wear her out. "Not as far as I'm aware."

"We will take our leave," says Cassandra. "We have tired you out with our visit."

"Before you go, come here, girl." Lady Rhoswen reaches out her hand to me and I step toward the bed.

"I know you," she says, taking my hand. Her eyes are warm as they search my face. "You're Aramoor's girl, aren't you? Bad business with your father. But you are all right with Cassandra?"

I curtsey, dropping my own gaze to the floor, as I try to extricate my hand. "Thank you, my lady, I am."

Lady Rhoswen holds on with a surprisingly strong grip, as she turns her attention to Cassandra. "I heard about the jewel," she says. "Very fortunate it came back to us."

"Very fortunate for Anice," is all Cassandra says.

Lady Rhoswen looks at me. "It was a good plan, from what I heard."

I bite my lip, trying to appear as innocent as I can. "Plan, my lady?"

She stares at me for a long moment before chuckling and addressing Cassandra once more. "Keep this one with you for as long as you can. And now, a kiss and off you go."

As Cassandra bends down to embrace her aunt, I step back, my mind working furiously. What has Lady Rhoswen heard about the plan that Cassandra and I had concocted to take possession of the Fire Star and flee?

Our plan had gone awry, thanks to Rennart Castle's former House Steward, Lorimer, who had attempted to steal the Fire Star for himself, resulting in the death of Lady Cassandra's loyal servant Sullivan.

The guilt that I feel over Sully's death will live with me forever. Had it not been for the plan – my plan – he would still be alive, probably back at Elderham Park, Cassandra's ancestral home, happy and content.

The question is, how does Lady Rhoswen know about all this? Reeve could not have told her, and he was the only other person who knew the full story except for –

"Myra," I whisper.

"Indeed," says Lady Rhoswen, demonstrating that her hearing has not been impacted by her illness. "Myra told me all about it."

"Myra?" Cassandra asks, and I remember that she

doesn't even know the woman who was so integral in helping Reeve and I to recover the Fire Star.

"Myra knows herbs," Lady Rhoswen says, before I have to explain. "She brings me tonics that soothe me, when she can sneak in around the so-called doctors, who seem to only want to put leeches all over me and bleed me."

I can feel my nose wrinkle at the thought.

"Why don't you send them away?" Cassandra asks, and we all laugh at the question.

"Imagine if I told your uncle I'd decided that I was going to ignore his apothecary friends and take my treatment from the wyld woman in the woods," Lady Rhoswen says with a smile. "It's simply not done. No, I must endure and trust that Myra can undo enough of the damage to keep me going as long as possible."

My fists clench at the thought of this lovely, brave, noble woman undergoing such awful treatments just because it is "what is done." Lady Rhoswen notices the movement and her gaze fixes upon me once again.

"Don't fret, young Maven. You cannot fight every battle at once. Keep your focus on what matters."

She pauses before adding: "And look after Reeve. He has so much potential – but he doesn't know what he doesn't know."

Her eyes close and, after a moment, Cassandra and

I realize we are dismissed as Lady Rhoswen drifts into sleep. As we creep from the room, the capped maid slips back inside, taking her place at the end of the big bed to await her mistress's command.

Cassandra and I are silent as we tiptoe down the hall, and my thoughts are gloomy, wondering if Lady Rhoswen will still be here on our return trip from Glawn. Wondering if *I* will still be here on our return trip from Glawn, or whether Anice will find a way to ease me from Cassandra's life.

"Don't fret," Cassandra says, seeming to read my mind. "It's only a week or two. By the time we get back, Lady Rhoswen will be on the mend."

She stops, placing her hand on my arm. "And surely Anice won't be as bad when she's away from everything and everyone she knows, except us? She'll have to be nicer . . . surely?"

It takes everything in me not to look at her askance but to reply in a reasonable tone, "Surely, my lady. She's been . . . under pressure, and I'm sure the change of scenery will do her the world of good."

CHAPTER THREE

"I can't believe my own mother would send me to this boondock on the buttock of the known world on purpose! You must send word to my father at once! He will never stand for me to be under such duress — and all alone!"

Reeve gritted his teeth as Anice continued to rail at Sir Garrick from the dark, warm interior of the carriage. Wrapping his cloak tighter around his legs with one hand, the other busy holding Sir Garrick's mount, Reeve couldn't believe they had stopped yet again. He wished, for the umpteenth time that day, that he was anywhere in Cartreff but on this bleak journey.

If only the confounded wind would stop blowing.

"Now, my lady," Sir Garrick said, as he stepped

closer to the door. "It is not much further to Glawn Castle. I know that you are not as comfortable as —"

"Comfortable!" Reeve winced as Anice's shriek rose above the whistling of the wind, but Sir Garrick stood his ground. "After a night in a flea-ridden bed in some forsaken hovel of an inn in the middle of nowhere? Stuck in this box on wheels for two days with only your wife and that maid for company!?"

"My lady," Sir Garrick tried again, but there was no stopping Anice.

"Why could my friends not have come with us?" she ranted. "We had the room to take them to Harding Manor, there were empty rooms at the inn — surely the Airl of Glawn has a few bedchambers to spare!?"

"My lady, we have discussed this before . . ."

Reeve tuned out as Sir Garrick went over the same reasons he had given Anice an hour ago when she'd asked the same question. And the hour before that. And the hour before that . . .

A sudden gust of wind blew up, startling Reeve's horse into a high-stepping dance, mane billowing like a flag. "Whoa, boy," Reeve said, gripping the reins, glad that Sir Garrick's battle-hardened mount had not moved.

Reeve was riding a gray courser from Lady Rhoswen's stables, having left the Airl's destrier munching on hay and having his ears scratched. The Airl had sent the horse to Harding to spend some time with Lady

44

Rhoswen's mares, hoping for a herd of little destriers come spring.

The gray courser had drawn the short straw and been sent to Glawn with Reeve.

As the gust died away to the steady, ever-present breeze that dried out Reeve's lips, irritated his eyes, tickled his ears and prickled his mood, Reeve heard Anice's querulous tones once more. The argument with Sir Garrick was still underway, albeit at a slightly softer volume.

With a sigh, Reeve edged both horses forward, unsurprised to hear Anice demanding once again to know why her friends could not have come.

Knowing that Sir Garrick could not explain to Anice that he was on a secret mission for the Airl and therefore did not need a coterie of young women under his charge, Reeve's patience ran out.

He leaned down from his courser and tapped Sir Garrick on the shoulder, pushing away the inner voice that gasped at his audacity as he did so.

"I think you should tell her the truth," Reeve said out loud, in his most confidential tone, willing Sir Garrick to play along and not simply knock Reeve off his horse for his insubordination.

"The truth!" Sir Garrick's dark eyebrows nearly hit his hairline. "Have you gone mad?"

Reeve swallowed, trying to maintain his confident

smile. "It's the only thing the Lady Anice will accept, sire. The only thing that is her due!"

"Reeve —" Sir Garrick's voice was a growl, but, as Reeve had suspected she would, Anice seized upon his words, flying down the steps of the carriage, her dark-blue gown swirling around her, tresses of her copper hair flying like snakes around her head.

"I demand that you let him speak!" Anice shrieked, the wind snatching her words and carrying them across the desolate landscape like arrows.

"Yes, do let him speak," Maven drawled from her seat just inside the door of the carriage, Lady Cassandra leaning over her like a common serving girl to watch the action. "We're terribly interested in hearing the truth."

Anice addressed her scorn toward the carriage. "Nobody asked you!" she sniffed, before turning her attention back to Sir Garrick. "But I do want the truth."

Sir Garrick assessed Reeve for a long moment.

Reeve tried his best to look as though he knew what he was doing.

All Reeve knew was that he needed to tell the Lady Anice something that would assuage her anger and frustration long enough to get her back into the carriage and keep her there until they arrived at Glawn Castle. The less time that he and the other outriders spent out in this wind, the better.

What exactly Reeve was going to say he had yet to

decide — but Sir Garrick didn't need to know that.

"Very well, Reeve," said Sir Garrick. "Be my guest."

The knight stepped back, the sweep of his arm indicating that Reeve should dismount and take his place next to Lady Anice.

Taking his time, trying desperately to think, Reeve swung his leg over the courser's back and slid to the boggy road, landing with a squelch. Deep wheel ruts stretched away behind the carriage to the horizon, where the stony hills met a sky as bleak as Reeve's future if he didn't get this right.

"My Lady Anice," Reeve said. He flashed his brightest smile as he stepped back on his left foot, stretched his right leg forward with toe pointed, opened his arms wide and bowed. It was a flawless courtly bow and, at the right feast, would have had the girls giggling and blushing.

As it was, the only response Reeve got was the sigh of the wind and the faintest titter from inside the carriage.

"Oh, do get on with it," Anice snapped, arms folded across her bodice. "It's cold out here!"

It was Reeve's turn to blush as he stood up straight and stepped closer to Anice. "Would you like my cloak, my lady?" he asked, feeling excessively gallant as he unpinned the heavy black fabric from his throat.

"No," Anice said, tapping her foot and smearing mud all over her navy slipper. "What I want is the truth so that we can all go home."

"Yes, my lady," Reeve said, as he crooked his elbow and held out one arm. "Perhaps my lady would walk with me a little way that we might speak in confidence."

When Anice hesitated, Reeve smiled in what he hoped was his most winning fashion. "Some things are best not spoken of before others," he said, hoping his face did not reveal that he was still trying to work out what those things might be.

"Oh, all right then," Anice said, uncrossing her arms and laying one delicate hand on his forearm, her bell sleeves fluttering around her wrists like butterflies.

As Reeve strolled her away from the carriage containing Maven and her judging ears, he felt Anice begin to shiver with the cold.

"My lady, I will not keep one as beautiful as you in the cold too long," Reeve said, and even as he spoke the words Reeve realized he'd found the key to his story. "For it is that very beauty that is at the heart of your solitary journey to Glawn."

Anice stopped dead, removing her hand from his arm. "And what, pray tell, could my noted beauty have to do with me being banished to the outer reaches of Cartreff without my friends?"

Reeve sketched her a tiny bow as though acknowledging the incisiveness of her question. "The truth is that the Airl has hopes of finding matches for Honora, Thora and, er . . ."

"Faith," Anice supplied, her pale brow furrowed as she tried to follow Reeve's words. Good luck with that, Reeve thought, as he tried to keep track of them himself.

"Yes, Faith," Reeve went on. "And so, the Airl, your father that is, wanted them to return to Rennart Castle without you, the brightest star in our fief, to eclipse them as he made the, er, introductions to suitable young men."

"My father said nothing of this to me," Anice said, hands on hips, remarkable green eyes narrowed as she considered his words.

"Well, er, no, he wouldn't," said Reeve, adding silently "because he knows nothing about it," before speaking aloud: "He knows that one as loyal as you would never see that the chances of, er, Honora, Thora and Faith are crueled every time you so much as walk into a room."

Anice bit her lip, half convinced. "It is true that I am far more beautiful than any of them," she said. "I can see his point. But surely I could have simply stayed at Harding Manor with Mother?"

Reeve allowed his gaze to fall to his feet. "The dear Lady Rhoswen did not want you stuck there by yourself, with illness stalking the manor," he said, and now his voice rang with truth.

Reeve peeked sideways to watch as Anice appeared

to measure and assess his story before finally, to his relief, giving a tiny nod.

"It makes sense," Anice announced, turning on her heel and flouncing back toward the carriage. "And it will not be for long. Three or four days should be sufficient to make nice and then we can return to Rennart Castle. I will notify Father by letter to expect us."

Reeve took note of the warning, knowing that Anice had laid down an ultimatum. She might cooperate for three or four days but beyond that . . .

Sir Garrick would need to walk a delicate line between diplomacy and efficiency to achieve Airl Buckthorn's goals in such a short time frame. Reeve shook his head, knowing that Sir Garrick was going to Glawn Castle with no clear picture of Airl Riding's loyalties, without an inside contact and with no trusted allies but Lady Cassandra, Reeve and Maven — all outsiders. The potential for putting a foot wrong and seeing them all, including Airl Buckthorn, up on charges of treason was very real.

After all, they were in Glawn on the hunt for allies to wrest ruling power from King Bren. Airl Buckthorn might be careful to say that the plan was to convince King Bren to accept "help" to govern Cartreff in a meaningful way. But, in effect, the Airl hoped to sideline King Bren before he bankrupted the kingdom or, worse, pushed the less fortunate citizens of

Cartreff to revolt with his careless and selfish behavior.

Sir Garrick rushed to stand by the steps, bringing Reeve's clamoring thoughts back to the windswept plains, and as Anice swept her skirts into one hand to lift them clear for her ascent into the carriage, she gave Sir Garrick an imperious nod. "Drive on."

Closing the door firmly behind her, Sir Garrick returned to Reeve, who had one foot in the saddle, ready to remount the courser.

"I have no idea what you said to her," Sir Garrick said, keeping his voice low, "and I suspect I do not wish to know, but well done, young Reeve. Well done."

With the tips of his ears burning from the praise, Reeve could almost ignore the tugging, mocking wind.

Almost.

The gray stone turrets of Glawn Castle loom at the end of the windswept road, as it feels as though they've done for hours. Such is the vastness of these tussocky, rock-strewn moors that we have been able to see the castle, looking tantalizingly close, for many hours as we creaked and swayed toward it.

Even Anice has finally given up lamenting her discomfort and whining about being so far from Harding Manor, and I still wonder what it was that

Reeve said to her all those hours ago.

Cassandra closed her eyes to both of us not long after that last stop, and has slept peacefully since, despite the long and winding potholed road that stretches behind us.

My view today, as it was yesterday, is of the places we have been. I am sitting opposite Cassandra, traveling backward on Anice's orders.

"Why sit three across when there is enough room to be comfortable?" she'd said early on our first morning, spreading her skirts across the seat as though to ward me off.

"Of course, my lady," I'd replied, not allowing my face to move a muscle, climbing over her to take my place opposite Cassandra, as though Anice had not been perfectly happy to sit four across with her friends only the day before.

For most of the trip, my eyes have been fixed upon the wild landscape, flat and boggy and peppered, as we approach Glawn Castle, with tall wooden mills such as I've never seen before. Unlike the stone waterwheels I have seen in the south, these sails are lattice and they seem too far from the castle to be useful in the milling of grain. I make a note to find out what they are used for — and why there are so many — as discreetly as I can.

Perhaps Reeve will ask for me. Such a question will always be taken more seriously from him than from me.

Even as I think of him, Reeve plods past on his courser. Gone is the smiling, teasing jauntiness of a few days ago. He is hunched down in his saddle, his cloak pulled close around him.

I do not envy him today — the pace of our travel has been brutal and the gray, biting weather uncomfortable enough to bear inside the carriage, where the wind whistles through the tiniest gaps.

A hitch in the pace of our horses draws my attention back to the road and I twist in my seat to look ahead, startled to discover that we are all but in the gates of Glawn Castle.

"My lady," I whisper, turning back and reaching to shake Cassandra's arm gently. "My lady, we are here."

She jumps at my touch, but recovers quickly to stretch and yawn. "Can you fix my hair for me?" she asks, sliding across the carriage to sit beside me on the plush seat and turning so that her back is toward me.

Her hair is braided and looped around her head like a crown for easy traveling, and it is a simple matter to unpin the plaits and unwind her tresses, which are now pleasingly crinkled from many hours in confinement.

"Oh, that feels good," says Cassandra, shaking her head. I know how she must feel. My own scalp is tight and prickly, though it will be many hours before I can unwind my own braids.

"I can leave your hair loose, my lady," I say, "but we should cover it. We do not know the Airl of Glawn, and he may be a stickler for etiquette. You are a married woman now."

"You should do it anyway," says Anice, watching us from the other side of the carriage. "Your husband represents my father and it would pay you to remember that. The rules may not have applied to Lady Cassandra of Elderham Park, but they most definitely apply to the wife of Sir Garrick Sharp, Knight Protector of Rennart Castle."

Cassandra does not respond to the dig, but I feel her body stiffen. We both knew that Anice would not hesitate to remind her cousin Cassandra that she had married beneath both of them, but knowing it and living with it are two different things.

"Perhaps the silver snood," I interject. "It is a nice nod to convention but it is also beautiful and luminous. It will let Airl Riding know that you are worthy of attention and respect."

The message is for Anice as much for the Airl, and Cassandra recognizes it immediately. "Excellent idea," she says. "But you will need to be quick."

I stand to retrieve the small trunk from the rack above my head, but as I place it on the seat, the carriage comes to a sudden halt and I am thrown backward, landing in an untidy heap across Anice's skirts.

"Get up, you fool!" she bawls, sounding very much like the fishmonger's wife, who was trying to drum up business outside our humble inn at an unearthly hour this morning. As I scrabble to regain my feet, Anice is trying to push me off, writhing in fury, kicking sideways with her little slippers and making an unholy racket.

I have had enough. As I stand, I take great care to ensure that her slipper is under my sturdy traveling boot, only for a second, and only with enough pressure to shock her into silence.

"Oh, my lady," I say, with as much sincerity as I can manage, "I am so sorry."

"You did that on purpose," Anice hisses, as she massages the toes that I have trampled. "You will pay for that."

"Don't be ridiculous," Cassandra snaps, as I open the trunk and remove the snood, taking care not to glance at Anice. "Anyone could see that was an accident. It has been a long day and you are overwrought, cousin. I should think that a long soak in a tub will bring some perspective."

"I will speak to my father," Anice continues, as though Cassandra has not spoken. "You see if I don't."

I do not need to look at her to know her porcelain complexion is red with rage, but again, I say nothing, concentrating instead on gathering Cassandra's luxuriant waves together and stuffing them into the cobweb-like silver of the snood. Once her hair is tucked inside, I draw the edges up, pinning the snood to the back of her head in a half circle.

Turning Cassandra to face me, I allow myself a smile. From the front, she looks like a painting of the Madonna, with her dark hair parted dead center and then disappearing in two shining waves into the glittering grasp of the snood, which is strewn about with sparkling stones.

I rebuckle the small trunk and put it back on the rack, pulling down the deep-emerald velvet cloak that has been carefully folded beside it. Shaking it out, I clasp it about Cassandra's throat.

"Keep your cloak on and no one will see how wrinkled your gown is," I say, dusting off the shoulders.

"Given that you arrived at my father's castle less than two weeks ago with no escort and no protocol, I am surprised you care so much," Anice scoffs, straightening her own skirts.

"A lot can change in a week," is all Cassandra says. "As you remind me, cousin, my husband is here to represent your father, as are we all, and it would not reflect well upon him if we were to step off on the wrong foot with the Airl of Glawn. So, I shall do my best to start off right — and so should you."

"I do not have a maid to help me," Anice grumbles, now smoothing her long tresses, which are, in truth, windblown after her earlier conversation with Reeve on the road.

"You are also young and beautiful and require little more than that," Cassandra replies, and I know she is right. Even windblown, Anice looks stunning. "I am sure that Maven would assist if you were to ask nicely."

"I could just order her to assist me," Anice snaps, her chin lifting as though for a fight.

"You could try," I hear Cassandra barely whisper, and I suppress a grin as Cassandra says, out loud, "She is not yours to order."

"Then I require no assistance," Anice says, as a footman in dark-gray livery with a deep-red hare outlined on the front pulls the carriage door open.

"Suit yourself," says Cassandra, before smiling widely at the footman and taking his proffered hand to support her out of the carriage.

Looking through the door, I see a row of hard-looking men standing to attention behind the footman, long dark-gray cloaks lined in deep red blowing around their ankles in the wind. To my surprise, even in the wind they wear broad-brimmed gray hats down low over their foreheads, fixed under their chins with a strap. It takes me only a moment to realize the hats would afford protection from rain and mist as much as from the sun.

Anice sneers at me before ostentatiously smoothing

her skirts and following Cassandra down into the courtyard. The footman glances inside the carriage, clearly sees no one of interest and closes the door, leaving me inside.

As the carriage rolls around to the stables and the servants' entrance, I sigh, knowing that I have many hours of unpacking and organizing before me, with no hot bath at the end of it.

I don't often miss my former life, but when I do the ache is sharp and usually involves rare moments to myself and memories of steaming water scented with lavender and a huge bed of my own with fresh linen sheets.

Pushing my thoughts aside, I gather the small trunk to my side and prepare to disembark the carriage. My Lady Cassandra may be ready to take on the Airl of Glawn in her silver snood but I have others to seek out.

Sir Garrick has made it clear to Reeve and to me that we are as much a part of this envoy as he and Lady Cassandra, and that it is our duty to keep our eyes and ears open in the kitchen and stables and among the servants of Glawn Castle.

The success of our mission depends on secrecy, and the first whispers of a break in confidence are more likely to be heard outside of the rooms where silver snoods are required.

"Are you all right there, lassie?" An older man, his tall, sturdy stance belying the countless wrinkles on his ruddy face, is peering inside the carriage, holding out one hand for me to grab for balance down the steps.

"I'm Winnock, house steward. I'm afraid you'll have to carry those trunks in yourself or wait a while — there's a . . . situation in the kitchens that needs sorting out before we can attend to your baggage."

I step down onto the cobbled courtyard, realizing as I do so that the carriage has been driven around the side of Glawn Castle and has come to a halt beside a tall pair of wood doors.

As I open my mouth to assure Winnock that I can manage, two of the hard-faced men who had greeted Sir Garrick and Cassandra at the front door clatter around the corner on their mounts.

"Any word, Winnock?" says the younger of the two, pulling his horse up hard beside us. Now that I can see him properly, I realize that he is only about twenty years of age, and it is his grim expression and burnished skin that make him look older.

Winnock shakes his head, and I can see that his long gray hair is tied in a ponytail low at the nape of his neck. I cannot help but compare his rugged, weathered appearance to the smooth unctuousness of Lorimer, formerly the house steward at Rennart Castle, now languishing in the dungeons of that same establishment charged with my attempted murder.

It still burns me that Lorimer is not awaiting the hangman's noose for the actual murder of Sully. I know that he did it, but to prove he did it I would need to confess my role in the disappearance of the Fire Star.

Worse still, Cassandra would need to confess her role in that crime, and that I will never allow to happen.

"I don't like this at all, Gerard," the younger horseman says, turning to the silent man beside him and bringing my thoughts back to the present. "It is most unlike Mistress Percy to abscond. Not when she knew we had important guests arriving today."

"She is a woman," Gerard responds, lifting his head so that I can now see his face clearly. "Everyone knows that they are unreliable."

He winks at me in such a way that I know I am supposed to see his words as a joke, but his pale-blue eyes are wintry under eyebrows so fair that they are almost invisible. I can see little of his hair under the broad-brimmed hat, but what I can see seems to be red bordering on orange. His hands on the reins are pale and freckled, the fingers short and squat, and the thin moons of dirt under his nails make me shudder.

"Miss, er, Miss, this is Gerard and Jonty of Airl Riding's personal guard," says Winnock, hurrying into the waiting silence.

"You are with Sir Garrick?" Gerard stares down at

me from his horse.

I bob a tiny curtsey. "I am Maven, maid companion to Lady Cassandra."

Though I keep my eyes on the ground, I feel the weight of Gerard's swift assessment.

"Winnock, Sir Brannon has decreed that we are to search for the cook until night falls. If Mistress Percy has wandered off the byways into the marshes searching for her herbs, we will need to find her soon or we will not find her at all. The welcome feast is to be delayed until we return. The Airl agrees."

Winnock nods, turning to enter the huge double doors without further word.

"Jonty, tell Hugh and Seb not to bother stabling their horses — you are to set off immediately. Turn your cloaks. She can't have gotten too far. Wasn't she last seen just after luncheon?"

"Well, yes, but —"

"But?"

"I don't think she'd wander off like that, sir," Jonty says, removing his hat to reveal curling blond hair, a shade more golden than Reeve's, before unclasping his cloak and reversing it so that the deep red is on the outside. "I think something's happened to her."

"Perhaps you don't know her as well as you think you do," Gerard says, with a yawn. "Anyway, it seems Sir Brannon has taken it into his head to agree with you – the Wolf only knows why. It's not like she's the first person to wander off onto the moors never to be seen again. Didn't go looking for that blacksmith's lad last year, now, did he? Consider yourself lucky that he's bent to send you out tonight. But I, for one, am going to offload this horse and find myself a tankard of ale."

Gerard pulls the rein to guide the horse away, but notices that Jonty has not moved.

"Well?" Gerard says.

"I don't understand –"

But Jonty's words are interrupted by a great thundering of hooves, and I step back as another guard hurtles around the corner on a huge gray destrier, his cloak, already "turned," blowing back to reveal its now dark-gray lining and the gray tunic beneath.

I am struck by the thought that these men would be almost impossible to see out on the moors with their cloaks turned to the gray side – and that this is not an accident.

Wear the red when they don't want to get lost. Wear the gray when they want to be invisible.

"Gerard, Jonty, we ride," the new man says, interrupting my thoughts. "Sir Brannon wants us back here before the moon rises."

The guard does not even bother to wait for a reply, wheeling his mount around and racing back toward the front entrance, no doubt to join the Knight Protector and the other guards.

Gerard and Jonty share a look. "All this fuss for a cook," muses Gerard, his disbelief obvious. "Airl Riding must really like her light touch with a loaf of bread."

Gerard chuckles at his feeble joke, but Jonty looks even more worried.

"Let's go," Gerard says, on the move before he finishes speaking, wheeling his horse about and clattering off, leaving behind only a pile of steaming horse manure.

Jonty is slower off the mark, his thoughts so far away that he all but jumps at Gerard's actions.

"She'll be all right, son," Winnock says to him. "Your aunt . . . she's one of the most capable women I know. Not many would try putting one over on her, and she doesn't suffer fools."

I file away the "aunt" and watch Jonty's wince dissolve into a rueful smile. "I know," he says to Winnock, quite as though I am not even there. "But she's getting on, you know, and, well, it's not like her to do this."

It is Winnock's turn to laugh, though it's more a choke. "Getting on," he says. "She's only just gone fifty – few more years in her yet, son."

"Says you," Jonty scoffs, though now there is a twinkle in his blue eyes, and I can see that he would be a good-looking man when not full of worry. "But I have no time to jest, I must away."

He nods to me and then is gone, taking care to avoid the manure left by Gerard's horse, for which I am grateful – flying manure would be the icing on the cake of a lousy day.

Winnock watches him go, the remnants of his smile fading back into his wrinkles.

"Your cook is important?" I venture.

Winnock appears startled by my question, and I suspect he has forgotten I am even standing here. I do not take it personally – people often forget that I am in a room. Once, it bothered me to be overlooked and underestimated, but I have discovered that it can have its advantages.

"So it would seem," Winnock responds, slowly, stroking his chin in such a way as to suggest he is more comfortable with a beard than being clean-shaven, as he currently is.

"Is her cooking really that good?" I ask, trying for lightness even as I consider all the options as to why the castle's elite guard would be allocated to find a servant. "It seems that such a search would not be made for just anyone?"

Winnock manages a weak smile. "True, though she does make a mighty fine hare pie."

I remember the symbol on the Airl's livery. "Hares may be plentiful around here, but so, I assume, are makers of fine hare pies?" I joke.

"Indeed, every family has a secret recipe," Winnock says, but it is clear his thoughts are now elsewhere. "The timing of this search is unusual . . ." Winnock breaks, and turns from me toward the doors. "The welcome feast . . . I must go."

He takes a few strides before stopping. "I am sorry, I forget my duty. I will send a footman for the larger baggage as soon as I can. Will you be all right with your smaller trunks?"

Winnock does not wait for my answering nod before he is gone, through one side of the huge wood doors, leaving it open behind him. With a sigh, I gather up the smaller trunks and boxes, balancing them as best I can. I make sure that Lady Cassandra's trunk, with its tiny Beech Circle symbol painted on the side, is on top and visible, before following Winnock's path into the yawning darkness beyond the doors, my mind alight with questions.

Is it a coincidence that Airl Riding's cook has gone missing mere hours before we arrived on our special, secret mission? And if it's not a coincidence, what possible link could there be between a cook in the wilds of Glawn and Airl Buckthorn's plans?

CHAPTER FOUR

"Wear it with the red outside so we can spot you if you wander from the path."

Reeve took the cloak from the burly guard, mumbling his thanks as he slung it around his shoulders and fastened it through the loop at his throat. Tucked inside the cloak's enveloping hug, he felt slightly better. It was surprisingly warm and lightweight for such a voluminous garment, flapping around his ankles in the breeze but otherwise providing excellent protection from the ever-present wind.

"And this," the guard said, handing Reeve a dark-gray, broad-brimmed hat, the same as the ones all of Airl Riding's men were wearing. "It will keep the rain off."

"But it's not raining," Reeve said, taking the hat.

The guard laughed. "Not yet. But you can be sure that the next squall is not far away. It never is."

Reeve put the hat on his head, and the guard reached over and pushed the crown down as far as it would go, which was to the point where it half covered Reeve's eyes.

"Keep it down on your forehead," the guard warned, "and tie it tightly under your chin. If the wind gets under it, the hat will all but take your head off."

Lifting the brim just enough that he could see out from under it, Reeve nodded, noting that Sir Garrick was now also garbed in the outer trappings of Glawn. It felt odd to see the blue fox of Sir Garrick's livery covered in deep red, but Reeve supposed it was better to be warm and easy to spot in the gloom than to worry about protocol.

"Ready, Reeve?" Sir Garrick asked, catching Reeve's attention.

"Yes, sire," Reeve responded, bowing his head as manners dictated and following Sir Garrick to where a pair of horses waited, saddled and impatient.

"Ready but not entirely happy, at a guess," Sir Garrick said to Reeve, keeping his voice down as they swung up onto the backs of their unfamiliar mounts. "Me too, if it's any consolation. But a woman has disappeared and, no matter how many hours we have been in the saddle today, that takes precedence."

"There is no question but that we must help, sire," said Reeve, trying to look like he meant it. Being a knight meant making sacrifices, and if he had to sacrifice his ability to sit comfortably for the next few days, well so be it.

"Good lad," Sir Garrick said, moving his mount closer. "It will also give me a chance to sound out Sir Brannon regarding our mission. The Airl's Knight Protector will have a good idea of where Airl Riding's loyalties lie, and, if I ask the right questions, I can get the lay of the land before bumbling in with Airl Buckthorn's petition. You ride with the younger guards and see what you can find out."

He urged his horse forward before Reeve could respond, leaving Reeve to wonder what those "right questions" might be. Reeve didn't want to say the wrong thing to the younger guards and tip off the wrong person about the mission.

Frowning, Reeve touched his mount's sides with his heels. As the horse walked forward, following the others toward the gates, Reeve risked a longing glance at the windows of the castle keep. After two long days out in the elements, Reeve had an overwhelming desire to be indoors, away from the assailing wind.

The high gray walls of the castle were forbidding, but Reeve could see the warm glow of lights already in some of the upper windows. The sun would not set for another hour, but even so it barely made an impression against the gloomy clouds that hung heavy in the sky. Reeve shivered as they left the enveloping stone walls of the courtyard and clattered across the creaking drawbridge over the moat, drawing his new cloak closer around him.

The aching emptiness of the marshy grassland beyond the gates evoked a sigh. Reeve would not deny a lady in trouble, but he couldn't help but wish that he and Sir Garrick had arrived just a few minutes after the search party had departed rather than a few minutes before.

"You'd better stick with me." The guard who had given Reeve his cloak and hat drew up beside him, and Reeve glanced at him gratefully. He fit the description of one of the "younger guards" Sir Garrick had directed Reeve to talk to, and seemed friendly enough now that they were underway.

"Thanks, I will, er —" Reeve prompted the man for his name.

"Call me Stanley," the guard said, and, turning in his saddle, Reeve noticed that Stanley's eyebrows were dark and heavy under his hat, and his eyes were almost black in color. "We only ever use first names."

Reeve sat up straight in his saddle. "Ever? Why?"

"Ever," Stanley said, cheerfully. "As to why, I think

Sir Brannon — who is always Sir Brannon — likes it because it reminds us who's in charge. From the moment we join Airl Riding's personal guard, we leave our family names and places behind. Our new lives begin on that day, with this new family. There are only nine of us — well, ten if you include Sir Brannon, but he's a cut above us."

Reeve considered this idea for a moment. "So, everyone in Glawn just knows you by one name? Isn't that a bit . . . casual?"

"I don't mind it," said Stanley. "Character counts much more than a person's name. That's what Sir Brannon says anyway. You get the respect you earn and it has nothing to do with where you're from or what your last name might be."

There was a short silence broken only by the plodding of the horses' hooves as Reeve considered Stanley's words.

"What's yours, then?" Stanley asked, breaking into Reeve's whirling thoughts.

"Oh, sorry, I'm Reeve of Norwood, squire to Sir Garrick, Knight Protector of Rennart Castle," Reeve responded.

Stanley chuckled. "Well, now, I figured you were with Sir Garrick, given I've never seen you before, but the rest of it is a mouthful, isn't it?"

"I guess it is," Reeve said, slowly. "But I quite like it.

My friends call me Reeve, but people who don't know me can . . . place me straightaway."

"There's pros and cons to that," Stanley began, but his response was interrupted by a shout from Sir Garrick.

"Reeve! Follow us!"

Reeve looked up to see that Sir Garrick and Sir Brannon had branched off to the left. Three riders suddenly rode off ahead at speed, and four others followed a barely visible path out toward a windmill on the right.

"Come on, then, young Reeve of Norwood," said Stanley, leaving Reeve to wonder about those pros and cons. "Wherever they go, we go, and we'll need to look lively to keep up with Sir Brannon. This, I suspect, is the true business of this little outing."

"True business?" Reeve asked, as Stanley guided his horse forward before stopping just a few meters ahead to address Reeve once more.

"I think Sir Brannon is more interested in speaking to your Sir Garrick far beyond listening ears than he'll ever be in finding a cook," Stanley said, frankly. "He likes to know what's what, does Sir Brannon."

Reeve frowned. "But what could be the 'what's what' of a honeymoon tour?" he asked, trying to keep his face as innocent as a babe's.

"Best we don't consider that too closely," Stanley

said with a grin. "More likely Sir Brannon is getting a feel for your master's character. Airl Riding is a big believer in character, and Sir Brannon is a genius at summing up any man. Or boy for that matter."

Reeve could feel his face flush as Stanley's gaze swept over him.

"Sir Brannon will find no fault with my master's character," Reeve stated. "He is the finest knight in the kingdom."

"Hmmph," said Stanley, looking over his shoulder at the rapidly fading backs of the two knights. "So we keep hearing. We'll be keen to see him in action."

Seeing an opening, Reeve asked, "And your Sir Brannon? What of his character? Is he hard? Strong? Loyal?"

"You would question the loyalty of a man you haven't met?" Stanley's affable face was marred by a deep frown.

Reeve chuckled, the sound feeble even to his own ears. "Not at all," he said. "I merely mention the characteristics of a fine knight."

"Well, I'd suggest you keep those mentions to yourself, young Reeve of Norwood," warned Stanley. "But now we must go — stay right behind me. Your horse will find its footing and it will be safer if you don't try to direct him. The moors are deceptive — what looks like solid ground may shift underfoot. Lay your reins across his neck and let him have his head."

Pushing aside a sudden image of his mount stumbling in the marsh and falling, Reeve did as he was told and then sat, heart in mouth, hands gripping the pommel, hoping that his horse was as sure-footed as Stanley seemed to think.

Stanley twisted in his saddle to check on Reeve, and his grin lit up his broad, flat face. "Don't fret, he's done this hundreds of times before."

"What's his name?" Reeve asked, swaying from side to side as the horse picked his way through the long grass.

"Oh, didn't anyone tell you? All the horses are called Rouncey."

Reeve took in his words with a frown. "Because they're all rouncies, they're all called Rouncey? Are the destriers all called 'Destrier'?"

Stanley nodded without turning back. "Sir Brannon likes to keep things simple. And it stops us getting too attached to any one horse in particular."

Reeve shook his head, wishing that Maven were here to exchange loaded glances with. He knew she would find the whole business with names, horses or otherwise, to be ridiculous.

But Maven was safe in the castle, no doubt in the kitchens tucking into a large bowl of warm, filling . . . something. Reeve was so tired and cold now that he couldn't even summon up an image of which warm, filling food he'd like to see most.

He winced when he thought of himself riding up and down beside the carriage just a few days earlier, showing off his freedom, knowing that Maven would have been gnashing her teeth. The shoe was definitely on the other foot now.

The further along the nonexistent path they went, the more convinced Reeve became that Stanley was right – Sir Brannon was not expecting to find the missing cook out here. He and his men were not really even looking. Instead, Sir Brannon was doing his job, assessing the visitor to Glawn before he could set foot inside the castle. Reeve hoped that Sir Garrick would tread very carefully as he attempted to find out what they needed to know.

Would Airl Riding and his community join Airl Buckthorn's plan to petition the King to reform his ways and take on a regent until such time as the petitioners felt he was ready to rule in his own right?

Given Stanley's reaction to the word "loyal," Reeve knew it was a delicate subject. Even the suggestion that King Bren was not up to the job was treason. And treason meant certain death for anyone involved.

But, from all that Reeve had overheard as Sir Garrick's squire, and all that he had seen firsthand in the past few weeks as he had traveled the roads of Cartreff, Reeve also knew that all was not well in the kingdom.

King Bren was more interested in entertaining his friends than in ruling Cartreff, and the people were suffering.

As the dark clouds above his head began to release their heavy burden of rain, Reeve tried to snuggle down into his cloak as he kept Stanley in view. Water dripped off the brim of Reeve's wide hat, and he sent a silent thanks to whomever it was that had come up with the clever design.

"This way, Reeve of Norwood!" Stanley shouted, and Reeve realized they were heading toward one of the dark windmills he'd spotted from the road on the way to Glawn. As they drew closer, Reeve noticed a deep, creaking sound and decided it was a good thing they were approaching the mill from the back — the huge, latticed sails on the front of the structure were whirling around at a frightening rate, the end of each arm almost touching the ground as it sped through.

Sir Garrick and Sir Brannon had already dismounted, and were heading, horses and all, through a tall back door that Sir Brannon held open.

"Come on," said Stanley, sliding from his rouncey.

Reeve hesitated. "Surely we won't all fit in there? Not with four horses?"

Stanley grinned, and Reeve once again couldn't help but grin back.

"It's bigger than it looks, I promise," Stanley said. "Just remember to never, ever approach a mill from the front. Even on the stillest day. The winds in Glawn are sudden and fierce, and many a man has been killed by a moving sail."

As Reeve followed Stanley through the door, the *thump*, *thump*, *thump* of the flying sails seeming to shake the building, he shuddered at the thought of being caught in their path.

Inside, as his eyes accustomed to the gloom, Reeve was startled to discover that there was no sign of Sir Garrick, and that the thumping sound was echoed in here by a deep, slow, bone-chilling creak coming from somewhere overhead.

In the center of the floor space, a thick, wooden pole disappeared into the low ceiling, but there was ample room for the four horses and for he and Stanley. The pole spun slowly, driven somehow, Reeve thought, by the windmill's sails. Curious as to how it all worked and what the purpose of the mill might be when there seemed to be no grain to grind, Reeve stepped toward the slow-moving pole.

"Leave Rouncey there." Stanley's voice rose above the racket, interrupting Reeve's examination. "Come this way."

With a wall of horses between he and Stanley, Reeve was unable to see where "this way" might be. Sliding around his mount, trying not to earn a flying hoof to the stomach or worse, Reeve discovered Stanley's boots disappearing up through a hole in the roof via a ladder.

"Ah," Reeve heard a deep voice say. "Stanley. Light that stove, will you? Sir Garrick and I have some things to discuss."

As he climbed up the ladder, Reeve realized that one slip would have him falling down onto the hard floor below.

Suppressing a shudder, Reeve completed his climb and popped his head through the square hole to discover a snug, if plain, circular room with a small stove, a table and several straight-backed wooden chairs. It was surprisingly light, thanks to a series of narrow windows, set in groups of four facing east, west, north and south. Anyone standing by those windows would have clear visibility to the horizon in any direction, but would be hard to see from the outside.

Hay bales lined most of the walls, save for an area of stone behind the stove, and the chimney had been bent so that any smoke would be drawn out of a narrow window nearby.

The huge, spinning pole from downstairs erupted through the center of the floor, and continued up through the ceiling above him, but this room was much quieter than the ground floor, perhaps thanks to the insulating hay bales. Another ladder was propped in the far corner of the room, indicating there was at least one more floor in this structure.

"Wait downstairs with, er, Stanley," Sir Garrick said to Reeve before Reeve could haul himself up through the hole. "We won't be long. It's clear that the cook is not here, and it will soon be too dark to look further tonight."

Reeve nodded and backed down the ladder once again, leaving the two Knight Protectors to their parley. Moments later, he was joined by Stanley, who managed to back down the ladder with a candle in one hand, which made Reeve think he'd done it once or twice before.

"Come on," Stanley said over the noise of the sails, and Reeve noted that he'd removed his hat, and his hair was so dark that Reeve could only make out his face in the gloom. "We can sit over there on the other side of the horses."

Reeve followed his new friend, and sat on the hard-packed earth floor beside Stanley. Even the four horses squeezed together didn't do a lot to absorb the racket from the mill, but Reeve realized he'd rather put up with the noise than wait outside in the wind. Unfortunately, the environment wasn't conducive to subtly pumping Stanley for information.

Reeve had a feeling, though, that Sir Garrick wouldn't consider a noisy, shaking windmill to be any kind of excuse for not at least attempting to follow instructions. He had to try.

Flailing about in his mind for a suitable opening line, Reeve turned to Stanley and discovered, to his amazement, that the guardsman had folded his beefy arms, closed his eyes and appeared to be snoring.

With a sigh that almost gutted the candle, Reeve settled back against the mill wall to wait. With any luck, Sir Garrick and Sir Brannon would conduct their secret discussion with efficiency and without any need for Reeve to race up that wooden ladder to his master's aid. He really wasn't sure he'd be able to manage the ladder at speed, knowing that one slip could end it all . . .

Then again, if things went badly with Sir Brannon, it wouldn't be a slip on a ladder Reeve had to worry about. In fact, a quick death in a windmill might be a blessing if the entire Rennart party were to be accused of treason.

CHAPTER FIVE

How can one place be so wild and lonely on the outside, and so insufferably dull and crowded on the inside?

Eyeing the deep-gray velvet curtains that hang on either side of the huge glazed window in front of me, I wonder if anyone would notice if I slipped behind them and hid for the rest of the evening.

Given the size of the pleats, I suspect not, but can I abandon Cassandra right now?

I turn from the window to take in Glawn Castle's Small Hall. At least, Winnock told me this was the small one when he gave me careful instructions on where to bring Cassandra for a (late) welcome reception that was planned and cooked by the missing woman before her unfortunate departure.

If this is the small hall, I am not overly keen to take in the grandeur of the large one. The ceilings soar above me, the walls feel as though they have been stretched beyond capacity and then covered in tapestries, and the flagstone floor is strewn with rushes and herbs and laden with tables, large and small, and chairs and stools.

Glawn Castle has proven to be an optical illusion, presenting a modest face with enclosing courtyard to the world. But once inside the unassuming stone entrance, one is drawn into an even larger central courtyard from which two enormous wings spread outward in a *V* shape.

There is more to Glawn than meets the eye.

A huge tapestry on the opposite wall draws my gaze and I take a moment to admire the skill of its creators, even as I wonder at the pedestrian nature of its design. It seems to depict a very similar view to the one I just saw from the window: the wide expanse of the moors, many stylized windmills and one or two small dark-brown squares that seem to have been placed to fill out the design.

I am absorbed in studying it when Cassandra wanders past, as though casually, as she "takes a turn around the room" with Airl Riding's wife.

Lady Adelina is a tall, thin woman, who wears her mouse-brown hair drawn back severely into a low bun at the base of her neck. It suits the oval shape of her face, though I suspect the style, which is affected by most of the women in this room, is more for practicality against the wind than fashion.

"You are well, Maven?" Cassandra asks with a frown, and I know that she has come to my side on purpose. "I was just saying to Lady Adelina what a shame it is that we can stay but three or four days here in Glawn."

My eyes are drawn to the other side of the room, where Anice is fluttering about, already at the center of a circle of younger women who are trying to engage her in their chatter.

"Quite well, my lady," I say, pasting on a bright smile as I bring my focus back to Cassandra. "I was merely admiring the tapestry. Oh, and the view."

I do not say which view, as Anice once again captures my attention, the swirl of her sumptuous pale-blue gown a perfect match for the satin slippers on her feet. It is one of six different day dresses she has brought with her for this short visit. I know this because she asked me to unpack her trunks for her, unwilling to leave the task to a castle servant lest "something go missing."

I say "asked," but we were both aware that I am not in a position to say no.

If I am honest with myself, I did not mind the opportunity to close myself inside her well-appointed dressing room, tending to her silent and beautiful garments while she and Cassandra shared cousinly confidences in the bedchamber. It may not have been the steaming lavender bath of my dreams, but at least it was quiet.

Now, though, I am chafing at my inability to leave this gathering and go to the kitchens. I am yet to contact any Beech Circle members who reside in the castle, and my curiosity at the cook's disappearance remains piqued.

While a missing cook is an inconvenience for those who employ her, it is a major problem for those who work in the kitchens. I can only imagine the consternation and chaos occurring downstairs — similar to that if a general departed the battlefield just as the horns sounded the first advance.

I have known several cooks, both at Aramoor and those I've met in the great houses of Cartreff in my time as Cassandra's companion, and I would swear on my mother's not-yet grave that any one of them would rather have died than leave their duties in such a fashion.

In this room, I am a party of one in considering the woman — even Cassandra appears to have forgotten her in the turmoil of trying to carry out Sir Garrick's orders to charm Lady Adelina and keep her busy while he carries out his mission. Looking at the good lady's pale face, thin lips and serious expression, I suspect that Cassandra has her work cut out for her.

So I alone shall consider the cook for now.

Lady Rhoswen seemed to think the cook is not a member of the Beech Circle, but it matters not. Our philosophy is to help all women and girls. I think that disappearing, for any reason, falls under that charter.

Plus, I concede, I am curious. I would like to know where she has gone – and why. Puzzles with missing pieces have always bothered me.

Unfortunately, I must wait for Cassandra to dismiss me from this hall before I can leave what I am now considering to be the *un*welcome reception. And Cassandra is so busy making nice that it may take some time for her to remember that Sir Garrick has also given me a task to undertake.

No, I cannot wait for Cassandra – it is up to me to have myself removed.

In the most socially suitable way possible.

"Yes, I was admiring the view," I say now, turning to Cassandra and Lady Adelina, quite as though an unseemly amount of time has not passed since my original comment and they have not moved on to discussing the exquisite shades of gray in the thick, woven rug beneath our feet.

They both start and Lady Adelina frowns, but I forge ahead. "I was wondering about the windmills," I say, in a "just too loud for polite company" voice. "How do they work?"

Cassandra bites her lip, and I can see she is torn between admonishing me for my interruption and her instincts that I am doing it for a reason. I smile at her as toothily as I can manage, and she subsides, watching me closely. I am not generally one for toothy smiles.

"The, er, windmills?" Lady Adelina echoes, her hands flapping toward her mouth as though I have insulted her. "How do they *work*?"

I continue to smile, but I notice that there is a widening circle of stillness around us. The other ladies in the room are becoming aware of the disturbance and are trying to listen in while giving the appearance of laughing and chatting gaily. It is not an easy feat to manage, but I feel that the ladies of Glawn have had practice.

"Yes," I continue, keeping up the pretense that this is a normal subject of conversation between two Cartreff women who've never met before. As though we are taught to question the whys and hows of the world and not simply leave it to the men in our lives.

"How do they work? What are they for? I have seen a windmill before but it was for the grinding of grain. You have so many, of different sizes, and yet I saw no sign of grain crops?"

I wonder if I have gone too far when her long nose wrinkles as though I have brought a bad smell into the room, but Cassandra steps in.

"You must excuse Maven," she says to Lady Adelina, grasping the woman lightly by the elbow and beginning to steer her away. "It has been a long day, and I fear that tiredness has gone to her head. I think what she means to say is that the windmills are very picturesque."

"Oh, yes, I see," says Lady Adelina, her forehead smoothing as the building frown melts away. "They are very pretty, aren't they? I am not originally from Glawn so I do not fully understand their purpose, but I have always enjoyed looking upon them from the castle."

"Indeed," says Cassandra, as they begin to glide away, and the pool of silence around us once again begins to fill with bubbles of natural chatter. I wait a beat and then Cassandra stops, as though having a sudden thought. "Perhaps you might return to my chamber and bring me my red shawl, Maven."

I allow only the tiniest smile to lift the corners of my mouth as I bow. "Of course, my lady."

As I make my way toward the door, remembering to restrict myself to a delicate stroll and not stride out the way I wish to do, I hear Lady Adelina ask Cassandra if she feels the cold.

"Not usually," Cassandra answers with a tinkling laugh that would surprise anyone who knew her. "But one can never be too cautious in an unfamiliar place, don't you think?"

Lady Adelina's response is lost in the murmur of

those around her, but I have received the message loud and clear, though I do not need it. I am always cautious — right up to the point where I am not.

Once in the hallway, I toy with the idea of collecting the shawl so I can return with it later, but decide that Cassandra will come up with an excuse for me.

Far better to use the time to find Lady Rhoswen's laundress and contact the Beech Circle. And if I should find myself having to pass the kitchens to do so, well, who would deny me a quick visit there to make myself known, as any visiting maid would do?

It takes only moments and a few discreet enquiries of passing servants to find myself on the broad stone steps that lead down into the labyrinth of tight hallways, winding their way to the working rooms of this castle.

The plate store, the servants' parlor, Winnock's parlor and the linen store are no doubt behind the closed doors I pass, but I follow my instincts (and my nose) to the spacious kitchen at the end of the hallway.

Entering the airy room, I am struck at once by the warmth, which seems to seep from every crevice and into my very bones. The source is an enormous fireplace spanning most of the far wall, a selection of bright copper pots hanging above the fire.

Beside the fireplace, a short hall leads to the wide back door that I imagine stands open on hot days to catch the ever-present breeze. Assuming they ever experience a hot day in Glawn. It was still warm when we left Rennart Castle a few days ago, but in this fief the chill feels settled and permanent.

I stand just inside the door, admiring the intricate brickwork of the fireplace surround and chimney. While the castle walls are all built in a uniform gray stone, the bricks are a patchwork of tones from dull red to deep gold, and bring a lightness to this space that is not present in the formal rooms above. More bricks are underfoot, arranged in a crisscross pattern, while thick dark beams overhead mark the soaring ceilings. Several dark doors to my left no doubt lead to the buttery, the bottlery and other storerooms.

A small team of servants, all clad in dark-gray pinafores and aprons that probably started the day white, are at work at two long tables, which are positioned at right angles to the fire so that no one may complain of cold.

All in all, it is the very picture of a well-appointed, industrious kitchen, the only thing out of place being the curling pale-brown feathers scattered here and there, as though overlooked in the cleanup after plucking.

But there is none of the raucous chatter or shouted orders that usually accompany the creation of a meal in such a large kitchen. Aside from loud chopping, the only sound is the slosh of water from the corner, where an unhappy boy is washing dishes.

"C'n I help you?" asks a short, skinny, freckled girl of about my age, rolling out dough with a lot of expertise and not a small amount of aggression. Her dark-red hair is tied back under a big white scarf, making her wide green eyes seem otherworldly.

"I am Maven, maid to Lady Cassandra of Rennart Castle," I begin, preparing to launch into the story I have concocted.

"Then you should be upstairs in the hall," the girl says, thumping the rolling pin into the unresisting dough, the action violent enough to wobble a large, yellow mixing bowl at the other end of the table. "Ring a bell. Someone will come."

The waves of resentment coming from the girl are palpable, but she focuses on her task.

"I am a servant, like yourself," I say, annoyed at her attitude. "Why would I ring a bell when I have perfectly good legs?"

The girl stops rolling and plonks her hands on her hips, releasing tiny clouds of flour. "Because you don't belong down here, particularly not right now."

Her voice wobbles on the last few words, and my irritation disappears. If the people upstairs have not spared a thought for the missing cook, it's clear that those down here have been thinking of little else.

"I am sorry," I say, walking toward her. "I heard about your cook and I'm sure you're all very worried. Some of my favorite memories are of kitchens and the women who run them, and I know what a hole you must have here in your midst. I promise I won't take up much of your time. My lady requires a posset, is all. I can make it myself, and be out of your hair."

She studies me for a moment before her rigid stance relaxes. "Thank you for your words," she says, before turning to the young girl next to her. "Sally, put some milk on to warm."

Without waiting for a response, she continues. "I'm Tillie, and Mistress Percy is a friend of me mam. A friend of mine. She seems gruff but, really, she's the kindest person. We're ever so worried about her, but nobody seems to care."

"But the Airl has sent men out to look for Mistress Percy," I say. "Sir Garrick and my friend Reeve have gone with them."

Tillie bit her lip. "Yes, but they went hours and hours after we last saw Mistress Percy. We couldn't get anyone to take us seriously. I knew she'd never ever just wander off when guests were coming – not with a reception and a banquet to prepare – but Gerard kept fobbing us off, calling her a silly old woman. But she's not like that. She's just not."

As her voice rises to a wail, a gray-haired woman shelling peas on the other table looks over with a frown.

"Tillie! Settle down – you know how you get, and you

know what Sir Brannon said. It's probably a mix-up of some kind. Get on with that pastry or they'll be eating crustless pies tonight."

Tillie grimaces, but resumes her vicious rolling.

I wait a beat before whispering. "When did you last see her?"

With a glance over at the woman with the peas, Tillie responds in a low voice. "She were here after breakfast because she asked me to go to the storeroom to find the treacle for the tarts she were making."

Tillie pauses, thinking.

"And?" I prompt, aware that pea woman is casting irritated looks my way.

"She were gone before lunch," Tillie continues. "I left the treacle with her, and went to the stables to — Well, never mind that. By the time I came back she'd disappeared. I think she was gone then — it were so busy in here, you know, that no one can really remember being the last person to see her."

Pea woman clears her throat loudly.

"If you can just show me where the herbs are, I'll make that posset," I say to Tillie.

Tillie leads me to one of the big doors, pushing it open to reveal a large pantry lined with shelves and with bunches of dried herbs hanging from the ceiling.

As Tillie turns to leave, I manage one last whispered question.

"She didn't finish the tarts, did she?"

Tillie stops, one hand to her mouth. "How did you know?"

"Her bowl is still there, isn't it?" I say, indicating the yellow bowl with a tilt of my head. "It's the only thing out of place in the whole kitchen, apart from a few feathers."

Tillie's eyes well up. "The filling mix is in there . . . Mistress Gyles wanted to finish, but Mam and me think, well, we think it's like it's waiting for her."

"Mistress Gyles?" I ask, reaching above my head for some dried mint and what I think might be borage.

Tillie nods in the direction of pea woman before she walks away, back to the waiting dough. I grab some ginger and lemon before heading toward the fireplace, where Sally is waiting with a small copper pot. "Have you some ale?" I ask, and the girl, who can't be more than ten or eleven, scampers off.

I put the ginger, lemon and saucepan on the table as close to the yellow mixing bowl as I dare, studying it closely. The wooden spoon is placed neatly in the bowl, as though Mistress Percy has just dashed into the pantry for extra sugar. There are no drips or spills around the bowl, and it seems the treacle filling is all but complete. I can see why Sir Brannon and the odious Gerard assumed she'd just "wandered off."

And yet . . . I can't help but agree with Tillie that a

woman who keeps a kitchen to this standard would not walk away with guests due. I glance around but everyone seems intent upon their tasks, so I edge closer to the bowl, examining the floor where Mistress Percy last stood.

Nothing.

Sally appears beside me, a tankard of warm ale in her hand.

"Have you got another mixing bowl?" I ask. "Preferably smaller than this one."

I nudge Mistress Percy's bowl in what I hope is a jocular fashion, and almost gasp when I notice that the movement has revealed the corner of a small piece of parchment tucked beneath the bowl.

As soon as Sally's back is turned, I grasp the corner with my nails and drag it from under the bowl, slipping the parchment into my pocket in one movement.

"Oi! What are you doing there?"

Pea woman is eyeing me with suspicion so I flash her a smile. "Just waiting for a bowl. Mistress Gyles, is it?"

She does not rush into the invitation to confirm her name, so I continue.

"I'll be gone in a moment."

Sally arrives, and I turn away from the inquisition and busy myself making a quick posset that, fortunately, Cassandra will never drink. I have never made one before and I suspect that my liberal use of lemon will make it unpalatable.

And the whole time I am grinding and mixing, I can think of just one thing: the crinkle of that slip of parchment in my pocket.

In theory, I should run straight to Sir Brannon and his guards with it, or even share it with Tillie and the others here in the kitchen, but something makes me hold my tongue. The disappearance of this woman on the day we arrive feels wrong. Whether it has anything to do with our mission, I do not know. But I know that I want to show this paper to Sir Garrick, or at the very least to Reeve, before I hand it to anyone from Glawn.

Just in case.

I squeeze another dribble of lemon juice into the steaming tankard, hoping Sally doesn't come near enough to notice the telltale chunks forming at the edges of the liquid.

"I'll be off then," I say loudly, to no one in particular, covering the curdled mixture with one hand as I make my way toward the door.

Tillie manages a weak smile, but I can feel Mistress Gyles's hard stare burning into my back even as I step out of the kitchen and into the hall.

Glancing around, I see that I am quite alone in the passage, so I remove my hand from the top of the tankard, almost gagging at the sight of the curdled posset with bits of dried herb floating on top. If I ever have to make another one, I will make a point of using less lemon juice. Or get Myra to show me how to do it properly.

I wish Myra were here right now, and not just for her posset-making abilities. I do not know the wyld woman well, but her strong, practical presence was a balm and an aid when the Fire Star went missing.

Myra reminds me of Berta, grandmother of the blacksmith at Aramoor — a woman who never left the small cottage the family shared, and yet who had more practical knowledge of the world than anyone I've ever known. Berta was probably born knowing how to make a posset — not that she'd ever thought it necessary to show me how to do it.

Among the many things Berta did think necessary, however, was revealing her association with the Beech Circle. Some might marvel at the trust she placed in me by sharing that information with a mere child, but I have met many young members of the Circle since and not one has ever given away her ties without the correct precautions.

"Can I help you with something?"

A brawny footman, laden with empty dishes, is frowning at me, and I realize that I am standing stock-still in the middle of the hallway with a rapidly cooling mug in my hand. Covering the tankard once again,

I smile, trying to look bewildered.

"Thank you," I say. "I am fine. I am searching for the laundry."

"It's that door behind you," he says, inclining his head to the left before brushing past me and continuing toward the kitchen.

I backtrack, open the door, allowing clouds of steam to escape into the hall, and enter, discarding the tankard next to a pile of linen on a big wood shelf just inside. Closing the door, I feel the steam settle over me like a falling mist, scented with soapwort and lavender and a base note I can only describe as diluted filth.

Through the mist, I see two women bent over huge wooden tubs, both dressed in the same uniforms as the kitchen servants, though these look limp and worn, the starch in the caps and aprons no match for the humidity. Each woman stirs steaming water in her tub, and, as I watch, a side door opens and an enormous dark-haired man lumbers in. He strains under the weight of two full buckets of water, which he pours into the closest tub, sending another cloud of steam into the air.

"Thank you, Evan," one of the women says, and he nods and takes the buckets back out the door, presumably for another top-up. The woman sighs, resting her head against the tall wooden ladle for a moment. I hesitate to approach when she seems so tired, but she also appears to be the one giving the orders, while the other girl is younger.

"Good morrow," I say, and the woman jumps, turning toward me. The girl, around my age, continues her steady stirring, though she eyes me curiously.

"I am Maven, maid to Lady Cassandra," I say. "Lady Rhoswen suggested you might have some, er, laundry tips for me."

I suppress a smirk at my words, conjuring up a vision of the majestic Lady Rhoswen discussing laundry tips.

The woman merely nods. "Of course. I am Ana," she says, wiping her hands on her apron, before turning to the girl. "Ida, I won't be a minute. These can soak until I return."

Ida continues her methodical stirring without looking up, as Ana joins me near the door.

"Welcome," she says, taking both of my hands in her slightly damp ones. As I clasp them, I realize how red and chapped they are, the skin rough beneath my fingers.

"I heard you had shown the symbol," Ana whispers, shifting the neckline of her gray tunic to one side to show a cotton shift beneath, an embroidered beech tree with its tiny robin picked out in white cotton near the shoulder. I smile, thinking that the Beech Circle must be entrenched across many levels of this castle if someone had seen the symbol painted on the side of

Cassandra's trunks. All at once, I do not feel as isolated in this strange, wild place.

Out loud, Ana says, "Come, I will take you to the linen store and show you what I mean."

I follow her out into the hall and to the next door, where she removes a key on a leather thong around her neck to gain entry to a small, quiet, dark room where the stacks of linen in shelves on all four walls muffle any sound of the outside world.

"No one will disturb us, or hear us, here," says Ana. "But we must be quick."

"Is this where you meet?" I ask, taking in the fact that there is but one tiny window in this small room, and it is an internal one. It lets in light from the larger room next door but no fresh air, probably to protect the dry linen from the mist in the laundry.

Ana laughs a lovely, gurgling chortle. "No, we are too many for this space, a dozen at least, though it changes from season to season. There is a small mill nearby, owned by a farmer's widow, and we meet there."

As Ana speaks, I study her face, which, though pale – as expected from someone who works indoors – looks as though it would darken to a deep brown in the sun. She seems to be around thirty years of age, and her lively, intelligent eyes are a deep brown, fringed by the darkest, thickest lashes I've ever seen. I can see only the very front of her hair under the big white headscarf, but it looks like it would also be dark and thick — perhaps even more so than Cassandra's. Her accent is Glawn, but there is a musical note beneath the harsh vowels, suggesting a childhood spent far away.

"The Circle is strong here?" I ask. A dozen members suggests so, but I know that while many hands can make light work, many voices can muddy waters, ensuring nothing is done.

"We have had some success," Ana says with a triumphant grin.

I have to ask. "The cook is not one of them? She has not made the choice to disappear?"

I suspect not, particularly with Lady Rhoswen's words in mind, but I have to be sure before I tread hard across the work of the Beech Circle.

Ana's smile fades. "She is not. We have been trying to find out when she went but no one saw. It is as though she disappeared in a puff of flour."

"You have no members in the kitchen?"

Ana winces. "Not one. I do have high hopes for the child, Sally, but they are all terrified of the assistant cook, Mistress Gyles."

"Most unfortunate," I say. "What about upstairs?"

Ana shakes her head again. "There is a real divide here between those who serve and those who do not — even the Beech Circle has been unable to breach that chasm."

I nod, unsurprised by the information. Lady Rhoswen would not have directed Cassandra to the laundry if there had been allies above stairs.

"Well, you have two there now," I say, touching Ana's shoulder. "We are here only a few days, but allow us the opportunity to assist if we may."

Ana's dark eyes narrow thoughtfully. "I will keep it in mind," she says. "We have a meeting in two nights' time and a few projects underway. There may be something you can do."

I allow a beat to pass as we both think of past Beech Circle projects we have each been involved with. Girls who disappear into thin air days before a marriage arranged to benefit everyone but them. Women who are taught to read and calculate so they may secretly assess the accounts abandoned by their husbands to corrupt estate managers. Older sisters who must find new homes when their younger brother inherits the family fortune.

"And what of you, Ana?" I ask. "Is the Circle helping you?"

It might seem odd to ask this of a complete stranger, but one thing I love about the Beech Circle is the way it allows us to cut to the quick of a matter. You say what you mean, you mean what you say. The complete opposite of most facets of life in Cartreff.

Ana's face falls. "Not yet," she whispers. "One day, but not yet."

I ask no more. If membership of the Beech Circle entitles me to forthright questions, it also entitles Ana to keep her counsel. If she wants to tell me more of her story, she will.

"Soon, then," I say. "For now, I will keep my ears open upstairs for news of Mistress Percy."

Ana is nodding. "And I will keep you apprised of anything I hear. Perhaps you will join our meeting at the mill?"

"I would like that. For one thing, I really want to see what those windmills do and how they work."

"Oh, I can tell you that," Ana says. "They're a surprisingly simple solution to the problem of all the water in the land around here. They act as a pump, pulling the water from the land and pushing it away into channels, leaving dry soil behind for farming."

Ana pauses, watching my face to gauge my interest and see if I'm following.

"So, the sails of the windmill drive a pump?" I ask.

Ana beams at my question, and I feel like a student who has pleased her teacher. "Indeed," she says. "I can take you out to one and show you if you like – there is a large one a short ride from here – but for now I must go back to my work. If I don't keep on top of it, the laundry pile at Glawn Castle multiplies like flies on a pat of butter in summer."

We exit the linen store and turn in opposite

directions in the hallway. It is not until I am at the top of the stairs that I realize two things: the first is that I've all but forgotten the parchment in my pocket, and I feel a surge of excitement at the thought.

The second is that I've left the posset on the shelves in the laundry . . . but that is probably for the best.

CHAPTER SIX

Reeve gave the boot he was holding one last wipe with the now-dirty cloth before placing it on the floor beside its mate, content that Sir Garrick would find his footwear shined to perfection. A fresh tunic was laid out on the bed, and the cozy bedchamber, decorated in the ever-present shades of gray, was spick-and-span, just as Sir Garrick liked it.

The Knight Protector's meeting with Sir Brannon at the mill had been swift, for which Reeve had been grateful, and the ride back to the castle in the fading light conducted in silence. With no opportunity to ask Sir Garrick what had been discussed, Reeve could only deduct that Sir Brannon and, by association, Airl Riding had proved open to Airl Buckthorn's petition – otherwise Reeve would right now be packing Sir Garrick's belongings for an even swifter exit from Glawn Castle.

In fact, on their return to the castle, both men had been drawn into the gathering of ladies, and Reeve had almost sighed out loud with relief when Sir Garrick had sent him to set the bedchamber to rights and prepare for the feast later that night.

Sitting on the thick, soft rug that covered the floor, leaning against the plump, high bed stacked with feather pillows, Reeve considered the dirty cloth in his hand, wondering if he should take it down to the laundry with Sir Garrick's traveling clothes. Deciding he could use the other side of the cloth the next day and save the laundress some work, Reeve opted to fold it back into the drawstring pouch in which he kept such odds and ends.

He was tying off the drawstring when a soft knock came at the door and Reeve jumped up to open it, thinking it would be Maven coming to swap stories of what they'd learned over the course of the afternoon.

He couldn't contain the startled "oh" that escaped when he saw who was on the other side.

"Expecting someone?" Lady Anice's amused tone didn't quite reach her green eyes. She was wearing a pale-blue dress and had clearly come straight from the gathering downstairs.

"Er, no," Reeve said. "I am only surprised that my lady is not with her cousin in the Small Hall."

Lady Anice rolled her eyes. "One can only drink so much watered-down ale and have so many conversations centered on the weather. Surely, even a squire would understand that. Besides, it is no longer afternoon and I needed a break before the feast."

She made to stroll past him into the chamber, but Reeve blocked her path. "Are you looking for Sir Garrick?" he asked. "Let me take you to him."

Lady Anice twirled one copper curl as she studied him. "It is not Sir Garrick I am here to see. I have some questions for you."

Stomach sinking, Reeve managed to keep his expression polite while his mind churned. Whatever Lady Anice wanted from him, it would mean trouble for someone. If Sir Garrick returned and found her here, in a bedchamber with Reeve, then the person in trouble most certainly would be Reeve.

Squires did not converse with airls' daughters alone if they wished to retain their position in a household.

"I am at my lady's command," Reeve said, with absolute honesty and a polite bow. "Why do we not walk a little as we talk?"

Lady Anice's smirk told him that she knew exactly what he was doing as she settled against the door frame. "Have you a pressing task to perform?"

Reeve's chuckle sounded uneasy, even to him, and he realized his nervous fingers were teasing at the drawstring on the pouch in his hand. The pouch.

"As a matter of fact," he said, dangling it between them, "I was just about to take this down to the laundress. I must hurry if I want to be back before Sir Garrick returns. I can escort you . . . somewhere on my way."

As he spoke, Reeve took a step forward and Lady Anice stepped back into the hall instinctively, giving him enough room to grab the door and pull it shut behind him as he followed her through. With a smile, he extended an elbow at the correct height, and Anice had no choice but to lay her hand lightly upon it.

They walked a few steps in silence, Reeve looking straight ahead, still trying to work out Anice's motivation for seeking him out, before she spoke again, her petulance at being outmaneuvered clear.

"People say you are so charming, Reeve of Norwood, and yet I find you churlish."

Reeve kept his pace steady, slanting a sideways look at her set expression. "My lady, perhaps I am unable to form words in your presence."

Lady Anice paused. "Understandable, and yet I have known you since you were seven, when you came to Harding Manor. It is not as though my presence is not familiar to you."

"We are no longer children," Reeve said, steering her along the hall. "I am a squire, you are Airl Buckthorn's daughter. I can think of no good reason why I have been bestowed the gift of your attention at this time."

Reeve felt the slight hitch in her step at his words and winced, wondering if he'd been too honest.

"Is it not enough that you are one of only three people I know in this barren place?" Lady Anice asked, her voice tight.

Though Reeve did not miss the "three," recognizing the slight to Maven, he settled for answering, "Perhaps."

They continued in silence until they reached an atrium where the hallways in this wing met, forming an intersection. Long, narrow windows set high into the stone afforded the space more light than in the hallways, but Reeve noted that the sun had almost set. Sir Garrick would soon return to dress for the feast, and Reeve needed to encourage Lady Anice to go to her quarters to do the same.

"Well, this is where we must part," he said, clearing his throat, preparing to take his leave and undertake his fake errand. "Thank you for the, er, chat, my —"

To Reeve's surprise, however, Lady Anice did not let him continue, turning to him suddenly with a high, girlish giggle, quite as though Reeve had just told the most humorous joke ever.

"You are very naughty," Lady Anice trilled, tapping

him on the shoulder for emphasis as she smiled up at him.

Confused, Reeve reverted to his training. "Why, my good lady, how could you say such a thing when it is you who drags a poor, lowly squire from his duties?" he parried, trying to infuse a teasing tone into his voice.

"Ah, how could I drag a squire who is so good on his feet? And yet now you will not even look at me?" Lady Anice continued, stopping in the center of the atrium, grabbing his elbow again and forcing Reeve to stop beside her. "Do you only flatter me when you want something? Getting out of the wind, perhaps . . ."

Looking down into her face, Reeve realized two things – first, he had not been as clever as he'd thought when he'd talked the Lady Anice back into the carriage on the road to Glawn, and, second, her voice might be light and charming but her green eyes were hard and glittery in the half shadows as she seemed to look past him.

"My lady," Reeve began, his mind churning with possible responses.

"Oh, never mind," she hissed. "You may kiss my hand to make up for your gauche behavior."

Reeve winced as her dainty hand shot up, almost hitting his nose. He had no idea what was going on, but he also knew he had no choice but to comply.

"Enchanted, my lady," he murmured. "Your forgiving

nature is but another jewel in your crown."

Brushing his lips across the back of her outstretched hand, Reeve caught a faint whiff of lavender before Anice snatched her fingers back with a triumphant smile.

"You overstep," she said, turning on her heel and striding away down the hallway toward her bedchamber. "That will be all."

Reeve was left flabbergasted in her wake. "But, I —"

Lady Anice did not look back.

Glancing around him, Reeve was glad to see the hallways were empty and that no one had witnessed the scene. Toying with the pouch in his hand, he realized he no longer needed to continue to the laundry.

Relieved, Reeve headed back to Sir Garrick's bedchamber to await the knight. With any luck, he might have a few moments to himself before Sir Garrick arrived to try to figure out what Lady Anice was all about.

Then again, that was not the work of a few moments.

Even after a long night spent tossing and turning, I cannot decide if I am disappointed, disillusioned or plain furious. I had thought better of Reeve of Norwood, going so far as to offer him a portion of my tiny reserves of trust, but watching him flirt so enthusiastically with Lady Anice in the hall last night makes me wonder if I am losing my judgment.

Now, hours after Reeve kissed Lady Anice's hand while I cringed in the shadows so he did not see me, I am still berating myself for not just walking up and saying hello to them both. But I know now, as I knew then, that I was not prepared to deal with Anice's triumph directly.

I know that she saw me there, even if Reeve did not. It seems that my instincts were right and she has, in her insidious way, noted the friendship between Reeve and I and taken it upon herself to insert herself in it.

I know what she is doing, and I can't understand why Reeve does not see it. Reeve, who can walk into any room at Rennart Castle and take its temperature in a moment. Reeve, who speaks as easily to the blacksmith and the kitchen maid as he does to Sir Garrick and the myriad lords who swirl around him, changing his language and even his stance to suit the conversation.

Reeve does not recognize what he does, I think. It is just part of who he is, a social chameleon who can make himself fit where he must. He has told me little about his earliest days as a page at Harding Manor, but the careful blankness of his expression when he does so gives me some insight into just how difficult it must have been to be sent from home at the age of seven to make his own way among strangers.

All the more reason, then, that Reeve should not fall for Anice's simpering and giggles.

Then again, Reeve still cannot understand why Anice is so hostile toward me for saving her from Brantley's plan.

No, Reeve may be adroit in the world of men but he has much to learn about the rules that govern my world.

He is not alone there.

What I cannot decide, even now, as I stalk down the cold, gray stairs with the faintest glimmer of dawn seeping through the high windows of Glawn Castle, is the outcome for Anice.

She must know that she compromises Reeve's position as squire to Sir Garrick if Reeve is seen to be courting her in any way. Is Anice looking to hurt me by having him sent away? Or is she so bored after less than a day here in the wilds of Glawn that she must entertain herself with mischief?

If that's the case, I for one am glad of our Anice-imposed three-day deadline. Imagine how much trouble she could wreak in a week.

Speaking of trouble . . . I finger the parchment in my pocket, the one that I found under the bowl in the kitchen, the one that I was rushing to discuss with Reeve when I came across him with Anice in the hall last night.

The one that I pushed back into my pocket instead, because I was so incensed by seeing the pair of them that I went straight to Cassandra's rooms and stayed there all night, feigning an aching head when she tried to entice me to join the welcome feast.

It was petty of me, I know, but sometimes I tire of putting a good face on things. Had Reeve seen me, he would have wanted to tell me all about his adventures to the windmill. Adventures that I was barred from because I do not wear breeches.

My face burns even now as I add this indignation to a long list, and I find that my feet are taking me toward the door to the courtyard and the stables beyond, almost without thought.

I stop under a corbel in the shape of a dragon's head. Carved high into the wall above me, the dragon appears to hold up one side of the stone archway, its fierce expression mirroring my inner turmoil. There are many dragons in the architecture here at Glawn Castle — leering out over the courtyard in the form of waterspouts; creeping above archways and window frames. It makes me wonder about the original Airl of Glawn and his feelings about the wildness of this landscape.

I touch the stone wall behind me, using the feel of the cold, hard rock beneath my fingers to ground me. In the years since my father's fall from grace and the disintegration of my family, I have learned to lock away feelings. It is hard to think straight when you're consumed by emotion, and my ability to think is the one defensive weapon I have – albeit a secret one.

Looking around to ensure I am alone, I pull the parchment from my pocket, examining it in the dim light. It is thick and smooth to touch, a sure sign of quality, but the words at the top of the slip read *Pease Pottage*. Beneath the title, which is written in a firm hand in black ink, is a list of numbers, the last of which seems to be only partial due to the positioning of the tear.

No matter how many times I have racked my brains since my first glance at the parchment, I have been unable to work out what it means. I have met many cooks over the past few years, and I know of none who can read, let alone keep a written record of their recipes.

Women in Cartreff don't keep books, and they certainly don't write them. Recipes are memorized, practiced, passed down from one to another and guarded fiercely.

Why then was this under the bowl of a cook in one of the most far-flung fiefs in the kingdom? Particularly written on parchment of this quality.

If Mistress Percy was a member of the Beech Circle, that might at least suggest that she could read and write, but Ana indicated that none of the kitchen staff have joined our ranks.

The door to the courtyard opens and I shove the parchment back into my pocket as two men push in, wearing the dark-gray cloaks of the Airl's guard.

"The wind cuts through me like a sword through faulty armor," one man grunts.

"Oh, come, now, you can do better than that," the other says, punching his arm. "Try this: it lashes my skin like I've rolled in a pile of hedgehogs."

"That makes no sense, Simeon — hedgehogs don't make piles."

"It doesn't have to make sense, it just has to —"

They see me standing near the door, and stop.

"Are you going outside, girl?" the shorter man asks me.

His question decides me. "Yes, I am," I say. "My mistress requires me to check on our horses in the stable."

The tall man chuckles. "You going to wake them up early, then, are you?"

I manage a smile. "Something like that."

The shorter man looks me up and down, appearing unimpressed with my plain brown gown and boots.

"You'll need something warmer than that out there," he says, and to my surprise unclasps the cloak from his neck before swirling it to land across my shoulders.

"The wind is more biting than a wolf's pup."

The other man slaps him on the back. "Good one, Simeon!" he says. "It's got more teeth than an asp!"

Simeon grimaces. "Asps only have two fangs, Aldwin," he says. "Anything's got more teeth than that."

Aldwin's face falls. "You're right," he grumbles good-naturedly. "You win."

I take the opportunity to interject. "Thank you for your cloak, kind sir. I will return it forthwith."

"No need to do that," Simeon says, turning back toward the entrance. "See that little door on the right there?"

Now that he points it out, I see a thin wood panel set to one side of the hall, so I nod.

"Find an empty peg in there and leave it on that. That's where we keep them. Hang yours now, Aldwin, and show her."

Aldwin obliges and, as he does, I see that the skinny door opens into a small chamber that spreads sideways along the wall. Like a hall behind the hall, set into the thick stone walls. I can see a few pegs, all with cloaks on them, through the opening, but Aldwin steps inside, disappearing for a moment or two before coming back empty-handed, having hung his up.

"I'll do that," I say, fastening the clasp at my neck and moving toward the courtyard door. "Thank you again."

As I step outside, I look up at the many silent windows that surround the courtyard – the two long wings that make up the bulk of the castle's layout create solid bulwarks against the wind along either side, but there would be little that could happen in this space that remained unseen. Someone would always be watching.

Reminding myself of this, I snuggle into my gray cloak and focus on the cold cobbles beneath my feet, keeping my face from any watchers above. Before the door bangs shut behind me, I can hear the fading voices of Aldwin and Simeon still trying to invent new descriptions for the wind, and I come up with a few of my own as the chill fingers of air blow around me.

Even here in the shelter of these two vast castle wings, the wind slips through.

I move toward the stables, positioned in the open space beyond the end of the two wings, along with the smithy's forge, the buttery and various other squat, shuttered stone buildings that contain the working heart of Glawn Castle. Passing a narrow stone staircase that leads down below courtyard level to a dark wooden door, I can hear the banging of pots and realize that this must be the outside entrance to the kitchen.

I wish the cloak had a cowl that I could pull up to cover my ears, which feel vulnerable in the dawn air, despite the long brown hair whipping around my face. I pause, wondering what I am doing out here in the elements, but I cannot suppress my drive to get out of the castle. To be on my own, even for a short while. To think through all I have seen and heard before another very long, trying day begins.

Cassandra will not wake for hours, so I continue to the stables. It takes a few moments to convince an indifferent stable hand that I need a horse to run an errand for my mistress. He knows that I am not a Glawn resident and seems not to care if I wander off to my death on the moors.

He does, however, care about the horse.

"Give him his head and he'll set you on the right path," he says, chewing a piece of straw as he tightens the girth around the horse's sleek, gray middle. "And watch out for the hares — they spring out of nowhere and they'll give Rouncey a fright. If you fall off, let him go home – he knows the way and it'll let me know that something's happened to you."

"Er, thanks," I say, allowing him to boost me into the sidesaddle he has fitted, before I am struck by a thought. "Is that why they were searching the moors for the cook last night? Did a horse come back without her?"

The stable hand looks at me for a brief moment, turning the straw around in his cheek. "Nope," he says, finally. "No horse. If she'd been on a horse, we'd have her by now because the horse would have taken us back to her. They're all trained for it, just like this one will take me back to you if you fall off. No, they're looking for Cook out there because she's not in here. If you're not inside these castle walls, there are few places to be in Glawn. A few of the mills are habitable, but most aren't."

There is a pause while he adjusts my stirrup so that I am perfectly balanced.

"Where exactly are you planning to go again?" he asks.

"I, well, my lady loves the fresh scent of meadowsweet, and I thought to please her by placing some in her room before she wakes," I improvise, hoping that meadowsweet, which grows like a weed across the fiefs of Cartreff, has also gained a foothold here.

"Good luck with that," the stable hand says, a cheeky grin spreading across his broad face.

"Oh," I say, allowing my face to fall. "Is there no meadowsweet here?"

He chuckles. "No, you'll find it, all right. I meant good luck with pleasing your mistress – I hear she's a bit of a handful, your lady."

I do not deign to respond, merely looking down at him from high and, chastened, he mumbles and scurries away, aware that he has overstepped. I may be only a maidservant, but as a visitor I am an unknown quantity to him, and he should know better.

It tells me more about the running of Glawn Castle than any welcome feast ever would. Sir Garrick will need to tread carefully here.

"Good sir," I call out, and he cannot ignore me, but his face as he turns back is mutinous. "Where grows the nearest meadowsweet?"

"Over by the big windmill," he says, waving toward the gates. "Onto the road, then left. It won't take Rouncey long to get there if you leave him to it."

"Very well, I will. Thank you."

Without awaiting his response, I click my tongue and Rouncey heads toward the gates, the wind rippling through his mane though our pace is slow.

Once on the road, I can see the dawn gathering on the horizon, and cannot stop the smile creeping across my face. The mix of open space, bracing air and freedom of solitude feels like a tonic.

Looking behind me, I begin to understand the layout of Glawn Castle, realizing that the openness of the land around it would make a surprise attack very difficult – anyone approaching would be seen from miles away. The smaller face it presents on this road makes it look a less inviting target, while the surrounding wings and tall stone walls that protect the courtyards at its heart give scale to the inhabitants.

It would be very easy to feel insignificant on the

moors of Glawn. Thick walls and smaller spaces offer solidity in a place where there is little.

For now, though, it is the openness that calls to me.

"Go, Rouncey," I say to the horse, who dances on the spot, picking up on my mood. "Let's see what that windmill looks like close up."

I direct him left and then let the reins lie loose across his neck, allowing my thoughts to drift along to the rhythm of his stately walk.

The wildness of the land out here, a cacophony of green and gray foliage, the golden brown of clay and the deep, dark peat moss, spikes of flowers in yellow and white and fading pink, suits my mood. Even the wind cannot dampen my humor, though I do wish I'd worn thicker hose beneath my dress. At least my full skirt has enough fabric in it to ensure that it does not ride up to expose my legs to the elements, and the borrowed cloak is generous and warm.

I could only be happier if I were riding astride, but I am content to manage within my restrictions. The good people of Glawn have enough to talk about without adding that to their roster of gossip.

The landscape, which looks flat from the castle windows, and even from the inside of a carriage, hides dips and depressions that surprise me, but not as much as the mist does. It rises up without warning once we have left the road, disappearing in the next hoofbeat, before building again. Looking down, I can see Rouncey picking a careful path in the bog, and I begin to wonder if I should turn back.

My head is clear now – is there any sense in getting lost?

Even as I have the thought, I realize that we have crossed a rise of some kind and the windmill lies before me, surrounded by the promised meadowsweet, the sky a wash of pale pink and orange behind it.

The windmill towers above me and I bring Rouncey to a halt a short distance from the dark-wood structure so that I might observe it. The huge white sails clatter around, pushed at pace by the wind, but the body of the mill is sound, impervious to the force of the sails. Even above the wind, I can hear the sound of water gushing, and I slide from Rouncey's back so that I can make my way through the sea of flowers around to the other side of the mill.

Taking care to stay well clear of the rushing sails, I walk to the edge of a channel that has been carved through the boggy landscape. Water runs into it, streaming from the bank in front of the mill.

Amazed, I watch the water appear from nowhere and then disappear into the green water of the channel, which is about as wide as three men standing on each other's shoulders. The land beneath my feet here is more solid than that on which Rouncey had been picking a path only a few minutes ago.

I bend down to touch the dark soil under my feet, finding it moist but arable, and I realize the mill is draining the water from the very soil, just as Ana had said.

Curious, I turn and make my way back to the other side of the mill, away from those dangerous, scything sails, where I find a door. Inside, it is dark and, as I pull the door closed behind me, the respite from the wind feels almost physical, so used to its constant battering had I become.

A huge shaft turns slowly in the center of the hay-bale-lined space. A ladder in one corner beckons me and I scamper up it, taking a moment to enjoy the space beneath my feet.

Upstairs, I take in a small room, but am drawn to a narrow window, which overlooks the path I have just taken. I can see Rouncey outside, enjoying a feast of the lush, green moss that seems to pop up all over the landscape, and watch the wind make patterns in the tall gray-green grasses. I realize the sun is now above the horizon.

My head is clear now and I should return to my duties.

I am turning from the window when a hare darts from the undergrowth near Rouncey and he stiffens, then rears up before bolting back toward the castle.

"No, no, no, no!" I am talking out loud, even though the horse cannot hear me, and I whirl around and run toward the ladder in a feeble attempt to – what? Even if I clamber down the ladder as fast as I can there is no way I can catch the horse now.

I can only hope the stable hand will be good to his word and will come looking for me when the riderless horse appears.

In the meantime, I will gather my meadowsweet and begin the long walk –

The sound of beating hooves interrupts my planning and I rush back to the window. One glance shows me that this is not Rouncey seeing the error of his ways and returning to retrieve me. Neither is it the stable hand coming to my rescue.

Instead, riding toward the mill from the opposite direction to which Rouncey bolted are five riders wearing the gray cloak and wide-brimmed hat of Airl Riding's guardsmen.

Is this a group out looking for the cook?

But no, these men are moving with purpose, not searching. And they are all but invisible in their gray cloaks.

My mouth dry, I decide to hide. These guards do not seem friendly and I do not want them to know I am here.

I send up a silent thank you to the hare that chose

that particular moment to send my horse home.

A proper look around the room reveals another narrow ladder in the corner leading to a square opening, high in the ceiling. As I tiptoe toward it and begin to climb, I hear the door on the ground floor open and the low muttering of men before boots sound on the hard-packed earth.

Breathing out to calm the rising clamor of my nerves, I concentrate on putting first one hand, then one foot, then the other on each rung of the ladder until, finally, I am able to slither up into the small opening and roll to one side just as I hear the first man's voice: "All clear."

My heart beats fast as I look up. The space here is smaller than below, and mostly taken up with a huge wooden wheel that spins around the center pole that rises from the ground floor. The wheel spins at what would be my waist height if I were standing, driven by the sails in the wind outside.

I lie still, breathing hard. The clatter and rattle of the sails is even louder in here, and I can just make out murmuring below me as chairs scrape across the floor.

I realize that to hear what is happening I will need to hang my head out over the opening a little – praying that nobody looks up.

I tuck my hair inside the neckline of my cloak, so that it does not fall in my face and obscure my view – or, worse, attract attention. Then I ease back onto my stomach and push myself forward so that my eyes, and ears, are over the opening.

I can't see the whole room, but four men are visible, faces obscured by the broad brims of their hats. All are listening to the fifth man, the one I cannot see, who is telling them off.

". . . don't care what you thought, you thought wrong. I am surrounded by harebrained jesters."

The men below me shift their feet, but only one is brave enough to speak, his response low and angry.

The fifth man strides over and grabs him by the cloak, hissing in his face.

"You are not paid to think. You are paid to do what you're told. And you were told to keep an eye on the cook. If you were doing that she would be in that kitchen right now, stirring up some form of flummery for the feast. Instead, she has disappeared. And with her —" He breaks off. "Did you search her quarters?"

The hats bob up and down as the men nod.

"There was nothing," says the same brave man who'd responded earlier. "Because there's *nothing* to find. She's a cook. Nothing more. And this is a waste of time."

The fifth man stills, and I am reminded of a big dog I once saw that seemed to gather itself into complete vigilance right before it attacked a rat. Still, it is all

I can do not to cry out when he steps forward and cuffs the outspoken man across the face. Blood drips on the floor.

"You go too far," is all the bleeding man says, but the other men step away from him as though he is contagious.

"Anyone else?" The leader stalks back to the table and uses the cloth laid upon it to wipe his knuckles. When no one answers, he drops into the nearby chair and puts his feet up on the table.

"Go then. We have only a few days, and I want that cook."

The other men shuffle toward the ladder, disappearing down it one by one while the leader sits in silence. I hardly dare breathe lest he hear me and look up. All I can do is hope that he follows the other men before the stable hand comes looking for me.

The other men have reached the door below, and I hear it slam shut, then the pounding of hooves as they ride away. I decide to try inching my way back from my position over the opening, hoping the sounds of departure will cover any noise I might make. Lying flat on my back beside the ladder, I catch my breath, trying to get more comfortable. Surely, he will leave soon?

But no. Instead, I am startled to hear the drumbeat of a horse's hooves approaching once more, and this time I nearly gasp aloud. If the stable hand comes looking for me here, it will be only moments before I am discovered.

I hold my breath as the horse stops outside the mill, noting as I do that even the wind appears to have dropped and, with it, the creak and wail of the sails. I hear a chair scrape in the room below as the door on the ground floor bangs shut again. The tread up the ladder is heavy, and I frown. The stable boy was not that big.

I roll back onto my side, trying to see down into the room without having to put myself out into the open, but I can see only one empty corner. Voices rumble, and I realize that the newcomer is another man, this time with a voice so deep that I am struggling to hear his words even without the howling wind.

". . . they say none of them know." The snatch of speech is from the fifth man, and the newcomer's response is snappish.

"I have sent them to find out. They know what's at stake."

The newcomer slams his fist on the table as he rumbles something in response, and I hear the fifth man's boots on the floor as he takes a step back.

"I'll check with Hugh."

Those are the last words spoken, and I listen in silence as the two men make their way down the ladder, out through the door and then ride away. Part of me is aware that I am lying on the second floor of a windmill in an unfamiliar landscape, miles from the castle with no means of transportation.

But the other part of me, most of me, if I am honest, is quietly gleeful. Something is amiss in Airl Riding's wild fief, and I have proof to take to Reeve (and therefore to Sir Garrick) of this fact.

Better than that, I have something to occupy my mind. Something that will take me beyond castle politics and Lady Anice and my current situation.

Something useful.

And, I have a name.

All I need now is to find a path back to the castle.

CHAPTER SEVEN

"It won't be much help," Reeve said, hating to watch the light dim in Maven's eyes when she'd been so excited about connecting a name with the strange gathering at the mill. "I spent time with them yesterday, remember. Hugh is about the most popular name in Glawn. There are three Hughs in the guard alone and they only use first names."

"What are you talking about?" Maven flopped onto the red, velvet-covered sofa beneath the window, looking at him as though he'd lost his mind.

Early morning sunlight streamed in, lighting up her brown hair with streaks of gold, as Maven ate the last bite of the hunk of bread in her hand.

Reeve had been surprised to find her waiting outside

Sir Garrick's rooms that morning when Reeve had crept out to get warm water for his master's morning wash. She'd had a pear in one hand, the hunk of bread in the other, and seemed to have been up for quite some time.

Now, Reeve filled her in on what Stanley had told him about the strange customs of Airl Riding's guards.

Maven frowned, smoothing down her brown skirts. "So they use first names, they interchange cloaks and hats and even horses . . . why would the Airl go to such lengths to cause confusion?"

"I think it's a loyalty and subservience thing," Reeve pondered, moving to sit beside her. "If a man has no family name and nothing of his own, he is only identifiable by his association to the Airl, right?"

Maven looked at him as though he'd grown a second head. "I think you might be right."

"You're not the only one who has ideas, you know," Reeve said, stung by the surprise in her voice.

When she laughed, Reeve realized it was the first genuine smile he'd seen from Maven in days.

"What were you doing out there, anyway?" Reeve asked. "I looked for you at the feast last night, but Lady Cassandra told Sir Garrick that you were resting in your rooms."

"I was unwell," she said, turning away, but not before Reeve saw her face drop. "I went for a ride this morning to clear my head."

"You were out on the moor alone?" Reeve spluttered.

"More than just the cook have disappeared out there, Maven. The guards told me how dangerous it is."

"The stable hand told me that the horse would find its way home," she responded, not meeting his eyes. "Anyway, if I had not been there, we would never have known about this plot."

Reeve got to his feet, needing to pace. "Are you sure it's a plot? I still can't see any reason why Airl Riding's guardsmen should be so worried about a cook."

"I think it's to do with this," Maven said, digging deep into her skirt and pulling out a small piece of parchment. Reeve studied it before handing it back.

"It looks like gobbledygook to me. A recipe? Perhaps the numbers are measurements?"

Slipping the parchment back into her pocket, Maven bit her lip. "I don't think so," she said. "I don't think the cook can read, for one thing."

Thinking about what he knew about Maven and the Beech Circle, Reeve frowned. "How can you be so sure about that? She may have, er, hidden skills."

But Maven shook her head. "Not this time," she said, and Reeve asked no further questions. His knowledge of the Beech Circle was limited and, while he had questions – many, many questions – he'd resisted following them up since the mystery of the Fire Star had been resolved. For one thing, he wasn't sure that Maven would answer them. But, mostly, he knew that the less he knew the better – for Maven, for her friends and for himself.

If the existence of a secret society of girls and women was ever to be discovered, the reality was that the consequences would be dire for anyone involved – and anyone who even suspected that existence and had not reported it.

Reeve was feeling more secure in his position with Sir Garrick after his role in recovering the Fire Star, but he was also a very new member of the Knight Protector's household. If Sir Garrick ever discovered that Reeve had known about the Beech, Reeve would be, at very best, sent home to his family in disgrace, and then most likely banished to sea to ensure he was no drain on Larien, his older brother and heir to the Barony.

And that was without Sir Garrick ever discovering Reeve's own secret.

"Are you okay?" Maven touched his shoulder, and Reeve realized he'd disappeared deep into his own thoughts and had reflexively clutched the tincture bottle on the chain around his neck.

The tincture that Myra, a wyld woman in the woods outside Rennart Castle, had promised would help him overcome his habit of fainting at the sight of blood.

A terrible habit, indeed, for a would-be knight.

"At the slightest hint of light-headedness, you must

unstopper the bottle and breathe deep," Myra had told him. "Keep it close and you'll be fine."

So far, he'd had no need to test the efficacy of her potion — and Reeve hoped it would be a long time before he did.

Now, he brought out a bright smile for Maven, knowing it was always the best defense against probing questions. "I'm fine," he said, and she nodded, looking unconvinced. Maven, he remembered, never seemed to need to ask probing questions. She had an unnerving habit of appearing to see right through him.

"I think we should at least tell Sir Garrick about that meeting this morning," Maven said, and Reeve was glad she'd shifted focus back to the problem at hand. "If nothing else, it shows that all is not as it seems here at Glawn, and I think that's information that he would need, given the delicacy of his negotiations."

"I will let him know," Reeve agreed.

"You should also show him this," Maven continued, withdrawing the parchment again and handing it to Reeve. "Without telling him that I came across the parchment or the meeting."

"How am I supposed to do that?"

"Oh, come now, Reeve of Norwood, I heard you were good on your feet," Maven said, patting him on the arm before striding away.

With a frown, Reeve watched her until she turned

the corner toward Lady Cassandra's rooms, which were next to Sir Garrick's.

Reeve walked the other way, the jug dangling from one finger as he headed down toward the kitchens. Had Maven truly stumbled across a plot within Airl Riding's guards? And if she had, what did that mean for Sir Garrick's mission?

The previous evening, as he'd readied for the feast, Sir Garrick had confided that his parley with Sir Brannon had gone well, with the Glawn Castle's Knight Protector indicating that Airl Riding would be open to signing Airl Buckthorn's petition. If Airl Buckthorn could gain a majority of airls on his petition, surely King Bren would take heed of the concerns of the leading families of Cartreff?

But Reeve knew that not all of the airls agreed with Airl Buckthorn's approach. Airl Broadfield, for instance, had expressed vehement opposition only the week before and was no doubt rallying his own faction together after his visit to Rennart Castle.

Finding out which side of the fence each fief might come down on was the true purpose of Sir Garrick's diplomatic mission, under the guise of a tour of Cartreff with his lovely new bride. There was safety in numbers when it came to petitioning the King, and, so far, it looked as though Glawn would be with them.

But perhaps Sir Brannon did not speak for the whole

of Airl Riding's guard? And if not, Airl Riding might find himself in a very precarious position in his own castle should any hint of his displeasure with King Bren seep out.

And then there was the question of the missing cook.

Had she simply wandered off mid-treacle tart or, as Maven seemed to think, was she part of a larger plot of some kind?

Shaking his head to clear the whirl of questions, Reeve realized he still had an empty jug in his hand and needed to get hot water for Sir Garrick. More importantly, he needed to figure out how to let Sir Garrick know what Maven had discovered without mentioning Maven . . .

"And then, while he was getting water for Sir Garrick, Reeve found a piece of parchment that had slipped into a crack in the kitchen floor, would you believe? He thought it might be related to the cook's disappearance and perhaps to a meeting that he overheard behind the stables last night."

I almost roll my eyes at the last, imagining those six men from this morning's meeting skulking behind the stables after dark while Reeve apparently listens in, but Cassandra is watching me closely — too closely — as she speaks, so I focus on the task of brushing the mud from the bottom of her fine-wool traveling gown with a stiff brush and say nothing. I know Reeve has made up this story, with him at the center of it, at my request, but I cannot help wishing that things were different.

"Maven, where were you this morning? You came in after I awoke."

I keep up the steady rhythm of brushing as I answer Cassandra.

"I went to see the laundress." This is not altogether a lie – I had revisited Ana once I'd returned from my excursion to the windmill.

The return journey had been unsettling. The castle itself was easy enough to find, given its prominence in the landscape, but without the sure-footed horse beneath me, getting to it had proved more difficult than I'd expected. Ground that looked solid gave way without warning, and my boots and the bottom of my skirt had been soaked by the time the stable hand had finally made his way out to find me.

It had given me a small insight into the fear and discomfort the cook might now be experiencing if she were wandering alone on the misty, windy moors. Even now, I cannot suppress a shudder at the idea of being lost out there in the dark.

That small insight was enough for me to want to make further enquiries about her and her movements, so I'd gone to see Ana. I'd also wanted to find out the directions for the Beech Circle's meeting place tonight.

I can feel Cassandra watching me as I brush.

"I see," she says, after a long pause. "And you were welcomed?"

Now I look up at her. "I was. The Circle is strong in Glawn, if not within the castle."

For, despite what the stable hand may have told me that morning, Glawn does not begin and end within the castle walls. The big mill I was in this morning is just one of many that are scattered across the moors, homes to farming families and men who do not like the company of others.

Cassandra looks relieved, and I know she is as glad of the suggestion of support here as I was.

"Well, anyway," Cassandra continues, leaning forward to smooth her deep-green hose before sliding her foot into a kid slipper of the exact color, "Garrick showed me the parchment, but I could not make head nor tail of it."

I place the brush on the floor beside my stool before standing with the gown. "You've told him you can read then?"

Cassandra laughs. "There didn't seem to be a lot of point in hiding it after he'd discovered I could play chess. But don't worry, I did not tell him where I learned."

Hanging the gown on the brass hook on the wall, I turn to face her. "You must be careful, my lady."

She will not meet my eye, focusing instead on putting on her other slipper. "I did not let him know the extent of my abilities," she says. "He thinks I can cipher a few letters, that is all. Besides, it is perfectly safe. Garrick will not betray me."

Cassandra lifts her eyes to mine, and I note how their deep green matches her gown – and how they shine. She has tumbled head over heels in love with Sir Garrick, the knight that only two weeks ago she'd railed against and swore she would never marry. Then, Cassandra had been willing to risk everything for freedom. Now, she ties herself more closely to Sir Garrick – and this confession underpins their ever-growing bond.

She is right. Sir Garrick will not betray her. Not when the bloom of love is fresh and he cannot believe his good fortune. But what of later? Then, the knowledge that his wife can read will be enough to sign her death warrant if he so wishes.

She knows this. I know she does. Like me, she has met Beech Circle members fleeing from husbands who are willing to use the secrets discovered through long years of marriage to free themselves of their wives permanently.

Still, Cassandra thinks this is the kind of thing that happens to "other people."

I, on the other hand, have a very different experience.

My own mother could not wait to disassociate herself from me once my father fell to ruin. Indeed, part of her blamed me for his downfall, arguing that guilt over teaching me to read, to write, to think for myself was what drove him to the gambling dens.

I cannot blame her for her feelings when I also blame myself.

I tell myself I should be grateful that she did not denounce me as a witch to the world.

"Maven?" Cassandra continues to eye me with curiosity, and I realize I am staring at her.

"Sorry, my lady," I say. "Catching fairy dust."

She smiles. "Fairy dust? I don't think I've ever heard you say that before."

I shrug. "Something my mother used to say, when I was very little and lost in thought."

Cassandra grabs my hand. "You are not much more than little now," she says. "It's so easy for me to forget that you are fifteen years old, Maven."

All of a sudden I feel weary. Sometimes *I* forget that I am fifteen.

"Fifteen is not so young," I say, managing a small smile. "I will be sixteen soon. Besides, remember Lady Ethelwyn? Promised in marriage at fourteen?"

"Rescued by the Beech Circle at thirteen and a half," Cassandra says, with an answering smile. "Among our finest work."

"I sometimes wonder how she fares in Talleben," I say, and yes, there is wistfulness in my tone. Had all gone to plan with the Fire Star I would have been able to visit Ethelwyn for myself.

"Last I heard she is well and happy in her placement," says Cassandra, standing and smoothing her skirt. "She will stay with the Sorbus for a few more years and then . . ."

"Then?" I ask, curious. I know that the Beech Circle assists members to a community in Talleben called the Sorbus, where women and girls choose to live without the influence of men. My focus has always been on that part – the getting away – but I know that Cassandra has asked many questions of other Beech Circle members about what happens next.

"Ethelwyn may choose to stay with the Sorbus forever or she may decide to take up employment, get married, or even return to Cartreff if that is what she wishes," Cassandra says. "That's the whole point of the Beech Circle, after all. Choices."

I murmur agreement, though I cannot conceive any reason why Ethelwyn would choose to return. Not when rumor suggests that her betrothed still seeks retribution from Ethelwyn's family for his "embarrassment."

"But now I have no choice but to appear in the hall for breakfast," Cassandra says. "You have broken your fast?"

I nod, having helped myself in the kitchens on my return from the windmill.

"Very well, I will promenade in the walled garden with Lady Adelina this morning, so once your tasks are complete here you are free to . . . look around."

"I will do that, my lady," I say, with a smirk and a curtsey.

"Just be careful, Maven," Cassandra responds, surprising me by walking not toward the door but to the large window. "Lady Adelina is most effusive in her admiration of the King's court, and I have not yet decided where her loyalties lie. It may be that she and the Airl are not the allies my uncle seeks. Or it may be that she is laying her praise a little too thick to be true."

I join her at the window, looking down through the crisscross pattern of lead that breaks the world into diamond shapes into the garden below.

The kitchen garden, I know after my exploration this morning, is situated within the great courtyard near the stables, away from the bedchambers of the Airl, his family and his guests. The walled garden we can see now is created between the outside wall of our wing and the huge, fortified, stone walls that enclose the castle.

The walled garden is Lady Adelina's private, sheltered outdoor space, a place in which she spends little time if her pale complexion, and that of the other ladies of Glawn, is anything to go by.

A wide path of soft green grass marks the border inside high walls of stone. Huge carved dragons sit atop the two corners that do not abut the walls of this building.

One glance at the plants that grow in the raised stone beds within the grassy border tells me that this is a garden for pleasure, not productivity: tall purple spikes of foxglove, fat roses in pale pink and orange, drifts of heather and, in the center, a tall shrub covered in blue flowers. It is a beautiful, cultivated sanctuary in this wild environment, and I wonder why Lady Adelina would not spend all her time there.

I can only think that the wildness of Glawn and the infernal wind have worn her down to the point where she rarely steps outdoors.

"You must be careful, too, my lady," I say, realizing that it would be easy to feel safe within the embrace of those thick walls, out of the wind, strolling in the sunshine. "Don't say anything that you would not want overheard."

While the main walls are tall and protective, there are quiet alcoves set into the outside of the drystone walls that provide the other two boundaries for the square garden – places where a listener could lurk, unseen unless someone happened to be looking out a window from above.

Cassandra frowns, turning from the window. "I'm

not sure that I'm going to be very useful to Garrick at all," she says. "I don't want to ask Lady Adelina too many questions about the King or her thoughts about the state of Cartreff for two reasons — one is that I'm afraid I'll say the wrong thing and get Garrick in trouble, and the second is that I'm not sure that Lady Adelina thinks about much beyond this castle. And why should she? They're so far away from everything here that very little of what the King does even affects them."

"The best thing you can do is just to listen," I say. "That's what Sir Garrick said we should do."

"I know," Cassandra says, with a pout, moving toward the door, "but I want to be able to do more than nod and murmur as we talk about the weather and she repeats to me what she's heard about the fashions of the court. You'll just have to do it for me."

As Cassandra picks up her Talleben gloves and steps through the door, skirts swirling behind her, I can't help but smile as I finish tidying the bedchamber and lay out her hairbrush and other essentials so that I am prepared to tidy her up for the late luncheon planned for today.

At last, I am ready to leave. After a quick glance in the mirror to make sure I don't have dust on my nose, I twist my hair back into a coil at my neck, Glawn style.

It's time to look around.

CHAPTER EIGHT

There was no sign of Maven at breakfast, so Reeve was unable to confirm with her that he had, to all intents and purposes, stolen the credit for her parchment discovery.

Trying to concentrate on serving Sir Garrick and Lady Cassandra at table, Reeve looked for Maven at the back of the hall, but it seemed she was content with the bread and pear he'd seen her with earlier.

Finally, Lady Cassandra and Lady Adelina pushed back their chairs, announcing their intention to visit the castle gardens, leaving only Sir Garrick and Airl Riding sitting at the high table. Reeve moved to stand closer to Sir Garrick, hoping to overhear a quiet discussion about the Airl's loyalties. But the men stuck to desultory chatter about the wind and horse care, and Reeve's attention wandered back to the half-full hall.

After his glimpse of the Small Hall yesterday, Reeve had expected the Great Hall to be, well, greater. In fact, it was not much larger than the hall at Rennart Castle, though its walls were heavily adorned with huge and costly tapestries, similar to some he'd seen in the smaller hall. When Lady Cassandra had admired them earlier, Lady Adelina had pointed out that they served the dual purpose of decoration and keeping out the ever-present drafts.

Several of the tapestries depicted, as Reeve expected, triumphant scenes of historic Cartreff battles, featuring knights, swords and horses. The ones that caught his eye, however, were a series along the exterior wall that seemed to be reflective of the views from the windows set into that wall. The first was a depiction of the courtyard, including several figures wearing the livery of Airl Riding. The middle tapestry was a broad work showing the grasses, wildflowers and windmills of the scenery beyond the gates. The third appeared to present a small farm holding, complete with sheep, ducks and a contented cow.

Each tapestry showed a level of artistry that Reeve had not seen before, and Lady Cassandra had pressed Lady Adelina for the name of the designer of the beautiful work.

Airl Riding had laughed. "No designer," he'd said to

Lady Cassandra. "They're just something that Adelina dreamed up."

Lady Adelina had blushed, looking down at her trencher, as her husband dismissed in a few words what must have taken years to complete, but Lady Cassandra was effusive in her praise.

"It is so clever of you to take your inspiration from the view," she'd said. "Most of the tapestries I see are more . . . fantastic in nature."

"They are still," Lady Adelina said, with a small smile. "Out there, everything is always moving, blown about by the wind. But in the tapestry, we can capture stillness."

Having never really considered tapestries before, Reeve now found himself looking at Lady Adelina's work over and over again as Sir Garrick and Airl Riding debated the finer points of stirrup length.

As they moved on to the ratio of oats in the daily diet of a destrier, a group of young women entered the hall in a flurry of chatter and color. Seating themselves below the middle tapestry, Reeve watched them whisper and giggle among themselves as they were served platters of fruit and cheese. They reminded him of Anice and her friends at Rennart Castle, sure of their place within these walls.

"Reeve!" Sir Garrick's sharp tone made Reeve snap to attention. "When you're quite finished staring, er, out the window, perhaps you could pass me that napkin?"

Looking down into the knight's amused expression, Reeve realized that Sir Garrick thought he had been staring at the girls – which, he supposed, he had, even if his thoughts were drifting.

"Sorry, sire," Reeve muttered, handing the knight a clean square of fabric.

"We are going to the stables," Sir Garrick said as he dabbed his lips. "I am sure you will be able to entertain yourself for a short time." His last words were accompanied by a meaningful look toward the table of young women, and Airl Riding guffawed.

Sir Garrick stood, and the two men strode toward the door. As they exited, the mood within the hall relaxed and the volume of chatter increased.

Reeve tidied the table, before walking toward the girls – but not for the reason that Sir Garrick thought. He was not going to entertain himself, he was going to inform himself. The sight of these girls and the memory of Anice and her friends had sparked an idea.

Reeve hadn't gotten very far the day before in questioning Stanley about Airl Riding's guards. But if Reeve had learned anything from the business with Brantley at Rennart Castle, it was that nobody watched the young men of a castle as closely as the young women did. If anyone would have an idea of the inner workings of the guardsmen, it would be this lively group.

If Reeve were to ask them outright what they knew, however, the girls would tell him nothing—because they would not think that what they knew was important.

Instead, Reeve would just do something he loved to do — he would talk to them. Most of all, though, he would listen.

He approached the table, and bowed.

"I am Reeve of Norwood, squire to Sir Garrick of Rennart Castle," he said. "I wondered if I might join your table."

"Well, now, Reeve of Norwood," said a small blond girl of about eighteen years of age, her pretty, open face dotted with freckles, "aren't you a charmer? Slide over, girls."

Her friends wriggled along the bench to make room for him on the end.

"Here," the blond went on, placing a trencher of poached fruit in front of him. "You probably haven't eaten yet if you've been serving Sir Garrick."

"Thank you," Reeve said, realizing he was hungry.

"I'm Margery," the girl went on, watching as he took a spoonful of fruit, before going on to introduce the other six girls at the table in a blur of names that Reeve knew he'd never remember.

He nodded to each girl while trying not to dribble pear juice down his chin.

"You are all in residence at the castle?" he asked.

"Yes, our fathers all have office with Airl Riding, and so we are stuck here in the boondocks of Glawn," Margery said, rolling her eyes.

"Ah, they are not with the guardsmen, then?" Reeve asked, slurping another piece of pear off his spoon to distract from his pointed question.

Margery giggled. "Nothing that dashing," she said. "Gerard is the oldest guardsman and, at nine and twenty, he's not old enough to be my father. Even so, he'll be looking for a new job in a year."

Reeve tried to hide his surprise. "The guards are all under thirty?"

Margery and her friends nodded. "Except Sir Brannon. They start at eighteen and move on by thirty."

Reeve frowned, spoon poised above the trencher. "Where do they go?"

"I don't know," Margery said, wrinkling her nose. "Wherever they can find a place, I suppose. I know there are some who would leave tomorrow to escape south to the court of their hero King Bren. But we'd all like that, wouldn't we, girls?"

The other girls giggled, and Reeve grinned. "Is it King Bren who draws you or the excitement of his court?"

"Escape is what draws me," Margery said, softly, and for a moment Reeve saw pain in her brown eyes, before she laughed again. "Though I do think Queen Margery sounds mighty fine."

As the girls teased each other about which of them would make the best queen, Reeve let the conversation drift around him, concentrating on his breakfast and smiling encouragement.

"Ah, you don't really want to be Queen Margery, what about Jonty?"

Reeve's ears pricked up as the girl with hair the color of chestnuts sitting opposite him spoke to Margery, who giggled.

"Phhhh, he'd be so lucky," Margery said. "Besides, if he has anything to do with it, he'll be sitting right beside the King anyway."

"Jonty?" Reeve asked. "Is that your sweetheart?"

Margery's smile was wistful as the girls giggled again. "He wishes," she said, leaving Reeve in no doubt that Jonty wouldn't need to wish too hard. "But I don't see him often, so perhaps I'm looking for an alternative ..." She winked at Reeve, who could feel the tips of his ears go hot as Margery's friends tittered.

"You can't throw him over now," the girl with the chestnut hair urged Margery. "His aunt is missing. He'll be needing support."

"He's the nephew of the missing cook?" Reeve asked. "I was out with the guard looking for her last night, but

I don't think I met him."

"That's right," Margery said. "She's cooked for Airl Riding for many years, but he's only been a guard for a short while."

"And there were some who weren't too happy about him getting the job."

Reeve was looking at Margery so did not see which of her friends had made the low-voiced comment, but he filed it away.

"I was led to believe that nobody knew too much about the guards," Reeve said to Margery, pushing his empty trencher away. "New lives begin here and all that."

"That's true of most of them, but we know Jonty," Margery said. "As I said, she's been the cook here for years, and he's been in and out of the castle visiting. That's one reason why some of the older guards didn't want him."

Reeve frowned. "The cook is so important to Airl Riding that he would go against his senior guards?"

"Well, she is an exceptional cook, you know, even the King tried to poach her," said Margery, with a twinkle in her eyes. "Not more than a year ago. He wanted her to go and work with her sister down in his kitchens. But she said no when the Airl offered Jonty a place on his guard. Right close they are, her and Jonty. Always whispering. I've even heard her telling him the family recipes, and how many men want to know about that?"

Reeve shook his head in wonder, though he was more startled by the idea of a cook saying no to King Bren than by the family recipe information. Margery looked as though she would say more, but the other girls were all giving her the kind of looks that said "stop talking," so she took a long sip of whatever was in her tankard instead.

Reeve knew that any more questions now would be obvious, so when the girls began teasing him about his dimples, he joined in, flashing them on request — though, in truth, he hated the tiny half-moons that appeared in his cheeks when he smiled.

Larien had always told him that no one would take him seriously with dimples and that he should "pinch them out." At four, Reeve had given it his best try until his mother had asked him why his cheeks were constantly bruised.

"We must go now, Reeve of Norwood," Margery was saying, drawing Reeve back into the conversation as the girls stood almost as one. "Lady Adelina is walking in the garden, and our fathers will expect that we will be seen to join her."

Reeve stood as well, moving aside to allow her out. "I might join the guardsmen in their training this morning," he said. "Perhaps I will attach myself to those planning their escape to King Bren."

Margery looked alarmed. "Don't say anything," she said, clutching his arm. "I spoke in jest. We are not supposed to know."

"I see," said Reeve, trying to look confused.

She looked around, noting that the other girls had all filed out from the table the other way and were heading toward the door.

"They are a tight group," Margery said. "I don't think they want more than five. Five fingers make a fist. That's how they refer to themselves."

Reeve nodded. "I understand," he said, with a bow. "I can see that a sixth finger would be out of place. I will say nothing. Besides, who would I say it to? You are my first friend here."

Margery gave him a long look before laughing. "Just like that," she said. "Very well, I will be your first friend. You're certainly easier to win over than the Lady Anice, who does not deign to be friendly with any of us."

Reeve winced, wondering just how unfriendly Lady Anice was being.

"Don't fret," Margery said, with a wink. "As she keeps telling us, she's only here for three days and then she'll leave us to our . . . what was it, 'backwater ways and be gone.' You're the one who has to take her with you."

With that, she was gone, leaving Reeve to mull over this thought. Pushing aside Lady Anice, he concentrated on what he'd learned about Glawn Castle.

Five men with aspirations to join King Bren? Surely, these were the men that Maven had overheard? But who then was the sixth man in the windmill? And what had the cook to do with any of this, particularly if, as Margery implied, her nephew Jonty was one of the five?

"Er, are you going to stand there all day?" An exasperated page boy in Airl Riding's livery looked up at him. "It's just that we're trying to put the hall to rights."

Reeve chuckled, seeing a reflection of himself just a few years ago in the boy's indignation. "Sorry," Reeve said, looking around him and noticing that an army of servants had descended. "I was just . . . on my way to the stables."

Reeve knew his first step had to be to watch the morning training of Airl Riding's guardsmen. In particular, he would watch Jonty closely. Now that Reeve knew the identity of one of the five guards who were loyal to King Bren, unearthing the other four wouldn't prove that difficult.

Sir Garrick needed to know that, no matter what Sir Brannon said, there was a group of guardsmen whose loyalty lay with the King. And if they got wind of Sir Garrick's negotiations, the entire mission could be in jeopardy.

And with it, the futures of Sir Garrick, Airl Buckthorn and maybe even Cartreff itself.

Five fingers to make a fist. But those five fingers needed to work together.

Reeve would watch to see who it was that Jonty trained with and, hopefully, be able to provide Sir Garrick with names.

I can see that Gerard has exceptional sword skills. The big, brusque man is fighting three of his fellow guardsmen at once, the sword flashing in the weak sunlight as he thrusts and parries, hither and thither, lighter on his feet than I would ever have imagined.

The perpetual sneer on his broad face has disappeared, replaced by a fierce concentration and, occasionally, even a bright smile as an opponent backs away, to be replaced by another.

In fact, all of Airl Riding's guards are well trained, working as one as they perfect their skills across different disciplines. In one corner of the courtyard, two men wrestle, throwing one another to the cobblestones with a ferocity that I fear will result in broken bones. Three others practice with bows, releasing arrow after arrow into a scarecrow that is stuffed with straw and dressed in rags, propped against a fence.

I cannot help but admire their skill as they hit their target time and time again, each allowing for the ferocious wind with a precision that illustrates hours of practice in such conditions. I wonder at the advantage they would have in a battle conducted on Glawn soil, where other bowmen would no doubt struggle with the wind.

"I had not thought to find you here." Reeve settles against the stone wall beside me. I have tucked myself against the outer wall of the garden, taking advantage of the shelter and shadow provided by one of the alcoves I had noticed from Lady Cassandra's window. The garden wall forms one side of this area of the courtyard, with the castle's exterior walls and the stables providing the others, creating an area at once open and yet outside of the daily life of the castle.

The perfect training area.

"They are skilled fighters," I say to Reeve, not bothering to answer his opening statement. "Airl Buckthorn will do well to have them on side should he need them."

Reeve glances left and right before answering. "I am not convinced they are on our side."

I say nothing, knowing he will go on. And he does, explaining what he has learned about the five guardsmen and Jonty.

"You have been busy," I say, raising my eyebrows at

him. "And the Norwood charm has been used to good effect."

Reeve bows and blushes. "I'm not sure that anyone would refer to my father as charming," he says with a laugh. "I fear that all due credit must go to Lady Rhoswen."

A shadow passes over his face at the mention of the good lady, and I know he is remembering her illness. "She has done well, it has to be said," I say, and there is no teasing in my voice now. "But those girls would not have been as open with me as they are when they flirt with you, Reeve of Norwood. And look what you have discovered."

Reeve frowns, his thoughts turning in a new direction, as I'd hoped they would. "I just wish I could figure out what it all meant – how the cook is tied into all this, for starters. I am looking for Sir Garrick – I'm hoping that if I tell him what I've learned, he might have some answers, but I'd like to be able to take him some names."

My eyes stray to the training soldiers. "Well, that's Jonty over there," I say, indicating toward the cook's nephew with a tiny nod. "He doesn't seem especially friendly with any of the others – if anything, he makes a point of moving from one thing to another very quickly."

Reeve is now also watching Jonty, who has joined the

wrestling figures in the corner. Interestingly, the other two seem to take particular pleasure in landing Jonty on his back each time.

"He doesn't look happy," Reeve observes, as Jonty staggers to his feet after a heavy fall, his anger obvious.

"No, he doesn't." Now Jonty is shouting at the other two, waving his arms. I can hear only snatches of his diatribe — "fit in," "not fair," "never asked for this."

As Jonty turns his back on them, the other two guards exchange looks, hastening to throw an arm each around Jonty's shoulders, talking to him in low voices. Gerard has dropped his sword and is watching the scene unfold across the yard.

"Maybe Jonty would rather be baking than wrestling," Reeve jokes.

I look at him. "What do you mean? Why would he? Just because he is related to a cook doesn't mean he wants to be a cook."

"Oh, just his interest in the family recipes."

I can almost feel my ears prick up. "What do you mean?"

Reeve explains what his new friend Margery had to say about Jonty's interest in the cook's recipes.

"He had her recite the recipes?" I say, my mind spinning as I think about that scrap of parchment. Pease Pottage. A string of numbers.

"Apparently," Reeve says, losing interest.

"Family recipes?" I prod. There is something here

and I feel the need to work at it, as though pulling out a stubborn baby tooth.

"Apparently," Reeve repeats, rolling his eyes. "Funny, isn't it, to think that we're probably eating the same food that King Bren himself eats?"

I frown. "How do you figure that?"

"Well, her sister works in his kitchens," Reeve says, looking at me like I've lost my mind. "Did I not mention that bit?"

"You did not," I say, keeping my voice even, my mind returning again to that scrap of parchment. "To clarify, the cook's sister works in King Bren's kitchens, cooking the same family recipes?"

As I speak, I can hear the echo of Lady Rhoswen's voice in my head, telling me that Airl Riding's cook is one of five sisters, all cooks in different parts of the country.

"She does," Reeve confirms. "He even tried to poach Mistress Percy to work with her sister, or so the story goes, but she said no and that's when Jonty came to be a guardsman at Glawn Castle."

I lean back against the wall. "Reeve, do you still have that piece of parchment?" I have realized what it is that seems familiar about what's written on that scrap.

He shakes his head. "Sir Garrick kept it. I think it's in his chambers."

"We need to go and look at it," I say, grabbing his hand.

But Reeve resists, pulling me back out of the wind. "Why do we need to do that? I came here to watch the training. I need to see if I can find out more before I go to Sir Garrick."

Breathing out, I try to stay calm.

"I think what's written on that parchment is the key to a code – or part of it anyway."

"It cannot be, Maven," Reeve scoffs. "The cook cannot read. How could she read the key to a code?"

"Keep your voice down," I hiss, hearing high, clear voices on the other side of the wall. Lady Adelina and her entourage. As I had suspected and warned Cassandra, the wall provides the perfect cover for eavesdropping – on both sides.

"It's the recipes," I whisper, lowering my voice even further as a blond girl in a blue dress slips out through the gate at the end of the wall and makes a beeline for Jonty. "The family recipes. There are five women working in kitchens across Cartreff who know those recipes."

Reeve looks bemused, his eyes following the girl, who has pulled Jonty to one side, one delicate hand on his arm as she speaks to him with some urgency. "And?" he finally says.

"Someone is sending messages via those recipes," I say, feeling very sure, but also understanding just how fanciful this could sound to someone else. "It's like a book code."

This gets his attention. "A book code?"

I give him a quick overview of how a book code works.

"So, you're saying that if I knew the recipe and had the key, I could decipher a message out of a recipe for boiled gammon? Or apple pie?"

"That's what I'm saying."

"But the recipes are not written down," he says. "How could you be sure that each sister makes them exactly the same?"

I stare at him. "Family recipes are precious things, Reeve. Cook and her sisters would not change a family recipe in any way. It's just not done. They are handed down word for word over generations, often the only thing that any of these women will ever inherit, and the only thing they have to give their own daughters. In many cases there are even special dishes or bowls that go with them, though I'd imagine that's not the case here with five sisters."

Reeve looks nonplussed. "How do you know so much about this, Maven? Do you have family recipes of your own?"

My laughter at the idea of my mother lovingly handing on a family recipe is harsh. "Not me," I say. "But every cook I have ever met has them, and guards them fiercely."

Reeve nods but his focus has wandered, once again

drawn to Jonty and the girl when she whirls around, hands over her face as though distressed, and scampers back through the garden gate leaving Jonty behind. He is staring at Reeve, his face a stern mask.

"What was that all about?" I ask. "What have you done to upset Jonty?"

"That was Margery," Reeve says to me in an undertone. "I believe she and Jonty are courting."

"Perhaps not anymore," I say as Jonty turns on his heel. "Did the famous Norwood charm break another heart?"

"Hardly," Reeve spits. "As I said, we mostly talked about him."

Leaning back against the wall, I watch as Jonty moves to speak with Gerard, a short, sharp conversation. "Be careful, Reeve," I say, as both men glance our way.

"I'm always careful," he says, though I can hear the tenor of nerves under his cocky response. "Perhaps Jonty is just the jealous type."

"Hmmm, perhaps," I say, with a surety I do not feel.

"Tell me more about this book code," Reeve says, changing the subject. "If you're right, is the cook in on it?"

I think a moment. "I don't believe Mistress Percy would even know it was happening," I say. "But what if she found out, Reeve? What if she was asking questions? Wouldn't that be a reason for her to disappear?"

Reeve looks across the yard to where Jonty is now standing in front of Gerard, his dejected pose suggesting that whatever Gerard is saying to him is not positive.

"Maybe," Reeve responds. "But it could also be that someone else has worked all this out and wants the recipe for themselves?"

I feel my stomach drop, remembering the discussion in the windmill the day before. Those men hadn't known the cook's whereabouts. So she'd either fled from them, or Reeve's "someone else" was definitely in the picture. Either way, the woman was in danger.

"I think we need to take what we know to Sir Garrick now," I say out loud to Reeve.

"What we think we know," he corrects. "It will have to wait – Sir Garrick is in the stables with Sir Brannon debating various points of horse feed. I don't think we can burst in there pointing fingers at his men. Perhaps you could get Lady Cassandra to send a message calling him inside for an essential cup of tea?"

I let his snide remark about Lady Cassandra's role in this mission slide. Reeve is an unusual boy, it is true, but the fact that he could make such a comment shows how little he truly understands the frustrating limitations of Cassandra's life. To be sidelined, restricted to taking tea, gossiping and embroidery, all the while knowing that her husband walks a knife's edge where one word in the wrong ear could have him accused of treason . . . *an essential cup of tea, indeed.*

"My Lady Cassandra is walking in the pleasure garden with Lady Adelina," I answer through tight lips. "To call for a cup of tea, essential or otherwise, with Sir Garrick at present would call undue attention to the pair of them. You know that they will not be expected to speak again today until the evening meal."

Reeve muttered something sharp under his breath.

"You will need to find a way to speak to him, Reeve," I say. "You're the only one who can."

I give him a push in the direction of the stables, where I can see the guardsmen setting up a quintain to practice jousting. Four men hold it across the crossbar, lifting it high while two men position the center pole, and they all push it upright, anchoring the pole deep within a hole in the courtyard. I am almost tempted to stay and watch, but the first knight is still putting on his armor and has not yet even mounted his horse, waiting for the stable boys to spread the sand and straw that will mark out the field of play.

"Where are you going?" Reeve asks, sounding miffed.

I look back over my shoulder, allowing myself a grin. "I have my lady's leave to look around, and that's what I shall do. Go watch the quintain practice — I'm sure

Sir Garrick will leave his talk of molasses and oats to watch Airl Riding's guards in action."

Reeve nods, and I watch him walk toward the practice area. The quintain pole is now solidly in position, a heavy sandbag dangling from one side of its wide crossbar. The armored guard is helped up onto his horse, a helm placed upon his head and lance handed to him. I pause to watch his first pass.

The guard settles the lance into the rest attached to his breastplate, allowing him to hold the enormous weapon close to his side, digs his heels into the horse and rides at full tilt down the marked-out list, or field of play, toward the sandbag.

Everyone near the courtyard stops at the sound of the thundering hooves, watching as the guard thrusts his lance at the sandbag – and misses, leaving it dangling in the wind as he hurtles past.

The bawdy commentary of other guards carries toward me on the wind as I turn away, heading toward the laundry, leaving this world of men behind. Ana's invitation to the Beech Circle meeting tonight is on my mind. At the heart of all of these questions about loyalty and codes and secret messages, there is a missing woman, an older woman, who may be lost or scared or both.

No matter what Sir Garrick may have to say about Reeve's revelations now, I intend to find her, and the only people I can rely on to help me do that are the members of the Beech Circle.

CHAPTER NINE

As Sir Garrick approached the quintain for the fifth time, Reeve was beginning to wonder if he was destined to spend not just the entire day standing out in the wind, but most of the evening as well.

Did these men never eat? Surely, they would need to dress for the feast soon?

As the morning had worn on and the time for lunch had come and gone, a steady stream of Airl Riding's guards had shown their skills with the lance. And then Sir Brannon, a spark of challenge in his eyes, had suggested that Sir Garrick might like to show them how it was done, and Reeve had known that the afternoon would be lost as well.

And so it had proven.

The only positive that Reeve could see was that Sir Brannon was as enthusiastic about the quintain practice as Sir Garrick. Each time Sir Brannon took a run, Reeve had used the brief scrap of precious time to tell Sir Garrick a bit more about what he and Maven had discovered.

Or thought they'd discovered.

Presenting it all, of course, as Reeve's own idea.

Sir Garrick had listened, but the more Reeve had gone on, the further together the knight's dark brows had drawn and the darker his expression had become.

"I cannot take this to Airl Riding," Sir Garrick had said, pushing one hand through his hair. "At best, he would think I had run to madness. At worst, he would take umbrage at the very idea he was fostering some kind of nest of spies within his walls, and send me back to Airl Buckthorn with a traitor's arrow in my back."

Reeve had hesitated, but knew he had to ask: "You are certain Airl Riding is with you?"

"I am," Sir Garrick had responded. "Brannon spoke true yesterday when he said his Airl wishes for different ... management of Cartreff. Riding and I spoke one-on-one late last night once all others were in their beds."

When Reeve gasped, Sir Garrick had raised an eyebrow. "You are not privy to all my secrets — which is for the best."

Questions crowded Reeve's mind but there had been no time to ask them, for Sir Brannon had approached, a triumphant grin on his face. "That's four from five to me, Garrick — dare you go again to best me?"

Even as he laughingly accepted Sir Brannon's challenge, Sir Garrick had gripped Reeve's upper arm, drawing him near.

"Find out more, Reeve," Sir Garrick had whispered. "But be careful. The ground shifts beneath our feet and we will need to watch our step if we are not to falter."

Reeve had said nothing as he'd followed Sir Garrick to where the horse master held a huge destrier. But, after assisting Sir Garrick into his armor, Reeve had moved through the crowd that had gathered to watch, maneuvering himself until he was standing near Jonty.

"You back again?" one of the guards standing near the cook's nephew said.

Reeve tensed as the group turned as one to look at him.

He'd been trying to discreetly hang about these men all day — a task that had grown more difficult as the hours had worn on, despite his best efforts to join their conversation. Every comment he'd made had been ignored, every question unanswered.

"It's the best viewpoint for the quintain," Reeve said, with what he hoped was a pleasant smile.

"Hmmm," the man replied, scratching his chin,

which was in need of a shave. "Nice dimples. I heard the girls enjoyed them at breakfast."

Feeling the heat flush his cheeks, Reeve turned back as the drumbeat of hooves alerted him to the fact that Sir Garrick was making his run. In light of Margery's chat with Jonty, the pointed comment about the girls could have been simple jealousy at play – or it could be more.

Whichever it was, Reeve took note. Maven's words about being careful echoed through his mind, as he watched Sir Garrick hurtle toward the quintain pole. Even the discomfort of being surrounded by hostile men could not distract Reeve from the poise with which Sir Garrick held his jousting lance, sitting lightly atop his mount.

Reeve knew from his own practice the strength and deftness required to keep a seven-foot pole steady and in position whilst riding at speed. Reeve's efforts often ended with him either dropping the lance or finding himself unseated as the unwieldy pole bounced around.

But he was getting better, which was all that mattered.

Sir Garrick, on the other hand, was a master. His lance barely moved as he adjusted his seat for its weight and closed in on the sandbag target. Some wag had painted the outline of a grinning knight on the bag, which moved gently in the stiff wind, despite the weight of the sand inside.

As Sir Garrick rode past, he managed to flick the lance with an enviable smoothness, despite its clumsy length, smacking the illustrated knight directly in the middle of his breastplate, setting the bag swinging from the impact.

"That's five from five," said the unshaven guard, spitting onto the ground beside his boots. "Best of the day."

"Sir Brannon got four," said a wiry man whose hair stuck straight up like a boot brush. "That's pretty good, Hugh."

"Not the best, though," Hugh responded. "Despite all his rules and his big talk."

Reeve began edging away, not liking either the growl in the big man's voice or that he was a Hugh. Possibly the Hugh that Maven had mentioned.

"What about you then?" Hugh grabbed Reeve's arm.

"What about me?" Reeve said, pointedly looking at Hugh's hand. "I'm going to assist Sir Garrick from his horse."

"You're his squire," Hugh said, not loosening his grip. "How about you have a go?"

Reeve swallowed. He was getting better at quintain, but he was nowhere near the standard of Sir Garrick.

"It's late," Reeve said. "Look, they begin to sweep up the list."

To his relief, the stable hands were indeed emerging

from the stables with brooms, ready to sweep away the sand and straw.

"I'm sure they can wait for one more run," Hugh said, his grip on Reeve's arm tightening. "You've been creeping about all day, listening in, watching as we show what we can do. Now it's time to see whether you fight as well as you flirt."

Flustered, Reeve allowed himself to be dragged along by the older man, with the other guardsmen following in a pack, until they reached Sir Garrick.

"Sir Garrick," Hugh said, a jovial and entirely fake lilt in his voice. "Young Reeve would like to have a turn and we've a mind to let him."

Turning from his horse, Sir Garrick raised his eyebrows. "You have faced the quintain before, Reeve?"

It was Hugh's turn to look surprised. "You don't know?"

"Reeve is newly in my service," Sir Garrick said. "But if he wishes to have a run, he may use my horse. Unfortunately, Sir Brannon and I are expected in Airl Riding's solar for a parley before tonight's feast. Perhaps you could await me in my chambers once you're done."

"Excellent!" Hugh's clap on Reeve's back almost knocked the breath out of him.

"I am in your debt, sire," Reeve said, with a small bow. "But my service to you remains my priority."

"It is only one run at the quintain," Sir Garrick said, with a laugh. "I'm sure I will cope without you for a short time."

"We may keep him longer than one run," Hugh said, and Reeve wondered if he'd imagined the threat beneath the joking tone. "He's practically become one of us today."

Sir Garrick chuckled as he walked away toward Sir Brannon. "I am not surprised. He has a knack for fitting in."

Reeve knew his face had gone pink at the praise, so he kept his eyes on the ground.

"Right, squire," Hugh said, and there was no friendliness in his tone now. "Show us what you can do."

"I —" Reeve looked around at the men who now surrounded him. In their uniforms they looked like a wall of gray, no friendliness in their faces. Reeve had the sinking feeling he had somehow erred in his questions today and that the safest place for him right now might be on Sir Garrick's horse.

"Very well, I'll have a go," Reeve said, trying to sound as though he was excited about the challenge. Rough hands helped him into some ill-fitting armor and boosted him up onto the big horse.

From here, Reeve could see that Sir Garrick had already left the practice yards and was rounding the corner of the walled garden, deep in conversation with Sir Brannon.

The ground looked a long way down, and Reeve

wished he was wearing a helm like the first knight, but there were none to be seen nearby. He couldn't help but feel that covering the expression on his face from Airl Riding's men might not be a bad idea — as would having some steel between his head and the ground should he fall off.

Most of the men were now moving away, positioning themselves along the list to watch Reeve's attempt at the quintain. Hugh had gone past them, heading for the quintain itself, and Reeve realized he intended to stand right near the sandbag, close to the point of contact.

Jonty fed the handle of the lance up to Reeve, who did his best to fit it into the rest in the breastplate of the armor and keep it close to his body, tucked under his right armpit. The point of the lance, way out in front of him and the horse, dipped and swayed in the wind, and Reeve gripped it underhand, trying to rest it in his palm and balance its weight. As he struggled to keep control of the length of the lance, the horse moved restlessly beneath him, spooked by the movement of the weapon.

Reeve slid in the saddle, upsetting his precarious balance even further, but he was managing to wriggle back into position when Jonty suddenly slapped the destrier's rump and the horse leaped forward.

Clinging desperately to the reins with his left hand and holding the lance with his right, Reeve heard vague shouts above the thunder of hoofbeats, but could see nothing beyond a blur as the destrier, having already done this many times that day, cannoned forward, straight toward the quintain.

Reeve's mouth was dry as he fought to maintain the balance of the lance, which jogged up and down with the rhythm of the horse. Now that he was here, he was going to do his best not to embarrass himself by dropping the lance before he even got to the quintain.

Biting his lip, Reeve bent down as low as he could in the stiff armor, trying to keep his eyes on the sandbag as he'd been taught. At best, Reeve had a fifty-fifty success rate with a lance, and he was desperately hoping this would be one of the times that the lance hit the target.

Closer and closer he rode, aware only of the sandbag, the lance, the horse. He was lifting the lance, meters from the target, when a sudden movement caught the corner of his eye. Distracted, Reeve inadvertently flicked the reins and the horse, confused, began to pull up. It was then that Reeve noticed that the sandbag was not dangling in the wind where it was supposed to be. Instead, it had been pulled to one side.

Reeve had time only to frown before he realized that the sandbag was now swinging outward straight into his path.

"No!" he shouted, as the startled destrier reared up with a whinnying shriek. Reeve fought to hold the horse as the heavy lance dropped from his grip, but a sudden jolt to the side of his head knocked him sideways.

Time slowed as Reeve fell to earth, and he saw the sandbag lazily swinging back into place above him before the world went black.

"Where do you think you're going?"

I want to pretend that I haven't heard but I know that will only cause me more problems, so I count swiftly to ten and turn to face Anice with a smile. She stands in the middle of the hallway, hands on her hips.

"My Lady Anice," I acknowledge, with the tiniest curtsey I can get away with. "I am on my way to the kitchens to fetch lavender tea for Lady Cassandra."

She looks stunning in a velvet gown the color of twilight, even with a suspicious frown on her face. "Why would Cassandra require lavender tea now? Is she not on her way to this tedious feast as I am?"

I do not sigh and roll my eyes like I wish to do. Instead, I bob again, as a good servant would. "She does not require it now. It will be waiting for her when she returns from the feast, to help her sleep."

Anice's lip curls. "Surely, her good husband Sir Garrick will tend to her sleep requirements. She has no need of you for that."

I will not give her the reaction she wants. "My lady

does like her tea."

"Hmmm," Anice says, advancing along the woolen rug, her long russet curls bouncing at the ends as she walks. "You know, the more I think about it, the less I can see a reason for you to be here. She has Sir Garrick. She has me for company – after all, I saw no sign of you today as we strolled in the gardens, maintaining tedious conversation with these women who know nothing. And any old maid can do her hair and fetch and carry."

I say nothing, and her eyes narrow.

"In fact," Anice drawls, "I can see no use for you."

Again, I say nothing, and she is suddenly right in front of me, her hand lifting my chin.

"No use at all," Anice hisses into my face.

Her hand is gone as quickly as it came, and she laughs lightly, strolling past me as though nothing has happened. "I have taken quite a liking to Sir Garrick's new squire," Anice says. "I think I will let him fall in love with me."

The fact that Anice has moved behind me makes it easier to hide my reaction, and I'm glad of that. Poor Reeve doesn't know what he's in for, though from what I saw only last night he may not mind.

There is a pause as I wait for her to keep walking away from me. I am happy to stand in the hallway all day if it means we do not have to continue this little chat. Anice, however, has not yet finished, and now I sense that we are reaching her true purpose.

"Yes, I think I might write to Papa and suggest that four's company and five's a crowd for this visit," she muses. "If it reaches him in time, he can have Sir Garrick send you back to Rennart Castle where you belong. If it does not, no matter, for we will leave here in a day or two and the letter will be in his hand when we return. He will be displeased either way and demand that Cassandra find herself another servant."

Companion, I whisper, but only in my head, for she is right. I am a servant, and I am at the whim of Lady Anice, Lady Cassandra, Sir Garrick, Airl Buckthorn and anyone else designated higher than me in the social standings of Cartreff.

Which is just about everyone.

I hear Anice's tiny, satisfied exhale and realize that my back has stiffened and my fists clenched at her words, giving her the exact reaction she sought. She knows how to hurt me and she knows that she can.

"Anyway, off you go to the kitchens," Anice continues, sounding happier than I have heard her all week. "You might as well be useful while you're still here. I'll keep dear cousin Cassandra entertained at the feast and let her know you are fetching her tea."

As Anice's footsteps skip lightly down the hall behind me, I count from ten to one, then again, and again, trying to calm my breathing and soften my tense body. Cassandra will not let Anice send me away without a fight, but Cassandra may not know about it until it's too late.

Anice does not know that we will not return to Rennart Castle when we leave Glawn. Sir Garrick may have to stick to her three-day deadline and leave Glawn to appease her – but we have many places to visit yet.

Will I still be part of the "we"? And if I am, for how long can I keep Anice at arm's length? How long before Sir Garrick has no choice but to bow to her demand that I leave them?

I flex my fingers and then clench my fists again, repeating the movement several times until I am sure I am in control of my body and mind once more. One thing I have learned over the past five years is how to control my anger, if only because I've realized that nobody cares about my anger except me. Why be ruled by something that matters to no one?

Instead, I either work it out of my system or stuff it deep down inside, where it fuels my loyalty to the Beech Circle.

Letting out one last deep breath, I turn and head down to my actual destination – the laundry. Ana has promised to take me to the Beech Circle meeting tonight so that I can glean more insight into the inner workings of Glawn Castle.

I had hoped to have spoken to Reeve before the

meeting, to find out what Sir Garrick thought about our theory about the cook and, more importantly, to learn what – if anything – Reeve's uncovered about Jonty and his friends. Given the amount of time he's spending with them, I'm expecting he'll have a great deal to report when next I see him.

I could see that Sir Garrick felt the same way when Hugh had informed him earlier that Reeve had asked to accompany the night's guard on their rounds of the fief if Sir Garrick permitted it. Sir Garrick had looked as surprised as I felt that Reeve had not come to seek leave to go himself. But Hugh explained that the guardsmen had been saddling up straight after quintain practice, and there had been no time for Reeve to return to the castle.

All I could think was that Reeve was following up a lead. Why else would he choose to ride around in the dark, in the wind roaring around the castle?

Sir Garrick had made a joke with Sir Brannon and Airl Riding about squires who made their own rules, but there wasn't much he could do but agree.

And so, I have no choice but to contain my impatience to find out what Reeve is so intent on pursuing.

The stairs are busy with servants bustling up and down, some staggering under the weight of huge platters covered in silver domes, others carting empty dishes back down to the kitchen. I pity the scullions who are no doubt already up to their elbows in hot, greasy water cleaning dishes, with a long night ahead of them.

I reach the laundry door, which is locked, but I can see a faint glow from beneath it. The handle rattles and the door creaks inward as I step through. The laundry is quiet, lit only by the candle in Ana's hand.

"I told the kitchen staff you were bringing me an emergency job," Ana says, her face ghostly in the pale light.

"If anyone asks I'll mention smalls," I whisper, holding up my empty hands. "That's usually enough to make them change the subject."

I join her as she giggles. "Come," Ana says. "It's not far, but we need to leave while the kitchens are too busy for anyone to notice. I need to be back in my quarters when everyone goes to bed."

She moves past the hulking laundry tub, which still smells strongly of lye and soapwort despite being empty, toward the back door.

"Where are your quarters?" I ask.

Ana groans. "Right at the top of the castle towers, under the eaves, where we feel and hear every gust of blasted wind. Men in the right tower, women in the left, eight to a room, so it's hard to hide."

I grimace. I might complain about my lack of time to myself now, but what Ana describes is the future that

Anice would wish upon me. I am about to ask more, but Ana puts a finger to her lips as she places the candle on the windowsill beside the door.

"Stay close to me now," Ana murmurs, "and no talking until we're well beyond the gates. The wind carries words like leaves on a stream and deposits them far beyond intended ears."

Ana turns to a hook beside the door, taking down two cloaks, and I recognize the dark gray of the guardsmen's uniform. I raise an eyebrow and she giggles again.

"Well, they do just leave them hanging about for anyone to borrow," she says. "I'll put them back when I get up for work in the morning, and no one will be any the wiser."

With that, Ana blows out the candle, and, mirroring her, I throw the cloak around my shoulders and follow her to the door, gasping as she opens it and a blast of cold air hits my face.

Ana hears me, and takes my hand in a reassuring grasp.

"We will not stay long tonight," she says. "I can feel the Wolf's Howl brewing, and we won't want to be caught out in that."

"I have heard it is strong enough to uproot trees and that people have been carried away by it." I cannot help but shiver at the thought.

Ana laughs, squeezing my fingers. "We haven't had

a really bad one like that for a few years. But even at its weakest it's enough to take your feet out from under you."

I hesitate on the threshold, torn between the lure of the Beech Circle meeting and the stillness of the air at my back. I'm suddenly aware how living in a place like Glawn could change a person – every task here is made more difficult by the wind. When even pleasurable activities become a chore, how much easier it is to stay home.

No wonder Lady Adelina likes to create beautiful landscapes in her tapestries – it's the only way to truly enjoy them.

"Come," Ana says, and I realize I've been hovering on the doorstep for several long moments. "The Beech Circle mill is warm and there will be cake."

"Cake?" I say, surprised, as she tugs my fingers and I follow her down the side of the castle wall.

"There's always cake," Ana confirms. "It's a rule of our group."

I smile, recognizing that each chapter of the Beech Circle has its own rules and rituals but a unity of purpose. Feeling lighter, I follow Ana quickly past the silent stables and beyond, to the small postern gate that allows a hasty retreat if the castle is ever under siege.

Once she has unlocked the gate and we are through it and onto the moor beyond, Ana begins to run, straight out across the fields. Every now and then, the waning moon shines for a moment or two between the scudding clouds and the effect is unsettling, shifting the shadows.

"How do you know where to step?" I gasp, thinking of the marshy ground beneath my feet that morning, grateful that I have pulled my hair back securely.

"You can't see it well in the moonlight but there's a natural ridge through here," Ana says. "Wait until you see where it goes."

We jog along for a few more minutes, with the wind blowing up our skirts, and then, suddenly, Ana stops. Stunned, I also stop and realize I am looking down into a dip in the landscape.

"You wouldn't know this was here if you didn't fall into it," I say, glancing behind me at the castle, ablaze with light, rising from the flat landscape. Even over the sound of the wind I can hear faint music. The feast is well and truly underway.

"Glawn is like that," Ana says. "It seems flat and knowable and then, just when you feel safe, it falls away beneath your feet. But we are not far now."

She leads me down into the dip, and then over a slight hill where I am startled to see a windmill.

"I never imagined you could hide an entire mill in this landscape," I say with a laugh.

"Lucky for the Beech Circle, the Widow Morris could," Ana says. "We can hide in plain sight here."

I stay close to her as we make our way toward the dark mill, which is silent save for the ever-present creak and rattle of the sails. I cannot see them in the dark, but as we are almost bent double by the wind I can imagine how fast they are spinning. I hope that Ana is sure of the way, for I don't want to walk into those sails.

A few minutes later, we are at the back of the mill, where Ana knocks three times, waits a few moments, then knocks again twice. The door creaks open slowly, revealing the warm glow of the room beyond.

"Ana!" An older woman with iron-gray hair and a cheerful, ruddy face opens her arms wide, and Ana steps into them for a long hug.

"Mistress Morris," Ana says, as she withdraws, "this is Maven, visiting from Rennart."

Before I know it, I'm pulled in for my own hug. "Welcome, Maven," Mistress Morris says. "Welcome."

As we step inside, my shoulder brushes the door and I realize that it has been lined with black fabric all around its edges to ensure that no light seeps out through the cracks. The windows are covered with curtains in rich, dark colors — berry, deep blue, a luscious green — and the floor with a wool rug so thick that I itch to remove my boots and run my toes over it.

The air is heavy with the scent of fruit and spice, indicating that the cake on the big, scrubbed wooden table is freshly baked.

The contrast between the wild weather outside the door and the deep comfort within could not be more marked, and the half-dozen members who sit around the table look relaxed and happy. In one corner, a brown-haired woman sits with a girl of around twelve or thirteen, both focused intently on the book open on the girl's lap as she mouths the letters to spell out a word.

Every Beech Circle has its own character, determined by the members and their meeting place. I immediately love the coziness of this one, as much as I love the awe-inspiring, carved, underground chamber near Rennart, and the secret room below Cassandra's family manor where our own circle meets.

As I remove my cloak and hang it on a hook by the door, I feel myself exhale. For the next few hours, I will be Maven. Just Maven. I will not have to hide what I know or think. I will have the opportunity to speak when I want to and to listen when I don't.

And when I leave, I will know another eight or more who are just like me. Eight or more who will help me if I need it while I am here in Glawn.

With a missing woman, a secret mission, a possible spy network and Anice threatening to send me home,

I can't help but think what a gift the Beech Circle is.

I turn back to the room, where the women are all looking at me with an air of expectation.

"I am so happy to be here tonight," I say, taking my place at the table. "I have been so worried about Mistress Percy and I know that if anyone has any idea where she might be, that person will be in this room."

My spirits fall when all present shake their heads sadly, including the girl in the corner.

"We have been looking, of course," says Mistress Morris, placing a slice of cake in front of me. "Asking questions, poking in corners, and we've searched every windmill hereabouts but there's nothing. It is as though the woman has been blown off the face of the earth."

"On a night like tonight she may very well have been," a tiny woman wrapped in what seems to be more patches than shawl says with a shiver.

"Eat your cake," Mistress Morris says to me, pushing a thick mug filled with hot tea toward me. "We will tell you all we know, all we have found, and you can tell us what they're doing up at the castle to find her. Somewhere in the middle, we may spark an idea that will lead us to the answers we seek."

I take a tentative sip of the hot liquid, savoring the warmth in my mouth a moment before swallowing, and begin.

187

"Quickly, now," Ana says, as we slip through the postern gate. "The feast will be ending and there will be people about." In any other fief, she would be whispering, but here in Glawn she is shouting in my ear and I can still only just hear her over the wind.

I am beginning to truly understand why they call it the Wolf's Howl as it moans and shrieks and wails. I cannot wait to be back inside the castle, out of its clawing grasp.

Sticking close to the shadows of the walls, we make our way to the laundry door, stopping to hide twice as rowdy groups meander past.

"Nearly there," Ana whispers, as we duck low beneath the kitchen windows to avoid being seen by the scullions, still washing endless dishes. Moments later, we are in the silent laundry and it is as though the past few hours did not happen – except that I am warmed from the inside.

"Go," Ana says, taking the cloak from me. "I'll put these away."

I smooth my hair and then, overcome by sheer relief, give her a fierce hug. "Thank you for taking me."

Ana laughs, as she steps back. "Thank you for coming. I think you have more than one new admirer tonight. Mistress Morris was so impressed by all that you had learned in such a short time."

I feel myself blushing and am glad for the darkness. "I was taught to listen," I say, not naming my father as my teacher. The Beech Circle is strong, but I am still careful about that information. The only person outside my family and Cassandra that I have ever told about the lessons that he gave me is Reeve.

Sometimes, I wonder at the trust that grew so quickly between Reeve and myself, but when I think of how desperate we both were to find the Fire Star and salvage our dreams, it is perhaps not surprising.

Thinking of him now, I say goodbye to Ana and, looking both ways in the hallway and finding it clear, exit the laundry. I should be back in Cassandra's chamber just before she returns. After I have settled her I will find Reeve, for we have much to discuss.

I know now that the guards at the gates saw nothing untoward on the afternoon of Mistress Percy's disappearance. No strangers had arrived, beyond us, and no unusual carts or carriages. No one had ridden out with a woman slung across their saddles, nor even a roll of carpet — I was impressed that Ana had even thought of that.

But when I'd asked if there was a chance the woman had simply been concealed somewhere in the castle, I'd been met with shaking heads. The girl I had seen being taught to read, named Joan, works at the castle as a housemaid and has seen nothing out of the ordinary, going so far as to pretend to lose her way all the way down to the dungeons with a bucket yesterday morning.

"Empty," she'd told me.

However, I have also learned that, as we thought, all is not well in the fief of Glawn. Ana and Mistress Morris confirmed that Airl Riding and Lady Adelina are both trusted and beloved. While they seem to me to be a pair of cold fish, each Beech member had nothing but praise for them.

"It's a harsh place," Mistress Morris told me, "and Lady Adelina struggled when she came to us from the south to marry the Airl. But she's one who's bent to the wind, rather than being broken by it. Found her ways, she has, with the tapestries and the like, drawing the other women around her. They're not used to company, is all. We don't get too many visitors up this way."

The guardsmen are, on the whole, a different story. They are distrusted and disliked, believing themselves superior to other castle and fief residents.

"They take what they want from the kitchens, from the laundry, from who knows where," Ana had confided, admitting to making sure she kept the laundry door locked most of the time, even when she was there. "But who would we complain to? They will always travel in groups of at least two or three, with those hats pulled down. It's not even easy to describe who it was you saw."

I tried not to ask too many questions about the

King, not wanting to flag my interest, even with the Beech Circle, but Mistress Percy came back into the conversation over and over again as we discussed different ideas on where she might have gone — and why.

Unfortunately, nobody had any solid ideas, though each member has gone home to further spread the word that she is missing. We decided that someone must have seen something and the further and more quickly news of her disappearance spreads, the sooner a clue must turn up.

Hopefully, Reeve had better luck with the guardsmen.

But when I get to the top of the stairs, the first person I see is a grim-faced Sir Garrick, deep in conversation with Sir Brannon and a man I assume to be Airl Riding.

It is my first proper look at the Airl, who is tall and thin like his wife, and clad, to my surprise, not in shades of gray, but in dark-brown hose, olive tunic and high black boots.

I realize I am staring and drop my gaze.

"Ah, Maven, just the person I wanted," Sir Garrick says.

I look up at him. "Sire," I say, with a yawn, trying to sound as though I'm just wandering in from a table at the very back of the feast.

"Is Reeve with you?" Now, Sir Garrick and the other two frowning men are striding toward me.

"Reeve? No." I don't even have to pretend to sound surprised. "I thought he had gone on night rounds with the guards?"

Sir Garrick's heavy dark brows lower even further. "He did, but has since disappeared."

It is my turn to frown. "The guards don't know where he is?"

"He returned to the castle with them on schedule, and told them he was returning to the feast for dessert," Sir Garrick says. "But he never made it."

"He must have become lost," Airl Riding says, sounding like someone who was repeating himself for the umpteenth time. "The castle grounds look different at night, and with the Howl brewing there are not many people about."

"Who was the last person to see him?" I blurt, and then kick myself. It is not the place of a maid to question the Airl of Glawn, and the mirror expressions of horror on the three men reflect my mistake.

I bite my lip, dropping into a curtsey. "My apologies, my lords, I forgot myself in my concern."

"Got a soft spot for the young squire then, have you?" asks Airl Riding, turning to Sir Garrick with a knowing smile. "Might need to watch those two."

I cannot look at Sir Garrick as he chuckles. I just hope he notices that Airl Riding has not answered my question.

"Ah, what it is to be young and impatient," Sir Garrick says, before sobering. "Still, the lass asks a valid question."

The Airl stops laughing. "You do not question the integrity of my guards, surely?"

I wonder if I am the only one who feels the world go still around us as a bridge of tension rises between the two men.

But I underestimate Sir Garrick.

"Not their integrity," he says, his tone jovial, even if his expression is not. "Their eyesight. It would not hurt to ask the last man to see Reeve for his thoughts on Reeve's direction."

Airl Riding relaxes. "This is true. Brannon, send someone to find out."

As Sir Brannon nods and moves away, Airl Riding is approached by Winnock with a question, and the two engage in deep conversation.

I think this is my opportunity to leave, but Sir Garrick stops me. "If you have questions, Maven, ask them of me first. Cassandra tells me that the Lady Anice made several suggestions at the feast that our party would travel more quickly if it were smaller – by one. Do not create a reason for me to send you back to Rennart."

I look at my feet, and sketch a curtsey, before turning away, feeling angry and defeated.

Sir Garrick, however, has not finished. "Mind you,

it would need to be a very good reason. Reeve spoke to me today about . . . his thoughts about the cook and her recipes," he says, giving me a sharp look as he says "his." "I find them . . . intriguing, and I also suspect Reeve has, er, discussed them with you. The thing is, Maven, I need more than speculation and I need it sooner rather than later if I am not to wander into a quagmire."

I pause mid step, listening hard.

"Sir Brannon will return in a moment," Sir Garrick continues, "and I have no doubt that whichever guard they decide to bring forward will tell us that Reeve walked into the night whistling happily and got lost between the stables and the front door. But you and I know him better than that."

I nod, and turn back to face him.

"Find him, Maven. I will stay here and listen politely to whatever story I am told, but you, you are free to go now. Go and find him."

"My Lady Cassandra —" I begin.

"I will swear black-and-blue that you left me and went straight to your duties should the need arise," Sir Garrick says, holding up his hand to stop me from speaking. "The Lady Anice may not see any possible reason for your presence on this mission, Maven, but I see it, more and more clearly each day. I have noticed that, in a strange way, you have more freedom to move about this castle than I do, and it opens up very interesting possibilities going forward . . . Use it now. I have a very bad feeling that Reeve needs us."

"Garrick!" Airl Riding and Sir Brannon are both stalking toward us, the guard I recognize as Gerard at their heels, and none of them are smiling. Airl Riding waves a piece of parchment at us as he approaches.

"A ransom note!"

Sir Garrick gasps, and I feel my head swim for a moment.

Who would kidnap Reeve?

CHAPTER TEN

Reeve had no idea where he was, but it was noisy, his head hurt and his throat was parched. Licking his lips, he willed his eyes open – but it didn't help much. He could hear the rattling clatter that he'd come to associate with windmills, but this was louder than anything he'd heard before.

But not as loud as the wind, which seemed to be screaming through his ears.

His back hurt, probably from lying flat on a wood floor. Shifting his weight to try to ease the pressure, he felt a sharp splinter burrow into his shoulder. With a frown that made his head ache even more, Reeve tried to roll over but couldn't. His legs were bound at the ankles and his hands were secured over his head by the wrist to the wall.

Reeve stilled, trying to make sense of what had happened. The last thing he remembered was riding Sir Garrick's horse, the quintain . . . Closing his eyes again, he pushed and prodded at his memory but could come up with nothing after that.

And now he was . . . here?

Squinting in the darkness, Reeve had a sense of a whirring movement above him, but could see nothing other than blackness. And he had no idea how he'd gotten here – or who had brought him here or why.

Trying to struggle against the ropes that bound him, Reeve was spent within moments. Cursing his feebleness, he tried to push down the fear and anger he could feel rising with every gasping breath. Even as a page, practicing with wooden swords and blunted arrows, the first lesson he'd learned was that every fight, every battle, every war, is won and lost in the mind before skill ever gets a look-in.

Giving in to fear now would not get Reeve out of this. Whatever this was.

But his training hadn't really taken into account just how overwhelming the grasping, clutching tendrils of fear could be.

Swallowing hard to try to ease his throat, Reeve lay still, trying to soothe his thoughts by relaxing his limbs. His head felt as though a blacksmith had laid it on an anvil and taken a hammer to it, and he thought he could feel bruises blooming on his right shoulder – which might also explain the dull throb in his back.

On top of all that, there was a maddening itch on his forehead, a dripping, trickling sensation, and he could feel the small tincture bottle lying down the side of his neck – two things he could do absolutely nothing about with his hands tethered.

Blowing upward in a concerted attempt to somehow relieve the itch, Reeve forced himself to concentrate on something else. Beginning with what he *did* know about his current situation.

Reeve knew he was close to a windmill, if not in one. But the space he was in felt different from the open rooms where he'd been yesterday. Smaller, more confined, much noisier, despite the fact that his arms were by his ears.

With a gulp, Reeve realized it was likely he was in the very top of a windmill, up where, as Maven had described, the wooden cogs, wheels and gears did their work. That might explain the whirring sensation above his head – and it also meant he'd best keep low down if he wanted to keep his head.

Not that Reeve could stand if he wanted to.

Given that his last memory was riding toward the quintain with Airl Riding's guardsmen watching, it was logical enough to assume that they had brought him here? And tied him up? But the more he thought about it, the less likely that seemed. Surely, Sir Garrick would have missed him if he hadn't returned from the practice yard? And what would they possibly hope to achieve by keeping him captive?

If Sir Garrick hadn't missed him yet, then he would do so soon and woe betide anyone who was involved in this affair.

No, there was something Reeve was missing.

Something big.

And he'd work out what that was very soon. After he'd closed his eyes for just a minute.

Sir Garrick has disappeared into Airl Riding's solar with the Airl, Sir Brannon and what looks like an army of guardsmen, leaving me alone in the hallway.

The ransom note was not for Reeve but for Mistress Percy, the missing cook. Someone is holding her and intends to kill her at noon tomorrow if Airl Riding does not deliver twenty silver pieces in a plain hessian sack to a location that Airl Riding is keeping to himself.

He has made it clear he will also keep his silver to himself.

"She is a very good cook," Airl Riding told Sir Garrick not ten minutes ago, explaining why he would not pay the ransom. "But for twenty silver pieces I could replace her with two cooks and a house steward for the next five years."

I searched out Jonty's face as the Airl made this declaration about his aunt, and for a moment he looked stricken before his face set into blank resignation.

I am more convinced than ever that he doesn't know where she is and that he has involved her in something she knows nothing about.

The men have gathered to confer on how best to manage the ransom situation, who might be behind this plot and what punishment they will receive once they're caught. It will no doubt occupy them for hours.

Sir Garrick's meaningful look as he left the hallway at Airl Riding's side leaves me in no doubt that he expects me to follow his instructions to find Reeve while Sir Garrick plays his diplomatic role in the unfolding crisis.

It's terribly late now, but I can think of only one thing to do. Remembering what Ana told me about her quarters, I make my way to the left tower, climbing countless stairs to the very top. It is freezing cold up here, and the shrieking wind seems to shake the very stones.

For a brief moment I consider knocking, but decide against waking all eight occupants of the room. Creeping in the door, I allow my eyes a few moments to adjust to darkness, listening to the wind rattle the windowpanes and the snoring from one side of the room that is even louder.

"Who's there?"

I turn toward the alarmed squeak and can see the outline of a girl sitting bolt upright in bed.

"It's okay," I whisper. "I'm looking for Ana."

"Third bed on the left," she says, lying back down.

"Maven?" I follow the sound of Ana's voice and sit on the edge of her narrow bed, which creaks beneath our combined weight. She is positioned directly under the high, arched window set deep into the stone wall, and the moon shines dully upon us. It seems the cloud has all been blown away by the Howl.

"What are you doing here?" Ana whispers, winding her long dark hair around her hand to pull it back from her face. Her eyes are huge and anxious in the moonlight, and her white nightgown seems to glow.

"I need your help," I say, grabbing her hand. "Reeve has gone missing. I need the Beech."

Ana frowns. "The Beech is not for the likes of him," she says.

I nod, knowing that I am asking a lot. The Beech Circle's mission is to help women and girls, not 16-year-old squires who, frankly, lack for little.

"You're not helping him, you're helping me," I say, and I mean every word. Reeve's friendship aside,

Sir Garrick's trust matters to me, particularly when combined with his warning about making sure I don't give him — or Anice — a reason to send me back to Rennart Castle. If I retrieve Reeve then Sir Garrick will have to ensure I stay.

But I cannot do that on my own in an unfamiliar place surrounded by uninterested people.

I need the Beech Circle.

"Please, Ana," I continue, when she looks unconvinced. "If I do not find him, my life as I know it will be changed forever — and not for the better. I know the Beech Circle will not forsake me."

Biting her lip, Ana nods slowly. "Wait outside," she says. "I'll get dressed."

Logically, I know I am not lost. Ana was right in front of me only moments ago. But the thick mist that blows around me has risen from nowhere on the howling wind, and I cannot take even one step for fear of it being the wrong one.

We have been out here for hours, a small group of Beech Circle members coming together and then splitting up, over and over in a pattern I cannot understand. We take it in turns to ride three horses between five of us, sometimes doubling up two to a horse, sometimes two walking to give the beasts respite. Twelve times now we've crawled through a windmill in the dark (a blessing to be out of the wind even with a face full of spiderwebs) before finding ourselves, empty-handed, in the elements once more.

The mist is a horrible, grasping creature of fog and damp that creeps beneath my clothes, stealing my breath with the sudden cold.

And it is here I stand now, unable to see Ana or, in fact, my fingers, which are outstretched lest I run into something right in front of me, aware as I am of all that is wild and lonely in this landscape.

What must it be like to be out here alone, not knowing which direction to walk, unable to call for help?

I think of that last wolf of Glawn, the one for whom this savage wind is named, and I wonder if it really is a myth, or if it wanders still, waiting for lost souls. Is that why people disappear forever, leaving no trace?

"Maven!" Relief floods through me as Ana's voice flies toward me, carried on the wind, drawing my wild thoughts back to the here and now. "We are here. Do not move. I will come to you when it clears."

I wrap my arms around my body and wait for the mist to pass, fighting the urge to move – anywhere, my body says, is better than here. But Ana and her friends have

203

passed the time, as we've trudged from mill to mill, all but bent double against the wind, regaling me of tales of those poor souls lost to Glawn's unhappy marshland.

When I'd mentioned that this was possibly not the best topic of conversation given Reeve's disappearance, they'd looked at me as though I'd lost my mind. It seems that Glawn folk are matter-of-fact about such disappearances, for the most part.

"To be honest, people are always wandering off," Ana told me during one of our mill searches, where it had been quiet enough for me to hear her. "You either spend your life inside the castle walls or take your chances, and most who are Glawn born and bred love the wild, clean air too much to remain indoors."

"So, you spend a lot of time searching?" I'd asked, surprised when she'd laughed in response.

"Not at all," she'd said. "People either come back or they don't. Sending others out after them usually just means you lose two or three people rather than one. That's one reason we were all a bit shocked when Sir Brannon rode off after Mistress Percy like he did. I mean, we all liked Mistress Percy, and her cooking is great, but he's never really paid her much attention before, except to demand a hot meal whenever he feels like one."

Reeve had already told me that Sir Brannon's search was more about sizing up Sir Garrick in peace than actively searching for the cook, so her words didn't surprise me.

"Ana?" I call now, my thoughts making me feel more isolated by the minute. "Are you there?"

There is no response above the howling wind, and now I begin to feel truly afraid, wondering if standing here in the dark and cold is really the best idea. They cannot be too far ahead of me? I can just —

Stay where you are. Ana's advice comes back to my mind again, and I take a deep breath to steady both my thoughts and my nerves. I can see how people are lost forever here. Fear makes us irrational, driving us away, somewhere, anywhere. It goes against every instinct I have to stay where I am when I want to flee.

I stamp my boots, trying to bring some feeling back to my feet, which are slowly turning to ice as the cold, damp ground seeps through the soles and under my hose. The movement soothes me, particularly when I begin to count each impotent step.

I have no idea how much time passes, but I am nearing two-hundred steps when I realize that the mist seems to be thinning. I hold out my hand at arm's length, relieved when I can make out every fingernail.

"Ana!" I shout. "Where are you?!"

"Over here!" The shout is faint, but my heart leaps in response. "Stay there and keep calling — we're coming!"

I begin by simply shouting "here" at intervals, but

realize that a steady sound will give them a better target. And so, I start to sing a song that I remember my father singing to me when I was a child and could not sleep.

"*I am here, darling one, right here,*
Right here, beside you, don't fear,
In the morning, in the evening, though the night is long,
I am here, darling one, in this song."

"That's a lovely song," says Ana, appearing beside me, and I manage a smile as she draws me into a hug. "But why are you crying? We would never have left without you."

I wipe my eyes, surprised when my hand comes away wet.

"Must be the mist," I say, stuffing away my feelings. She gives me a long look and then nods.

"It's not far now to the next mill, and the dawn will break soon. Stay strong, Maven."

I manage a laugh. "I will because I must. What choice do I have?"

CHAPTER ELEVEN

Reeve was dreaming of rivulets of rain running down windows and the deep blue of the vast lake near his family's manor in Norwood ... He awoke with a start, licking his dry tongue over parched lips, blinking at the weak sunlight striking his face through a tiny crack in the stone wall opposite where he lay.

Was it morning? How long had he been lying here?

The faint glow in the room was enough for him to see that, as he'd thought, he was lying beneath the huge gear wheel in the top of a windmill. The gale outside seemed to have eased to a dull roar, though the great sails were still careening on and on, around and around, driving the wheel above him.

Reeve's head hurt so much that he wished he had not

woken up. At least while asleep, he had respite from the noise and the horrible, aching dryness of his throat.

But if he was awake, he at least had a chance of escape.

Reeve tested his bonds again. Still tight, no matter how hard he pulled and strained against them.

"Aaaugh!" Reeve croaked in frustration, barely able to hear himself over the noise of the gears. If only the infernal wind would stop for a moment, he might have a chance to at least shout for help, but there was no point in that.

Suddenly, Reeve stilled. Turning his head, he pressed one ear to the floor. Yes, there was movement below him. Voices. The scrape of wood across the floor.

Was he in the mill where Sir Garrick had met with Sir Brannon? Who would have brought him here? Had they come back for him?

Reeve could feel his heart thumping, a rushing sound in his ears. He tugged hard against the ropes that bound him, but they held firm, each arm outstretched and tethered to the wall behind his head.

Helpless, he listened as the tread of boots began climbing the ladder beneath him . . .

The floor beside Reeve opened up with a sudden bang as a ladder was shoved up through the trapdoor, just inches from one outstretched arm.

Stomach churning with anger and fear, Reeve could

only listen as the footsteps continued, one rung at a time. Footsteps that were sure and . . . light?

To his astonishment, Maven's face appeared through the hole in the floor.

"There you are!" she said, quite as though they were playing hide-and-go-seek. "At last. I can't tell you how many of these ladders I've been up in the past few hours."

Maven leaned back down through the hole. "I've got him!" she said, sounding triumphant, and Reeve heard a quiet cheer from below. A quiet, high-pitched cheer. "We've got him!"

"I'm so glad to see you," Reeve croaked. "But why did it take so long?"

Maven looked affronted. "Do you have any idea how many windmills and other hidey-holes we've been in and out of before the sun even came up?"

"We?" Reeve couldn't help but ask.

"We," Maven said firmly, not answering his question as she hauled herself up into the dark room, crawling across to him to stay under the gear wheel.

"Aren't I in that big windmill near the castle?" he asked, as she began to work on the ropes that bound him hand and foot.

"You most certainly are not," Maven responded, untying his right wrist and massaging some feeling back into it before folding it by his side. "It's true they all feel the same once you get up here, but you're a long way from the castle. I would never have found you but for . . ."

"The Beech Circle," Reeve finished, with a whisper, feeling tears well up as pins and needles began to prickle up and down the arm by his side.

Maven nodded as she moved to his other arm. "Apparently, this is a local trysting spot, far from prying eyes — one of many. The residents of Glawn do like a good tryst, it seems. But enough discussion, we need to get you out of here."

She leaned over the hole in the floor. "Ana, can you hand me up a water flask? He's not in a good way."

With both arms by his side now, Reeve could only concur. They'd been tied in one position for so long that he could barely lift his fingers, and the prickling sensation was almost unbearable.

He turned his head as a beautiful, dark-haired woman popped up through the trapdoor.

"Ana, meet Reeve, Reeve, Ana," Maven said, focused on easing the rope from his second ankle. "Keep your head down, Ana, or that wheel will take it off."

Reeve summoned up a smile for his rescuer, a smile that became genuine as she climbed up into the room and unstoppered the water flask before holding it to his lips.

"Not too much," Ana said, as he lifted his head to

gulp greedily at the water. "You'll be sick, and I think you've got enough to deal with."

Taking a small sip, Reeve winced as his forehead throbbed with pain.

"That's a nasty cut you've got there," Maven said, settling on the other side of him and dabbing at his forehead with the bottom of her skirt.

Cut? Reeve blanched as he looked down at his shirt, at the floor around him, at Maven's skirt. There was blood everywhere. His blood. It was his blood that he'd been feeling trickling down his face. His blood that had created that terrible itch. A little river of his blood.

"Oh no," Reeve moaned, scrabbling frantically at his neck for the tincture bottle that Myra had given him. If he could just grab it, open it, drink it, he might be able to stave off —

"Reeve, are you all right?" Maven was leaning over him, waving a hand in front of his face. A hand streaked with blood.

Reeve's world went black.

"What are we going to do with him now?"

Ana and I have slapped Reeve in the face. We've poured water over his head. We've shouted his name.

But he won't wake up and I am beginning to despair.

Having found him, I am worried I will lose him forever.

I saw him trying to grab the tincture bottle that Myra had given him, but I can't pour it down the throat of someone who can't swallow.

At least now I know what it's for. Myra was careful to keep Reeve's secret, even from me, but it doesn't take a genius to see his reaction to blood and put two and two together.

I can see why he would not want word to get out about this. His ambitions to be a knight, to be a man of his own means, would be crueled in an instant.

For now, though, his ambitions are not as important as his health.

"He breathes," says Ana, grabbing my hand to stay my panic. "I think he has just fainted."

"We have to get him out of here and smuggle him back inside the castle," I say. "We can't take the chance that someone will come back for him."

As I say the words I am aware of just how difficult it will be to move Reeve. He may be on the smaller side for a 16-year-old squire, but he's bigger than the five of us are and, in his current state, he's a dead weight.

"We have the horses," I continue. "We'll have to put him on a horse and —"

"And what?" Ana laughs, without humor. "Ride him back through the gates? That'll be inconspicuous. Whoever put him here put him here for a reason, and

I'd think you'd want it kept fairly quiet that you've recovered him."

Even as I acknowledge that she's right, an inkling of an idea is forming in my mind, sparked by her use of the word "inconspicuous."

"That's exactly what we need to do," I say, thinking out loud. "We need to ride him in through the front gates, inconspicuously, with us, in a group."

Ana laughs again. "I'm not sure you've grasped the meaning of inconspicuous."

"We're going to dress him so he blends in," I say, with a grin. "The other girls are day workers at the castle, right?"

Ana nods, not looking convinced.

"Good," I say. "We're going to clean him up and dress him like one of them."

"Like a girl?" Ana is incredulous. "Will he ever forgive you for that?"

My grin becomes a wide smile. "Possibly not. But if we get away with it, he'll have to."

"And if we don't?"

I don't want to think about that. Someone wanted Reeve out of the way and was happy to leave him here without food or water, seemingly to die. Whether it was to keep Sir Garrick occupied in a search, to send a message or for some other reason, I'd rather that someone didn't know Reeve has been rescued just yet.

"We will," I say, with more confidence than I feel. "But we'd better get on with it. I'd rather be well away from here before anyone else shows up."

Between us we drag an uncomplaining Reeve so that his feet are positioned by the ladder, the whole enterprise made endlessly more difficult by having to stay under that ever-spinning wheel above our heads. Looking down, I see three pale, scared faces peering up at me.

"Ruby," I say, speaking to the oldest girl, who is about the same age as I am and has the strong, stocky build of a farmer's daughter. "Can you take the ladder away for a moment and drag that bed over so that it's under the hole? We're going to have to try to lower him down there and I think we'll need a softish landing place."

Ruby directs the other two to start moving the bed while she removes the ladder.

"Are you ready?" I ask Ana, and she grabs hold of Reeve under one armpit in response. Together, we push him, feet first, toward the hole in the floor. As soon as his floppy legs go over the edge, I begin to feel his weight and I'm careful to stay close by his side so his back doesn't arch too much. There's no point in rescuing him if we break him in two in the process.

Moments later, Ana grunts and we lurch forward as Reeve dangles in space, held only by his armpits.

"Ready?" I shout to Ruby and the others below, as

I feel Reeve begin to slip through my fingers. "We can't hold him."

"Got him," Ruby answers to my relief as he slides out of my grasp.

I hear a loud squeaking thud as he lands below, and I slither forward to hang over the edge to see what's happened. To my surprise, Ruby is lying on the bed under Reeve's prone body, looking startled and winded.

"I had him by the leg, to sort of guide him down, but it turns out he didn't need much guiding," Ruby half laughs, half groans, and I can't help but chuckle myself, but only for a moment.

"Can you two get him off her so you can get the ladder back up?"

The other two girls rush to do as I ask, and within minutes Ana and I are making our way down the ladder.

"Right," I say. "We need to dress him. Do any of you live anywhere near here?"

Ruby nods, and I'm relieved, because of all of us, she's probably closest in size to Reeve.

"Can you swap clothes with him and then go home and change before going to the castle?" It's a big thing to ask someone you've only just met, but she begins to untie the red woven belt around her long, gray woolen shift. As she lifts the hem of the shift to pull it up and over her head, I see a rough, white cotton chemise beneath it.

"We'll need the chemise but you can keep your hose and boots," I say, as the two younger girls giggle. "Ana, help me undress him."

We make quick work of Reeve's soft black tunic, easing it off his unresisting arms and over his face. At first, I try not to get blood on it, but I soon realize that the collar is soaked with it.

"I'm so sorry, Ruby," I say, handing it to the girl to cover herself. "It's in a horrible state. Maybe wear it inside out so that the blue fox is not as obvious."

Ruby is slipping it over her blond curls as I turn to Ana, who has removed Reeve's boots.

"I'll do his breeches," I say. "If you pull the chemise over his top half, I can take them off under that."

I am conscious of sparing Reeve some dignity in this process — and also, frankly, there are some things that friends do not need to know about each other.

Working in tandem, pulling and lifting, we soon have Reeve decked out in his new finery and I realize that, with his shorn hair, he still looks like a boy in a gown.

"Ana, I'm going to need to borrow your kerchief," I say. "And I'm afraid that I'll probably need to replace it later because there's still a lot of blood in his hair."

"It's okay," Ana says, unwinding it as she speaks. "Airl and Lady Riding provide them as part of the uniform, so I'll grab another from the laundry. But you should at least try to wash his hair first – the blood won't take long to seep through."

She's right, so I waste precious minutes pouring water over Reeve's head, emptying the flask but managing to at least clear up some of the blood. I turn to Ana, still holding the scarf.

"Can you put it on him? It needs to look like everyone else's."

Minutes later, Reeve is as ready as he'll ever be and, I have to concede, with his short hair covered and his face framed by the artfully arranged kerchief, he makes a passably pretty girl.

Not that I think I should *ever* tell him that.

"Okay, let's get him out of here," I say, worried that whoever left Reeve here will come to check on him soon.

"Easier said than done," Ruby mutters, but she volunteers to go down the ladder to the ground floor first, waiting halfway down to help maneuver Reeve's legs again. Apparently, having Reeve fall on her wasn't all that bad . . .

Between us, we get him down the ladder and out of the windmill doors, where our three horses watch us with great interest as they munch on the sparse grass around the stumpy trees to which they're tied.

I climb up onto my horse and pull Reeve up in front of me, laying him across the neck of my horse and keeping one hand on him to try to hold him in place. It's horribly awkward, but what choice do I have?

When we get closer to the castle, I will need to try to arrange him across the saddle in front of me, but for now he flops like a sack of potatoes.

"Ruby will take one horse home and get changed as fast as she can," Ana says. "The rest of us will have to take it in turns riding this other one between us."

"We'll have to take it slowly anyway," I say, before turning to Ruby. "Try to hurry back to meet us before we get to the castle gates. The more of us there are, the easier it will be to hide him among us."

Ruby takes off at a gallop into the rising morning mist and, as she disappears, I'm pretty sure I can hear a loud whoop. I smile, realizing that Ruby has discovered the freedom afforded by a pair of breeches.

"Right," I say to Reeve, who shows no sign of hearing me. "Let's get you to bed."

CHAPTER TWELVE

"What's the matter with your friend? Had a bit too much fun last night?"

Reeve could hear the rough voice as though from far, far away, and decided he must be dreaming again. For that could not be horsehair beneath his cheek?

"Something like that." With a start, Reeve recognized Maven's voice, very close to his ear, as a hand patted his head.

"You lot are late for work," the rough voice growled. "The Airl's not going to be too happy with you."

Reeve's head hurt and there was a strong scent of horse in his nostrils. He wiggled, trying to get comfortable, and the hand on his head pressed down hard, holding him still.

"Probably not," came a cheerful voice from somewhere ahead of Reeve, and he thought he recognized Maven's friend Ana who had come —

His thoughts stopped. Last time he'd seen Ana, he'd been lying in that dark space and there was —

He gulped, not wanting to think about the rest, but unable to stop.

Blood. Lots of blood. His blood.

Reeve swallowed, as hard as his horribly dry throat would let him, knowing that he'd passed out, fainted dead away, at the sight. Right in front of Maven and a woman he didn't know at all.

But where was he now?

"Anyway, you're only making us later," Ana said, her tone teasing. "You don't want to be responsible for having us all lose our jobs?"

"Wouldn't be my fault," the rough voice said. "Blame your pretty friend."

Pretty friend? Reeve frowned, wondering who the guard was talking about.

"You might want to at least pull her skirts down a bit," the man went on. "She's showing a bit of leg there. No hose on a cold day, tsk, tsk."

As Maven's hand moved from Reeve's head and he felt her bend down and tug at something near his knee, Reeve froze. It was him the guard was talking about. Him. In a skirt that was showing too much leg.

A skirt!

Suddenly, Reeve was wide-awake. He tried lifting his head, but the movement sent his mind spinning. As he closed his eyes again, he felt Maven's weight on his back as she leaned forward to whisper in his ear.

"Stay still," she hissed. "We haven't come this far to have you ruin everything now."

Unsure exactly what he was ruining, Reeve nonetheless complied, mostly because he was so confused and so tired he didn't know which way was up. He felt the horse move beneath him and heard the steady *clip-clop* as it made its way sedately across the cobbled courtyard. Reeve tried opening his eyes again, but the cobbles were a blur, making him feel sick to the stomach, so he closed them again.

"Where's the best place to take him?" Reeve heard Maven ask in a low voice.

"He's still watching so we'll have to go toward the stables," Ana answered. "But you and I can slide off with him at the laundry door, and the girls will carry on with the horses. Once we're inside, though, it's up to you."

There was a moment of silence. "Enjoy these last few minutes of rest, Reeve," Maven said. "I need you on your feet once we get inside."

Reeve managed to grunt in response and then focused on the *clip-clop* sound, until it came to an abrupt halt and he felt Maven slither off the horse behind him.

Without her supporting arm, Reeve felt himself slide sideways, landing in a crumpled heap on the ground at her feet. He was vaguely aware of the sound of giggling as the horses moved away.

"Come on then, miss," Ana said, grabbing him under the armpit while Maven hauled him up by his other arm. "Let's get you inside to rest."

The two girls stood on either side of him, one of his arms across each of their shoulders. Reeve could feel the wind, fortunately only a light breeze today, blowing on his bare legs, and the strange feeling of fabric brushing against his boots. Now that he was upright, he realized how tight the top half of his gown (for surely that's what he was wearing?) was. One deep breath and he'd split the side seams, for sure.

Where in the world had the shift come from — and what did he have on underneath? Reeve felt a rising tide of heat wash over his face — more to the point, who had changed him out of his own breeches?

"Don't worry," Maven said, as they moved toward a small door set into the wall. "Your modesty is quite safe, isn't it, Ana?"

Ana's laugh was a gurgle in his ear. "Quite," she said, and Reeve wondered why he didn't feel reassured.

As they entered the steamy laundry, however, Reeve realized that his modesty was a small price to pay for the fact that these two girls and their friends had rescued him from the horrors of that dark, noisy room.

"I think we should clean him up again before you take him anywhere," Ana said, with a huge yawn.

"Thank you," Maven replied, reaching across his chest to grasp Ana's shoulder. Reeve was surprised to hear the tremble in his friend's voice.

"You would do the same for me," Ana responded, her eyes bright, and they both nodded, as though there was no more to say. As members of the Beech Circle, there probably *was* no more to say, Reeve realized, before wondering just how wide the network really was. Were they in every castle, every fief, every village in the land? He was astonished that it could have gone undetected, and flourished, long enough to grow so large.

It made him wonder just what else Cartreff's airls and knight protectors had overlooked.

"Come," Ana said, walking Reeve and therefore Maven toward the big tub. Easing him down onto a bench beside a pile of folded napkins, Ana grabbed one and dipped it into the cool water that filled the big washtub for the day ahead.

Reeve squirmed a little but could not find the strength to resist as Ana removed something that was wrapped around his head, and then wiped at his scalp with the napkin. Reeve winced as the napkin instantly turned pink.

"We're going to need a few of these," Maven said, picking up another cloth and copying Ana's movements. "At least the cut on his head has stopped bleeding."

Reeve swallowed but said nothing as the two girls dabbed gently at his face and neck. From the way they dragged the wet napkins down either side of his face, he could only imagine that the blood had run in rivers down his skin and dried there.

"I don't think we can do much more with your hair," Ana said. "You'll need a good bath to get the matted blood from it."

She turned to Maven. "It is fortunate indeed that the guard on the gate was so distracted by his bare legs, because his face would not have passed close inspection."

Maven laughed as Reeve winced at the idea of his legs hanging out of his skirt. "Don't fret," Maven said to him. "He'll never see them again so chances are he'll never recognize you."

As the two girls giggled at his discomfort, Reeve focused on the positives. He was here, he was safe, and, with the blood cleaned up, he wasn't likely to pass out and bare his legs again any time soon.

Now, he just had to hide somewhere while they figured out exactly who it was that had tied him up in that windmill. And what they hoped to achieve.

"Where will you take him?" Ana asked Maven, as

though reading Reeve's mind.

"My Lady Cassandra's room," Maven said, instantly, and Reeve knew that she'd been considering this question long and hard on their journey back to the castle. "He is dressed for it and I don't think that anyone will look for him there."

Ana laughed. "And your lady? Will she welcome a bleeding boy in a skirt?"

Again, Ana spoke aloud what Reeve was thinking. The only time he'd been in Lady Cassandra's rooms was that very first morning they'd met, when the Fire Star had gone missing.

"She will," Maven said, and there was no doubt in her tone. "But we'd best be on our way before the castle gets busy. Thank you for your help, my friend."

"Godspeed," Ana said, as she helped Reeve to stand and settled his arm once again across Maven's shoulders. Reeve felt Maven sag as she took all his weight, and he tried his hardest to stand as upright as possible.

Ana turned away and went to open the other door in the laundry, the one that would take them into the castle proper, sticking her head through it to check the hallway. "All clear," Ana said. "But Ida will be here any minute so you'll need to hurry. You'll be okay?"

"We'll be fine," Maven said, and Reeve took strength from her solid, positive tone. "We have to be."

Taking heart from the "we," Reeve staggered out into the hallway with her, concentrating on staying on his feet, listening to Maven's orders to step left, right, up or down, his vision swimming and his head whirling.

Reeve was vaguely aware of a stifled shriek of surprise and the sensation of falling through a door, before he was finally lying on his back on a firm pallet, the scent of violets filling his nostrils as he closed his eyes for just a moment . . .

"You looked surprisingly good in that kirtle."

Reeve winced as Sir Garrick's words brought him back to the present, and he opened his eyes on the knight's grinning face.

"Oh, don't take on – it's good to know. Chances are we might need a spy in the future and who'd ever suspect?"

Reeve didn't quite know how to answer. Three parts of him were in awe of Maven and her friends for managing to get him to safety, even though he'd been out cold. The other part wondered if she – and Sir Garrick and Lady Cassandra – had to enjoy the process quite so much.

"I don't plan to make a habit of it, sire," he finally managed. "It's a bit breezy."

"Leave him be, Garrick," Lady Cassandra said, entering the small dressing room that adjoined her bedchamber. Reeve had been dozing on a pallet — Maven's, probably — for several hours, only waking when Sir Garrick had clomped in a few minutes before. "He's been dozing on and off for several hours and I'd imagine he's in no mood for your witty asides."

Sir Garrick laughed. "At least you admit they are witty."

"At least Reeve admits that skirts are breezy," Lady Cassandra countered, looking thoughtful. "I am surprised that the women of Glawn have not taken up a more practical form of dress, in the same way that they have their own fashion for hair."

"You would have them in breeches?" Sir Garrick asked, his eyebrows almost hitting his dark fringe.

"I would have them in what makes them most comfortable," Cassandra said, firmly. "It would not surprise me if we were to discover that they wear well-fitting breeches beneath their gowns."

Sir Garrick looked at her, his face soft with fondness. "Is that your secret weapon for warmth?"

Cassandra laughed, turning up the hem of the deep-red wool gown she was wearing to reveal another, less full, layer of fine wool beneath. "When we learned we were to travel to Glawn, Maven remade an old kirtle to create a heavy petticoat," she said. "I can tuck this around my legs when I sit, even as my gown spreads over the top."

"Very resourceful girl, that Maven," Sir Garrick said, looking thoughtful. "Where is she, anyway?"

"I've sent her to find a footman to bring hot water for Reeve," Cassandra said. "I nearly fell over when I saw the state of him. All that blood. How fortunate it was that Maven happened to speak to that farm girl who'd heard strange cries from that mill . . ."

Reeve's mouth went dry, and he hoped she would move on from that subject with haste.

"Yes, fortunate indeed," said Sir Garrick, and Reeve saw that his master was once again serious. "Do not fear that I have overlooked that fact, Reeve. I sought merely to lighten the atmosphere as we must try to present a normal appearance. We are far from home and surrounded by potential danger. It will not do to tip our hand."

Cassandra frowned. "I think it's a bit late for that, wouldn't you say? Reeve is not in this state by accident. It looks to me as though our hand may be tipped – or will be once whoever did this to him goes back to find him."

"Sire, what if this is about the cook and her sisters . . .?" Reeve croaked.

"I have not forgotten our conversation," said Sir Garrick, "but nothing has changed on the question of proof. We do not know if your situation is to do with our mission here or . . . something else. Were you not sat with a group of young ladies yesterday, Reeve? Could it be that you have made someone jealous?"

"Surely, this would be an overreaction to one public conversation?" Lady Cassandra said, before Reeve could respond. "I did hear whispers of Reeve's dimples among the young ladies yesterday, but nothing more. Perhaps it was more about engaging your attention, Garrick. After all, if Reeve was to go missing for any length of time, you would not be parleying in the Airl's solar, you would be looking for him."

Sir Garrick frowned, seeming to take on the import of her words, before crouching down beside Reeve. "What is the last thing you remember?"

"The quintain," Reeve said immediately. "I was riding toward it."

Sir Garrick's frown deepened. "So, you do not recall going for ales after the session with Airl Riding's men?"

Reeve thought so hard that his head began to ache. "No. All I remember seeing is the sandbag swaying in the wind as I rode toward it."

"I see," said Sir Garrick, rising, his brow furrowed. "Then it seems the guards may have not been honest and I must make further enquiries."

"Be careful," Lady Cassandra said, her hand on his arm. "If Reeve was taken as bait for you, then . . ."

"Always," he responded, placing his hand over her own. "Careful is my middle name."

Lady Cassandra shook her head. "Cornelius is your middle name," she said, managing a laugh at his wince. "Be careful anyway."

"I shall attend you, sire," Reeve said, struggling to rise from the pallet, his vision fading at the edges as he did so.

"You shall not," Sir Garrick said, crouching once more to push Reeve gently back upon the pillow. "You need to rest, young squire. Rest and work hard to remember all you can. It would be for the best if you are not spotted in public yet."

Reeve couldn't keep his eyes from closing. "I'll just be a few minutes," he said out loud, aware of Sir Garrick's quiet chuckle, but unable to rouse himself enough to respond as darkness descended.

CHAPTER THIRTEEN

It is amazing what a few hours' sleep will do for the body and mind. I have never been one to linger in bed, sleeping only five or six hours a night, even when I lived at home with my family and could have slept all day had I wanted. But between the missing Fire Star, the travel to Glawn and the events since our arrival here, the past sennight has pushed me hard.

I can only thank a higher being that I am not Ana right now, up to her elbows in lye soap and mountains of laundry after the busy night we had.

Cassandra had met Reeve and I at her chamber door, and helped me to put him to bed. True to his word, Sir Garrick had told her where I was, but that had not stopped her fretting about my absence all night, and she was heavy eyed as we tucked Reeve in.

"Now, sleep," she'd said to me, pointing at her own bed. "The finest mind fails without rest, Maven, and I am worried that I rely too heavily on yours."

I was so weary I hadn't even tried to argue, simply falling into the pillowy softness of her high, four-poster bed as she drew the curtains around me to keep out the light and the prying eyes of any castle servants, who might attend to her that morning.

When I'd awoken, the morning light filled the chamber and I could hear Reeve snoring through the closed door to the dressing room beyond. Rolling from the feather mattress to the floor took effort, but I needed to see for myself that he was on the mend.

"He is fine," Cassandra had said, as soon as my feet had hit the floor. "You have done well by him. No one will imagine that he is here."

She had dressed herself and combed her hair back in the sleek Glawn style, which suits her, showcasing as it does her extraordinary green eyes. *She does not need me anymore.*

The thought had hurtled through my mind in an instant and I'd batted it away, but now that I am on my own, following Cassandra's direction to fetch hot water, I take it out and examine it more fully.

Anice is right, I concede with a sinking heart. With Cassandra's growing relationship with Sir Garrick providing far more fulsome company than I can, and her own innate ability to look after herself, even if she does not yet trust it, Cassandra has no real need of me.

A heaviness settles over me as I tread toward the kitchen, wondering just how long it will take Cassandra herself to realize this.

I try to shake off the feeling, and I'm reaching for the remnants of that lingering, well-rested joy I felt earlier, when I round the corner to the stairs and all but bump into a wall comprised of Airl Riding's guards.

"Excuse me, good sirs," I say, keeping my gaze on the floor and bobbing to show a respect that the stories told by the Beech Circle last night will not allow me to feel.

"Be on your way, girl," a rough voice rumbles, and my skin prickles in recognition. Is this the deep-voiced man from the windmill?

I peek up from beneath my hair to take closer note of who has spoken, but all I see are four men in identical clothing, none of whom are looking at me and none of whom are easily identifiable as the man who spoke. Sir Brannon I recognize, along with Jonty, but not the other two.

Was it one of them?

"Beg pardon, sire," I say, hoping to prompt the voice to speak again, but it is Jonty who turns to me in exasperation.

"Just go," he hisses, "can you not see we are busy? The cook is in the clutches of kidnappers, we have plans to make and you are distracting us with inanities."

I try to look flustered as I hasten down the hallway, but I am, in fact, deep in thought. I could swear that the man who spoke prior to Jonty was the sixth man in the windmill, the one giving the orders.

I peek back over my shoulder at the guards, who are huddled together, listening as Sir Brannon mutters to them.

Sir Brannon? Have I ever heard him speak?

I cast back through my mind for an occasion when Glawn's Knight Protector may have had cause to talk to me, but can think of none. I pause mid step at the top of the stairs.

I must be sure. If Sir Brannon is the sixth man, then he knows all our secrets and Sir Garrick is at risk in this castle – and, by association, so is my Lady Cassandra.

Not to mention what might happen to Airl Buckthorn and all at Rennart Castle should news of our mission reach the King's ears.

Taking a deep breath, I turn and retrace my steps back to where the men are still talking, and I stand there, fidgeting with my fingers until Jonty notices me again.

"What is the matter with you, girl?" he spits.

"'Scuse me, sires," I say, "it's just that I'm not from

234

here and I'm not sure of the way to the buttery. My lady has asked me for a cask of wine for her room this afternoon."

Jonty rolls his eyes and lifts his hand as though to cuff me, but Sir Brannon grabs his wrist.

"No, Jonty, the lass cannot help being lost," he says, and I almost freeze at the sound of his deep tones. It is definitely the man from the windmill, and I almost forget to smile at him.

His dark eyes fix upon me, and all I can see in them is my own tiny face reflected back in his pupils.

"Can you?" he asks, his voice now holding an edge of menace.

"Er, no, sire, I cannot help it," I say, bobbing another curtsey, trying to ignore the fact that the hallway is empty of friendly faces and my knees are shaking. "I am a long way from home."

"Indeed," Sir Brannon rumbles, his expression still intent, and I wonder if he is buying my "lost maiden" act even the slightest bit. "I'll tell you what, Jonty here will escort you to the buttery — after all, I'd hate for you to, er, stumble into any areas that might prove dangerous for you."

Now all four men are frowning at me, and there is a small voice in my mind telling me that a sensible person would turn and flee at this point.

"I'd be ever so grateful," I say, batting my eyelashes

at Jonty and knowing that the breathlessness in my voice will be put down to flirtation, not fear. "My friend Reeve has still not turned up, you know, and the moor seems endless."

Sir Brannon gives me one last lingering look.

"Make sure she gets there," he says to Jonty, eventually. "We can't have two of them disappearing off the face of the earth."

I am processing the fact that our plan has worked and they think Reeve is still missing when Jonty takes me by the arm, none too gently, and makes to "guide" me away, but Sir Brannon holds a hand up to stop him.

"Have you news of Sir Garrick's squire?" he asks me, and this time his intense stare feels as though it is probing behind my eyes.

"No, sire," I say, hoping I appear pale and worried. It is not a stretch. I am feeling worried, but my concern right now is for myself, not for Reeve, who is no doubt sleeping soundly upstairs.

"Sir Garrick searches for him?" Sir Brannon probes.

"As far as I know, sire, but I am merely a lowly maid."

"Hmmm," Sir Brannon says. "And yet last night Sir Garrick joined us in our meeting regarding the ransom note, allowing his own squire to be absent from his duties to do who knows what. I am not sure how they run things at Rennart, but that's not how we do things here. It makes me wonder."

The other guards mutter assent, and I focus on holding my expression blank. Sir Brannon is looking for any change, and I cannot allow him a reason to doubt me further. I don't know what is happening here at Glawn Castle, but I do know that I need to speak with Sir Garrick as a matter of some urgency.

"I'm afraid I don't know about that, sire," I say. "I went to my Lady Cassandra as soon as Sir Garrick left with you."

"Hmmm," he says again.

"Can I take her now?" whines Jonty. "I have no time to play nursemaid to a maiden."

"Take her," Sir Brannon agrees. "And mind you deliver her directly to the buttery. I will go to the hall and speak with Sir Garrick."

He turns on his heel and strides away, the other two men behind him.

"Come on, then," Jonty says. "I've got better things to do than this."

"I'm sure I would find my way with directions," I say, all but skipping along beside him to keep up, such is his haste to be rid of me. "I know you must be worried about Mistress Percy. Has Airl Riding changed his mind about paying the ransom?"

"Sir Brannon says he has not," Jonty says, stopping in his tracks. "All we can hope is that the kidnappers will negotiate."

I blink, my mind whirling. "What makes you think they would do that?"

"Sir Brannon thinks that they have decided to go high with their demands to then get what they really want, a much lower figure," says Jonty, beginning to walk toward the buttery once more.

I follow at a slower pace, forcing him to stop and wait for me, my tired mind spinning with questions. Jonty grabs my elbow and begins to hurry me along, making me aware that I had come to a standstill on the stairs. I don't have much more time with him.

"I still don't understand why anyone would kidnap a cook," I say, extricating my arm by pretending to stumble and grab for the wall. I know that I am probing too deep but also that I may never get another chance to speak to this man one-on-one.

Which is not to say that I will allow myself to be manhandled by him.

Fortunately, Jonty doesn't seem to mind my interest in his aunt.

"I can't think of anything," he says, as we reach the lower floor, but his voice is unsure and he will not meet my eyes.

I decide to push a little bit. "No secret family recipes that people would kill to own?" I ask, keeping my tone light.

Jonty's laugh sounds nervous. "Not that I can think

of," he says. "Why would you think that?"

"What else could a cook have that would be worth all this attention? Particularly if she is the only one who knows them."

The silence between us draws out and, as it does, my last sentence rings in my head and I almost stumble again. I have been working on the assumption all this time that Mistress Percy is the only one who knows her recipes, but what if that is not the case? Even a head cook must delegate sometimes?

And if someone else knows the recipe, then can I test my theory about the book code?

"Hey, hang on! It's this way." As Jonty takes my elbow again, I realize that my steps have been racing headlong in tandem with my thoughts and that they're taking me toward the kitchen.

"Ah, sorry," I say, allowing him to guide me out a side door toward the buttery.

"It seems you truly would be lost without me," Jonty says, and I hear a note of relief in his voice that suggests that my momentary lapse has allayed his suspicions.

I giggle half-heartedly, preoccupied with my thoughts as I wrestle with the idea of who might have learned Mistress Percy's recipes. As we cross the courtyard, I am struck by the image of a dour face watching my every move in the Glawn kitchen.

Mistress Gyles, who sits and watches and glowers.

If anyone in that kitchen knows the recipe for Mistress Percy's Pease Pottage, it will be Mistress Gyles.

Even as I have the thought, however, and picture her face, I know that the old woman will never tell me.

No, not me.

But I can think of someone she might tell.

I turn to thank Jonty, who barely bothers to acknowledge me before stalking off, our moment of fellowship over now that he has done his duty. I duck inside the buttery door and find myself in a cool, tidy space with a stone counter at one end that's currently unattended.

"One moment please," a gruff voice shouts, and I notice that the trapdoor leading to the cellar is open. I breathe a sigh of relief. I don't really need a cask of wine, I just needed a destination for my walk with Jonty.

"No matter," I shout back. "I'll return in a moment, good sir."

I stick my head out the door to check that Jonty has gone. The courtyard is clear, so I pick up my skirts and walk as quickly as I can back toward Lady Cassandra's rooms, my thoughts churning like the sails on a Glawn windmill.

If we know the recipe, we can use the code to break the message. If we know the message, we can use it to work out exactly what's going on in Glawn Castle and who might have Mistress Percy.

Once we know who has her, we can figure out where she is.

But time is short.

The ransom note has given a deadline of noon today, just three short hours away.

It will not leave Reeve much time to work his charm on Mistress Gyles.

CHAPTER FOURTEEN

Half of Reeve was buoyed that Maven placed such trust in his ability to charm the elderly ladies of Cartreff. The other half feared that she had set him an impossible challenge, particularly given how tired he was and how much his head hurt.

He had tried to explain that to Maven, but she had been immovable. "Don't tell me you can't make that work for you, Reeve of Norwood," she'd said. "Sir Garrick needs you to do this."

"Sir Garrick told me to stay out of sight," Reeve had countered, but it was not enough to stop Maven.

"Out of sight of the guards," she'd said. "No one in that kitchen even knows who you are or that you're supposed to be missing. You just need to sneak in there, do your best work, and sneak back here again."

"But my face — Maven, look at me!" Reeve hadn't even needed to try to look pathetic, knowing that the bruises on the side of his face were blooming even if the blood had been washed from his hair.

"Oh, come now, you can use that to your advantage," Maven had responded. "Make them feel sorry for you!"

Reeve knew that he was doomed. If Maven was convinced this would help Sir Garrick, then Reeve was bound to get it done.

Which is why, having crept like a thief in the night down to the kitchen, ducking at every sound, Reeve now found himself getting his hand slapped by the pretty redhead he could only assume was the Tillie that Maven had told him to seek out.

"I told you not to touch the oatcakes," Tillie said, the teasing lilt to her voice belying her words.

"But my head aches so much and they are so delicious," Reeve said, with a smile, knowing that the dreaded dimples would appear as though by magic even as his head throbbed. "The touch of lavender in them is artful."

"Artful, is it now?" Tillie scoffed, her gray skirts swinging as she put her hands on her hips. "And, the state of your head aside, what would a strapping squire like you know about herbs in cooking?"

"Not much," Reeve admitted truthfully, blushing a

little at her use of the word "strapping." Only a tiny girl like this could ever consider him of enough size to be strapping. "But I am always eager to learn."

"Well, it's not me you'll want to be chatting up with your compliments then," Tillie said, dusting her hands with flour and turning back to the huge bowl of dough she was kneading. "Go and tell Mistress Gyles you find her lavender artful. She'll be that thrilled, particularly as Mistress Percy doesn't usually let her have a say."

"Mistress Gyles?" Reeve asked, as though he didn't know exactly who she was talking about. He popped the last piece of oatcake in his mouth with a flourish, realizing as he did that he could happily eat another six of them, it had been so long since his last meal.

Perhaps lavender had medicinal properties.

"Over there," Tillie said, sending little clouds of flour into the air as she waved at the woman stripping the skins from fat beans near the fire and keeping a weather eye on proceedings in the kitchen.

Dusting a trace of flour from his own hands, Reeve crossed the flagstone floor and bowed to Mistress Gyles. "May I sit with you a moment?"

The woman did not even look at him, continuing her work with the rhythmic expertise born of years of practice, much of her face hidden by the white cap she wore.

"It won't matter whether I say yes or no," Mistress Gyles said. "You've got the feeling about you of one who will sit anyway."

Reeve frowned at her words. "No, my good mistress, you have that wrong," he said, continuing to stand. "I await your permission, and if I do not receive it I will not press."

Now, Mistress Gyles stopped, pinning him with a shrewd gaze. "I do believe you mean what you say," she said, eventually. "Which makes for a change. Sit. Tell me, why is your head bandaged and a bruise blossoming on the side of that pretty face?"

Reeve looked around and snagged a nearby three-legged stool, which he drew up beside her at the table. He decided not to play games with her, as it seemed she valued his honesty so far.

"I ran into the quintain and do not remember much after that."

She studied him, the rhythmic movement of her hands never pausing. "I see. Bit more practice required then. And what is it you want from an old woman like me?"

"The cook's recipe for Pease Pottage," Reeve said, baldly, keeping his voice low.

For a moment, the rhythmic podding faltered, but then Mistress Gyles continued her repetitive task. "And why would a young squire, particularly one in a state like you, ask me about a thing like that?"

Reeve considered his response, before deciding

that the truth of it was all he had to offer. "I think that it might help me to find her," he eventually said.

"Hmmm, do you now?" Mistress Gyles said, placing the bowl of beans on the table and turning to look directly at him for the first time. "And what makes you think I would know it? Mistress Percy guards her recipes fiercely and entrusts them to no one."

Reeve did not miss the bitterness in her tone, or the narrowing of her pale blue eyes. At close glance, he could see that Mistress Gyles was not as old as he'd first imagined – perhaps in her fifties – but she looked as though circumstance or the Glawn wind had worn away her life force. Probably both.

"I think you see a lot more than perhaps Mistress Percy might think," he answered now, praying that Maven was right before forging ahead. "Anyone who brings out the precise marriage of lavender and oat as you have done in those biscuits is worthy of running a kitchen of her own."

But Mistress Gyles laughed at him, a harsh, croaking sound. "Oh, you think so, do you? Decided that after one bite of biscuit, have you?"

Reeve blushed, worried that he had overplayed his hand, but she reached over and patted his shoulder.

"As it turns out, I do know the recipe, young sire. Haven't I sat here and watched her make it year after year, turning her back on the kitchen as she put in the secret ingredient, overlooking the fact that I'm always here, in the corner, in full view?"

Mistress Gyles leaned back in her chair, her expression triumphant.

"And you will tell me?" Reeve asked, carefully.

"I cannot for the life of me understand how you think it will help to find the poor woman, but yes, I'll tell you. I won't take over her kitchen this way. Not like this."

Reeve nodded, though Mistress Gyles seemed to be gazing past him at something only she could see.

"But will you remember it, young man?" she asked, her gaze snapping back to him. "Or will you need to write it down like that nephew of hers does?"

"You have seen him do it?" Reeve asked, with a frown.

"Oh yes," Mistress Gyles said, with that croaking cackle. "It seems Glawn is full of young men with a sudden interest in cooking."

Ignoring the subtle invitation to tell her more, Reeve suddenly realized that he had not brought anything with him on which to capture the recipe. Mistress Gyles seemed to sense his dilemma.

"Wait," she said, rising slowly and disappearing into the pantry for a few moments before returning with a clean square of muslin, a goose feather and a small clay pot of dark liquid. "That should work for your purposes."

For one horrible moment, Reeve thought she had brought him blood to write with, but the scent from the pot soon filled his nostrils.

"Is that wine?" he asked.

"Yes, though no one would drink it now it's that thick. But it should hold shape enough in the weave of the fabric."

Reeve dipped the hard, pointed end of the goose feather into the liquid and pressed it into a corner of the muslin to test her theory. The small dot smeared outward a little, but otherwise held its shape.

"Ready? Let's begin."

Reeve wrote carefully as she recited the recipe:

"Five big handfuls of dried peas
Three fingers of butter
One spoon mint
One spoon parsley
One spoon marjoram
One spoon savory
Pinch salt
Pinch pepper

Place peas into a pot and cover with fresh water. Bring to the boil, skimming off scum that rises. Lower the heat and simmer for at least one hour or until peas are very tender.

Drain peas. Mash well. Stir in butter and herbs."

Mistress Gyles stopped speaking, and Reeve read over what he'd written.

"That's it?" he asked, perplexed. "I thought it would be more complicated."

Surely there couldn't be a secret message hidden in this?

"Wait a minute," Reeve added, tickling the side of his nose with the goose feather while he thought. "Which of these is the secret ingredient? The one you said she turns her back to add."

Mistress Gyles raised an eyebrow. "Well, now, it could be any of them. How much do you know about Pease Pottage?"

"Not much," Reeve admitted. "Only that I like to eat it."

Her cold stare assessed him once again, and he noticed a silver-gray curl slipping from under her white cap. "The secret ingredient is not in the Pottage but in the biscuits Mistress Percy serves with it. Legendary, they are. She would never serve Pease Pottage without them."

Reeve thought a moment, his mind racing. "And did, er, her nephew ask for that recipe, as well?"

Mistress Gyles nodded, crossing her arms over her white apron, which Reeve noticed had no marks or stains on it. "Apparently, it's been handed down the generations of that family since the last Goresgin invaders were ousted from our shores. Though I have my suspicions that not all were ousted ..." Her expression was suddenly far away again, and there was a moment of silence while she smiled to herself.

"Um, might I ...?" Reeve waved his feather above the muslin, which was only half covered in his writing so far, to bring her attention back to the task at hand.

The cook rolled her eyes and began reciting once more:

"In a bowl, mix:
Two handfuls stone-ground rye flour
Three handfuls oats
One handful bran
Spoonful each of pumpkin seeds, sunflower seeds,
   flax seeds
Pinch salt
Pinch caraway

In a jug, mix:
Spoonful honey
Three ladles warm water

Slowly add honey water to bowl. Stir to paste. Stand. Roll into small balls and flatten as thin as you can. Dot all over with a fork. Cook in hot oven for ten minutes. Remove. Allow oven to cool. Return biscuits to cool oven for another hour or so. Remove and cool completely."

"What's caraway?" Reeve asked, as Mistress Gyles's voice faded away.

Mistress Gyles laughed. "You're not as silly as you look. That's the secret ingredient — the Goresgin brought it with them but it's not common in Cartreff. A few families on the coast keep stocks of it — as I said, I have my suspicions that more than one Goresgin invader decided he'd stay in Cartreff all those years ago."

The kitchen door suddenly banged open and, though he had his back to it, Reeve froze. If he was spotted sitting here, who knew what could happen? Reeve had no desire to be dragged back to that mill again, for any reason. Thinking quickly, he dropped the feather, which drifted to the floor.

"What hey!" a man's voice called out. "Look lively and bring six hot breakfasts to the courtyard, quick smart. The guards are here and we're hungry."

Ducking under the table as though to retrieve his quill, Reeve twisted until he could see the man speaking — one of the guards. Reeve thought he was one of the Hughs, a short, stocky man with large, strong hands. From Reeve's limited perspective, it seemed that every person in the kitchen had frozen, heads down, hoping not to draw the man's attention.

"Jump to it," Hugh bellowed, menace in his tone. "You know how we don't like to be kept waiting. You don't want us to come in here and complain now, do you?"

Did Reeve imagine the quiver of fear that ran through the kitchen before the bustling began, double the pace it had been before the man arrived?

"Thought not," Hugh said, an ugly, smug sneer on his face. "We'll be waiting."

Reeve waited until Hugh had left, banging the door behind him, before emerging from beneath the table and blushing under Mistress Gyles's knowing look. "Anyone would think you didn't want to run into Hugh," she said. "Which makes me wonder . . ."

"I, er, didn't want to be teased about my failure at the quintain," Reeve said. "I got quite enough of that yesterday."

The old woman smirked, before nodding. "There's not many who are keen to run into Hugh. Nor any of those others. Now, have you got what you wanted?"

Reeve looked over all that he'd written on the muslin cloth, wondering if Maven was going to be sorely disappointed when she saw what he had. True, he now had a secret recipe for Pease Pottage should they ever need one, but as for solving the mystery of the missing cook . . .

"Not what you expected, young squire?" Mistress Gyles's gimlet gaze was still fixed on him.

"Well, it's a recipe for Pease Pottage," Reeve said, standing up with the muslin square held gently between two fingers so as not to smudge it. "That's probably what I expected."

"Indeed," Mistress Gyles responded, seeming to lose interest in him as she reached over to grab her bowl of beans again. "Just don't tell anyone else about the caraway. Mistress Percy would have my head for that."

"If we find her, she may be too grateful to care about such things," Reeve said, with a laugh.

"If you find her," Mistress Gyles agreed, without looking up. Feeling himself dismissed, Reeve quietly took his leave, with a quick wave and smile at Tillie on the way out.

Now, he just had to get back to Lady Cassandra's rooms without being spotted.

CHAPTER FIFTEEN

"Five fingers the scum rises bran caraway cook remove completely."

Reeve is repeating his words, his disbelief making his voice squeak.

"It doesn't make much sense, Reeve," Cassandra agrees. "Is it possible that those numbers are not what you thought? Or that perhaps Cook's recipe differs from that of her sisters in some way?"

Cassandra, Reeve and I have agreed to keep up the pretense with Sir Garrick that the code idea is Reeve's, and to keep my ability to read from him at this time. I have known Sir Garrick only a week or two and I am not yet ready to trust him with my life. Reeve is uncomfortable with the deception, but understands the peril I am in.

Right now, however, I am confused. I was so sure about the book code idea.

"My lady," says Reeve, risking a quick glance at me, "I have it on good authority that family recipes are sacred and that each sister would give exactly the same version of this dish."

I stare at the muslin square spread out on Cassandra's bed, hoping I've just made a mistake with the order of the code, but no. No matter which way I look at it, if my idea about this code is correct, then this is the message.

Assuming, of course, that Mistress Gyles has remembered the recipe correctly. She is not, after all, a family member, for all her brooding and silent observation of Mistress Percy's methods.

But book codes rely on key words, so we should be able to figure this out . . .

"Wait," says Reeve, clicking his tongue and coming to stand beside me. "Five fingers?"

He bites his lip, looking thoughtful.

"Remember, Margery talked about five fingers with regards to Jonty and his friends."

"Margery?" Sir Garrick asks.

"One of the young ladies you sent me to speak to yesterday, sire," Reeve says.

"Ah," says Sir Garrick. "And she mentioned five fingers?"

"Yes," said Reeve. "There are five guards, closer than the others, and great admirers of King Bren."

Sir Garrick is pacing the room. "Read those words again."

Reeve repeats the list of words. As he does so, with the idea of "five fingers" as a useful phrase, I start to think about where the periods might go if this were a proper message.

Five fingers.

"The—scum—rises," I say out loud, slowly, not looking at the muslin, trying to make it seem as though I am just remembering this from Reeve's earlier words.

Sir Garrick stops pacing and fixes his heavy dark stare on my face. "Go on."

"Bran makes no sense," I say, my frustration rising. "But what if the bit after that was 'caraway cook'?"

Reeve grabs my hand in his excitement. "Carry away cook! Remove completely! Maven, that's it!"

Sir Garrick takes a seat on the small, velvet-covered stool beside the bed. "It's a directive to kidnap the cook," he says in wonder. "But who are 'the scum,' and what of 'bran' right in the middle?"

"Sire," I say, with a little curtsey to soften the blow of what I am about to say. "I feel as though the scum may be . . . you. Or us. Or opposition to the King, that is to say."

He surprises me by throwing back his head and

laughing loudly. "You're right! By gad, we are the scum."

"You needn't look so pleased about it," says Cassandra, her forehead lined with delicate wrinkles. "And what of bran?"

I clear my throat, knowing that what I have to say next will not produce hearty laughter. "I think, my lady, that it perhaps refers to Sir Brannon," I say quietly. I am remembering that deep, growling voice in the windmill.

As I suspected, this sobers Sir Garrick immediately. "He cannot be involved. He has been supportive of my discussions with Airl Riding these past few days."

For a moment, no one says anything as we consider the import of those words, before Sir Garrick groans. "But then, who else? He runs the guard with a firm hand, they do exactly what he says, and who else would Bran be? You are right, Maven, it must be him . . . And that means that he has at his disposal all the details of our discussions, and, more importantly, a full list of who it is that moves against King Bren. If he sends a message . . ."

And suddenly some of the pieces fall into place for me. "He cannot send the next message," I say, thinking out loud. "Because he does not have the cook."

"What do you mean, he does not have the cook?" Sir Garrick is back on his feet, hands on his head. "This message instructs him to hide the cook."

"It does," I say, pausing and tucking my hands in my pockets for they tremble a little at the idea of pushing back against a man of Sir Garrick's stature, even if I do like him. Pushing back means showing him that I can think.

"Well, go on," Sir Garrick says. "Maven, I know you are . . . resourceful. I have no intention of sharing any thought or evidence of that resourcefulness with anyone outside this room, I promise. Trust me with your thoughts."

When I hesitate, unable to break the habit of a lifetime, Cassandra turns to smile at me, offering silent support and encouragement. I am not alone, I realize. We are all in this together — and all in danger.

"He was the sixth man at the windmill," I say to Reeve, who is the only one in the room who knows what I'm talking about. "I recognized his voice in the hallway this morning."

I turn to Sir Garrick, quickly filling him in on the meeting, explaining that five men had arrived first and then the sixth had shown up — angry because the other five did not know where the cook was.

"So, you're saying that the five had instructions to take the cook but that she was already gone?" Sir Garrick asks. "And Sir Brannon was the one giving them the orders to unearth her at all cost? Because he needed to know where she was to send a message back via this . . . book code?"

I nod, understanding now the consternation in the group at the mill. To have been instructed to hide the cook but then to have her disappear . . . the key to their code system . . .

Reeve groans, plonking on the bed. "But the ransom note? If Sir Brannon and the Five are behind the book code and they don't have the cook, who does? Does someone else in this castle know about the Five and all the rest?"

Sir Garrick looks grim. "Sir Brannon has been sent out to arrest whomever it is that comes to collect the ransom at the appointed time, so we may have the answer to that soon enough."

I stare at Sir Garrick. "Sir Brannon is in charge of the ransom?"

"Well, yes," Sir Garrick says. "He is the Knight Protector, after all. Airl Riding would trust no other."

"Will he go alone?" Reeve asks, and I can see that he has caught the direction of my thoughts.

Sir Garrick nods, looking worried. "The note specifies that only one person is to approach a certain shepherd's hut. Only Airl Riding, Sir Brannon and I know where the meeting is to take place. Brannon will take the ransom money as bait, but he will not give it over. Instead, the kidnapper will be arrested and . . . inconvenienced . . . until they tell Sir Brannon where the cook is being held."

I walk to the window, gazing down at Lady Adelina's walled garden as I try to order my thoughts.

In the garden below, I can see a group of girls strolling together without a care in the world, the pinks, lavenders and lemons of their brightly colored gowns picked out like jewels against the green of the grass. I wonder what they talk about while we are closeted in here discussing kidnapping, betrayal and treason.

"I think," I say slowly, as I spot Anice's copper-colored hair at the center of the group, "that Airl Riding will not get his ransom money back. In fact, it would surprise me if Sir Brannon returns to the castle at all — and the Five will disappear with him."

I turn back to the room to three puzzled faces.

"They will take the money and run," I clarify. "If we are right, Sir Brannon and his men have not been able to send a message to their network about everything that Sir Garrick and Airl Riding have discussed. And they will be desperate to get that information to the King."

Cassandra gasps. "Do you think Airl Riding knows about it? Has he been lying to Garrick since we got here?"

"I would bet my life that he does not know of Sir Brannon's treachery," says Sir Garrick, taking her hand. "Let's face it, I already have bet my life on it, and yours, too, Cassandra. Airl Riding is a man of honor who cares deeply about protecting the people of Glawn. His conscience is sorely pricked at the idea of turning against the King – as is mine, if I must be frank – but his sense of injustice on behalf of this kingdom is stronger."

Part of me wonders at Sir Garrick's certainty, but I also know that he is one who has survived – and thrived – in the noble houses of Cartreff because of his ability to take the measure of other men quickly and with confidence.

His ability with a sword has also helped, but perhaps the two go together . . .

"But why take the money?" Reeve interjects.

"They can't send a message," I say. "I don't think they have any more idea than we do about where Mistress Percy is, and they can't send a secret message about Airl Buckthorn's petition without her. Twenty silver pieces is a lot of motivation for them all to ride off and take their message directly to King Bren."

"How would they think they could possibly get away with such a thing?" Sir Garrick wonders. "Surely, they know that Riding would send someone after them as soon as he realized they'd gone."

"But they are six elite soldiers and they would have a head start," I say. "Once gone, who would Airl Riding send to look for them? More than half his personal guard is involved. Nobody knows their full names, and they all look the same to most of the people in the community."

Reeve is on his feet. "They will change clothes, split up, ride south to the capital and arrive with silver to swell the King's coffers – that's what I would do. Once there, they are safe – and we, most certainly, are not."

"Brannon cannot simply ride away!" Sir Garrick is now looking thunderous. "The others may be interchangeable but he is far too recognizable. Plus, he is bound by his oath of loyalty – Airl Riding would have grounds to hang him if he breaks it. For him to disappear is tantamount to signing his own death warrant."

Sir Garrick's words stop me in my tracks, for he is right. The oaths of men are taken very seriously. They can lie, they can cheat, they can kill, as long as they do it in the name of their airl.

But one breach of that word . . .

Sir Brannon is a better player than that. He would not show his hand in this game so easily.

"I think Sir Brannon will arrive back without the ransom and with a sad story about how the kidnapper eluded them and how he had to bring in reinforcements and send the Five to take up the chase. He will give them the excuse they need to disappear, and will quietly slip away while everyone is distracted."

Sir Garrick is now striding toward the door. "I must inform Airl Riding immediately of all that we have learned this morning. Reeve, with me — and get my sword."

Reeve blanches a bit, and I know that following this order is the last thing he feels like doing. The foray to the kitchen took it out of him and he is still recovering from last night's ordeal. But he will not say no to Sir Garrick.

He, too, has sworn an oath.

CHAPTER SIXTEEN

"Where is Mistress Percy in all this?" Cassandra asks, plonking on the bed beside the muslin square as the door bangs shut behind Sir Garrick and Reeve. "What will happen to her?"

"I don't know," I say, feeling sad for the woman who has been caught up in this business of men and may pay a heavy price. As the stakes for Airl Riding rise, his interest in the fate of a cook will fall even lower — if that's possible.

"And what of us?" Cassandra goes on. "What are we to do? Part of me wants to pack our things and get us all in the carriages and out of here as soon as possible."

"Anice's deadline is upon us, proving Lady Rhoswen right — after all, she did say Anice would provide us with the perfect excuse to leave if we needed to do so," I say. "But until Sir Garrick gives us the word, we must carry on as though nothing is happening, so that we don't tip off anyone who may be watching us. Which means you must soon meet Lady Adelina for luncheon and I . . ."

My voice trails away as I consider my next move.

"You?" Cassandra prompts.

"I am going to go back to the kitchens. Mistress Percy disappeared from there, but it seems that Sir Brannon either did not take her – or somehow lost her soon afterward."

It is this conundrum that has me bewildered. If Sir Brannon does not have the cook – and everything I think I know says that he would like to have her but does not – who does?

And why would anyone want her out of the way? Who else would benefit from her absence?

Even before I have finished formulating that second question, I see a face in my mind.

"Why are you nodding?" Cassandra asks, her head cocked to one side.

"I have an idea about who might have made the cook disappear and why," I say, and cannot contain my smile.

"Is it Jonty?" Cassandra asks, and I pause, testing the idea, as she continues. "I just wondered whether he might have felt bad about using her the way he did and spirited her away to keep her from Sir Brannon's plans?"

Even as I agree that it's a good theory, I discard it, remembering Jonty's bleak face during our conversation this morning. Unless he's an accomplished actor, Mistress Percy's nephew has no idea where she is.

"Unless he was willing to force her, he would have to have given her a good reason why she had to go," I say out loud to Cassandra. "And from what I've learned of Mistress Percy, even the best explanation in the world would not have convinced her to walk out at the time she did."

Cassandra nods. "She would have waited at least until after the feast. But if you know who has her and where she is, maybe we shouldn't find her until after Sir Brannon is safely dealt with?"

"I'm not sure where and I'm not even sure how it happened," I confess with a laugh, "so you can rest assured that we have a moment or two. But I will not wait for the machinations of men to be over before saving a woman who may be hungry and frightened."

"You're right," Cassandra says, with a weak smile. "I don't know what I was thinking. I'm just – scared. It's one thing to be trying to rally to set things in motion for the good of Cartreff, but quite another to face the wrath of the King should our plans be discovered before they can be properly put in place. We could die, Maven."

Tears well up in her eyes with those last bald words,

and I break with protocol to give her a hard hug. "I know, and I'm scared and worried, too. But I have faith that Sir Garrick and Airl Riding will be able to contain this, and I have to have faith that we, and the Beech Circle, if necessary, can rescue the cook without harm."

"Then go," she says, all but shoving me to the door. "Tarry not a moment longer. I will cover for your absence, if necessary."

"I think it more likely that I will need you to help me explain everything to Sir Garrick — assuming that I am right," I say, pushing down the rising sense of unease I feel. Sir Garrick has gone haring off after Sir Brannon, and much hangs on what happens at the shepherd's hut. If I am wrong about that, I am wrong about everything — and I will be begging Anice to send that note to Airl Buckthorn recalling me to Rennart Castle where I will hide with shame for the rest of my days.

If I am even allowed to do that.

But I cannot sit about and wait to find out, not while Mistress Percy remains unaccounted for.

Pulling the door to Cassandra's chamber gently behind me, I make my way once again to the castle laundry, nodding and smiling in what I hope is a congenial fashion at anyone I pass. There is no sign of the Airl's guardsmen lurking anywhere about the place, and no sign of whispering groups of servants, either.

Which either means that Sir Garrick and Reeve have

not yet ridden out in pursuit of Sir Brannon, or that they will not do so. So much rides on what Sir Garrick says to Airl Riding – and on how it is received.

I cannot think about that now, though, and try to control my rushing thoughts as I open the laundry door, waiting a moment for the clouds of steam to clear before stepping through.

"Ana!" I wave and receive a friendly wave of greeting in return, before Ana holds up one finger, indicating I should wait a moment. I watch as she uses a thick wooden paddle to stir the water in the vat before scooping out a garment and handing the paddle to Ida, who inspects the garment, shakes her head and steps up to take Ana's place at the tub.

Ana wipes her hands on her limp apron as she comes toward me. "How's your friend?" she asks, as we move to the relative quiet of the linen shelves.

"He's fine," I say, "thanks to you."

I can see the blush even though her face is already red from the heat of the laundry.

"Thanks to the Beech, you mean," Ana says, and I smile.

"So, what can I do for you?" she asks, casting a glance over her shoulder to where Ida is stirring the tub while keeping one eye on us.

"This might seem like a strange question, but I was wondering what you know about Mistress Gyles?"

Ana doesn't hide her surprise. "She's all right. A bit dour, but she's been here since she was a scullery maid, so everyone puts up with her. She's part of the furniture – like Evan."

"Evan?"

"Yes, you remember – the tall man here the other day with the cart. He helps out here and there throughout the castle, but Ida and I find him very useful in the laundry. He's been here since he was a babe, as well."

My mouth goes so dry that I'm almost unable to ask the next question. "Are they close, then? Mistress Gyles and Evan?"

Ana laughs. "Close? I don't think I'd use that word, but neither of them has anyone much else, so I think they sort of make do with each other. But if you want to know anything about her, Evan would be the one to ask. Not that he says much."

I pause, rolling her words around in my mind. "What does he do, here in the laundry?" I ask. "I saw him pushing that cart for you the other day, but is that what he does?"

Now, Ana is frowning. "Why are you so interested in Evan? I know he's big but he's harmless. We've never had any trouble with him at all."

"I don't know," I say, uncertainty making my voice shake. "I'm just following an idea."

Ana gives me a long look before responding. "He doesn't really work in the laundry, per se — it's just what he does while he's waiting on his traps."

"Traps?"

"He traps hares and other bits and bobs for the table — particularly important in the winter months when the roads can be impassable, so our table is limited to what's nearby."

"Ana! I could use a hand over here." Ida's querulous tones suggest she's had more than enough of watching us whisper in the corner.

"I have to go," Ana says, turning from me. "There's a lot to do today and it's not fair to leave Ida with it."

"Just one more thing — what do you mean by bits and bobs?" My question comes out sharper than either of us expects.

"Oh, you know," Ana says, waving her hand about and looking fed up. "Birds — grouse, mostly. Mostly when he goes out to check the hides before Airl Riding goes hunting."

The hides. And now I have a sudden memory of the three strange little square structures on Lady Adelina's tapestry — those dark-brown squares in among all the windmills.

"One last question, I promise," I say, when Ana looks as though she would walk away. "Can you remember the last time Evan checked the hides?"

She stares at me. "Yes. It was the day you arrived. Mistress Gyles had to step in for Mistress Percy to make the grouse pie for the feast from the birds he brought back."

She turns away again and, this time, I let her go, remembering the kitchen as it was on that first day, full of feathers from plucking, Mistress Percy's bowl left, waiting, on the preparation table . . . And I feel a tiny click in my mind.

"Thanks, Ana," I shout, charging out of the laundry.

My only thought, as I hurry back upstairs, is to get to the Small Hall to have another very close look at Lady Adelina's tapestry and the location of the hides. Then I'm going to have to face the moors again. This time on my own.

"Wandering about aimlessly again, are we?"

It is all I can do not to roll my eyes and walk on at the sound of Anice's voice behind me, but even now, in the midst of a crisis, I know I cannot simply ignore her. I cannot give Anice any proper reason to send me away.

And so, exhaling so hard that my hair wafts from my forehead, I turn and face her with a curtsey, discovering she is, as always, surrounded by other girls. In her own way, Anice could be a great asset to Sir Garrick's mission if only she could be trusted. Young women – and men – flock to her, drawn by that dangerously fascinating charisma she exudes, even if they do not always like her. I am reminded once again of a cat, but this time a sleek, beautiful house cat, petted and feted right up until the moment it turns and scratches your eyes out.

"Not at all," I say. "The Lady Cassandra has sent me to the hall. She wishes me to take close note of Lady Adelina's tapestries, that we may create something similar for Rennart Castle."

Even as the lie falls glibly from my tongue, a small part of me despairs of what I have become over the past few years. My ten-year-old self was open and inquisitive, honest and thoughtful.

Look at me now.

"Hmmm," Anice says, a tiny smile playing around her mouth. "Run along then, like a good servant. My cousin might as well make the most of you while she can."

The other girls titter as Anice sweeps by me, forcing me to one side of the hallway as they pass. I am troubled by her last words but have no time to dwell on them now.

After a quick visit to the hall to refresh my memory, I grab a cloak from the side room, turning it so that the dark gray faces out. Today, I wish to blend in.

Then, steeling myself, knowing that the mist may rise and I might once again experience the intense loneliness I felt when caught in it last night, I slip through the castle gates, choosing a moment when the two guards on duty are sharing a joke. As I dash in the direction of the first hide, I congratulate myself on the success of my quiet escape.

Hours later, as I trudge toward the third and last hide, I am feeling much less clever. In fact, I am feeling lost. Today, there is no mist and the Wolf's Howl is more of a whimper, but even so my boots are waterlogged, my hem a muddy mess and my sense of direction as scattered as my thoughts. All I can do is follow the picture in my head, which leads me away from the big windmill where the Five had their meeting.

Adding to my mood is the knowledge that with every step I get further away from the castle, with no Ana to guide me back and no stray horse to alert anyone that I'm missing. The last person to have seen me if I don't return will have been Anice – who will probably tell them I ran away and good riddance.

"Just a few more minutes," I promise myself, dragging my unruly thoughts under control. Some might ask why I risk so much for a woman I've never met, but no one else seems willing to do it. I turn and check that I can still see the big mill behind me and, reassured, trudge forward.

Is it the memory of women like Mistress Percy – the warm, nourishing women from my past – that drives me on? Or is it the question of whether there might be somebody to do the same for me if I were one day lost?

Perhaps both.

Five minutes pass, then ten, and the mill is disappearing into the tall grasses as the horizon rises behind me when, suddenly, I stop, squinting ahead of me. The sway of the grasses makes the structure difficult to make out, so blended into the landscape is it, but the sun is high enough that it casts a solid shadow.

Exhilarated, I run forward, freezing as a hare hurtles out of the grass ahead of me and bounds away.

Catching my breath and laughing at my racing heart, I watch it crash through the grass before I dash toward the hide. Prying open its back door, I peer into the gloom inside . . . and smile. Curled up at the bottom of the hide lies a small, gray-haired woman, her sharp, desperate eyes glinting in the half-light above a dirty gag, her arms and legs bound by thick rope.

"Mistress Percy," I breathe, as I crawl inside to remove her gag. "I'm so very happy to see you."

"I have no idea who you are," she croaks, "but I've never been so glad to see anyone in my life. Now, get me back to my kitchen at once. I've a bone to pick with Nell Gyles."

CHAPTER SEVENTEEN

"What have you to say for yourselves?"

Reeve flinched at Airl Riding's thunderous demand, and the five men standing before him shuffled their feet as their horses, tied to a rail nearby, shifted restlessly.

"I, well," began the guard Reeve knew as Hugh, though he was not the menacing presence he'd been when Reeve had last seen him on the quintain list. Now, Hugh looked as cold and tired as Reeve felt, standing beside the shepherd's hut that had been designated as the ransom drop.

"What could they possibly have to say?" boomed Sir Brannon, and Reeve saw Hugh wince as he stared up at the Airl, still on horseback and looming over Hugh,

Jonty and the others.

After Sir Garrick's meeting with the Airl that morning, things had played out much as Maven had posited. At first skeptical of Sir Garrick's theory about Sir Brannon, the Airl had been forced to investigate the situation more closely when his Knight Protector had returned to Glawn Castle without the cook and without the ransom.

The kidnappers, it seemed, had eluded him.

When Sir Brannon had suggested five guardsmen ride out to chase the "kidnappers," Airl Riding had taken Sir Garrick's advice and agreed to it — but had then surprised Sir Brannon by deciding a short time later that the Airl, Sir Garrick, Reeve and a handful of outriders would revisit the designated ransom drop — this shepherd's hut — for "clues."

Sir Garrick had raised a cynical eyebrow at Reeve when Sir Brannon immediately suggested he would join them, despite his fatigue.

For Reeve, the suppressed fury on Sir Brannon's face when they'd arrived at the shepherd's hut to discover the Five saddling up to ride off with Airl Riding's silver had almost been worth riding out onto the moors again. It seemed that one of the horses had stumbled on the uneven ground, bruising its hoof, and they'd been held up, wrapping the foot in cold, wet rags, unable to make their escape.

They'd been arguing among themselves when the Airl's party had ridden up to the hut.

"They have nothing to say," Sir Brannon hissed now at Hugh, before turning to address the Airl. "It is outrageous that you would even consider accusing your loyal guard of crimes of any nature, let alone the kidnapping of a woman, at the behest of complete strangers, particularly those who carry treason in their traveling trunks. We hereby all relinquish our posts and will take our leave now."

He turned his back on Airl Riding and signaled to Hugh and the other guards that they should move toward their mounts. But the Five did not move, watching the Airl uncertainly.

"You are going nowhere!" the Airl bellowed, and Sir Brannon hesitated, while the other guards who had ridden out with the Airl — Gerard, Stanley and the other two Hughs — moved up to form a line behind Sir Brannon, effectively cutting off any escape in that direction.

"These men have been caught red-handed with the silver in a place that none knew was the designated ransom drop except you and I. You, Sir Brannon. I didn't tell them —"

"Because it was they who conspired to steal from you, my lord," said Sir Brannon, oozing outrage and pointing to the five men. "If you are to punish anyone, punish them!"

"Now, wait a minute," said Jonty, pushing his way to the front of the group on the ground, now huddled together. "That's not how it went at all. You're the one who came up with the whole idea. You're the one who got me in here as a guard — and it was all about my aunt. She wouldn't give you what you wanted because those recipes are just for family. My family."

"Be quiet!" Sir Brannon roared. "Lies, all lies, concocted to cover up for your family network of spies, disloyal to the very house in which you live. I don't even know where your aunt is."

Jonty's face fell. "Yes, well, none of us does, do we? Not after you *lost* her. Hugh took her to the bridle room, just like you asked, and she was happy enough to wait there to talk to you, but then — poof! Gone like a gust of wind."

"Pah!" said Sir Brannon, drawing himself up in the saddle with outrage. "How could I have lost her when I never had her in the first place? My last visit to the bridle room was with Sir Garrick yesterday and there was no sign of any cook there."

"Because you'd already lost her by then!" shouted Jonty, almost in tears.

Airl Riding held up his hand, and Jonty took a step back. "So, you're saying, Sir Brannon, that you never had anything to do with the so-called Five Fingers and are not using your position to undermine this household and my position."

"That's exactly what I'm saying," said Sir Brannon, his dark brows angry slashes of belligerence, "and you won't be able to prove otherwise because there's no proof to be found."

Reeve had to admit, with a rising feeling of nausea, that there was a note of sincerity in his voice. Could Maven have been wrong about the sixth man? And if she was wrong about that, was she wrong about everything?

"Very well," said Airl Riding after a long pause, during which Reeve swore even the wind stopped and the landscape held its breath. "There is no point discussing this here. We will return to Glawn Castle."

He turned to Gerard. "Get these five mounted up and see them securely returned — we will ride ahead to prepare a warm, er, welcome for them."

For a few minutes, confusion reigned. For a moment, it looked as though Hugh might make a run for it, and Gerard, Stanley and the other loyal Glawn guards rode forward to round up the Five and force them toward their waiting mounts. Sir Garrick, Reeve and the Rennart outriders were pushed aside to make way, but the sudden movement startled the horses tied to the rail, setting them to kicking and stamping as the men around them shouted.

The horse on the end, the one with the wrapped hoof, pulled hard on its rope, managing to break the loose tie as it tried to run off, eyes wild with fear and pain. Reeve urged his own horse to follow. He managed to catch up to the limping horse quickly, and grabbed hold of the reins that were slapping against its neck.

As Reeve rode back toward the others, every ounce of strength focused on trying to keep his own mount and the loose horse under control, Reeve heard the sound of pounding hooves – headed his way.

With the loose horse tugging and snorting in fright beside him, Reeve could barely manage to glance up, but when he did Reeve wondered if it was possible for a heart to stop. For riding straight at him at full speed atop his enormous destrier was Sir Brannon, his face a twisted grimace of reckless fury – and he showed no signs of swerving.

As his own mount pinned its ears back and tensed beneath him, preparing to run, Reeve fought to hold on to the reins of the injured horse as it tried to pull away, kicking and squealing.

And still Sir Brannon came at them, as though he'd decided to take all his anger and frustration out on Reeve and the poor, innocent horses.

"Yah!" Sir Brannon shouted, and now he was close enough for Reeve to see his eyes, alight with a wild glee.

It was too much for Reeve's horse, which reared up, muscles bunched, throwing Reeve to the ground. Landing on his side with a bruising thud, still clutching the reins of the injured horse, Reeve could only watch in pain as his rouncey bolted.

Catching an agonizing breath, Reeve curled himself up, trying to protect his head from the flashing hooves of the injured horse. Hearing the heavy hoofbeats drawing nearer, Reeve wondered if Sir Brannon would simply ride over the top of him, killing him once and for all.

At the last minute, however, Sir Brannon urged his destrier to switch direction, dug his heels into its side and raced away across the moor, his gray cloak billowing behind him.

"Sir Garrick!" Reeve yelled, staggering to his feet, cursing at the pain that surged through his side. "He's getting away!"

Airl Riding shouted to his men, and Reeve saw Gerard and one of the Hughs break away from the confusion around the hut to begin the chase, but Sir Brannon had a big head start and was riding without heed for sense or safety.

With a sinking heart, Reeve couldn't imagine the two guards would catch him — not without putting themselves and their horses at risk of death. Even as he watched, Reeve could see that Sir Brannon was surging further and further ahead, hardly visible now in the gray landscape, no doubt heading south and carrying all he'd learned about Airl Buckthorn's plans to Airl Broadfield — and hence to the King.

Which meant anyone associated with Airl Buckthorn

would be labeled a traitor and sentenced to die. Including Reeve.

For a small woman who is on the thin side for a cook, Mistress Percy is remarkably heavy. Or perhaps it is just that even a spoonful of sugar would become a burden if one had to all but carry it miles across unfamiliar terrain.

"It's not far now, love," she says to me again, and while I appreciate her attempts to keep my spirits up, the reminder that there is still a way to go does not help me. But it will do us no good to give up.

"You are doing very well," I say to her, shifting the position of my arm around her waist to bring her more upright against my body. Her own arm is across my shoulders, and I am taking as much of her weight as I can, aware that she is weakened from two nights on the moor. The hide provided shelter, it is true, and Evan had brought her food and water, but the terror of being inside that tiny structure during last night's Howl has left its mark.

We are approaching the big windmill, slogging our way through the tall grass. The hares seem to have come out after last night's Howl, perhaps taking advantage of the lighter wind today to do whatever it is hares do, for we have been startled several times by their sudden appearance, each reducing us to fits of giggles.

I am glad she is still laughing.

The slow creak and whine of the windmill's sails is getting louder, and I am looking forward to a rest within its dark confines when I become aware of the thunder of hooves. Peeking behind me, I spy a lone horseman charging toward us, swathed in the gray cloak of the Airl's guard.

"We must hurry," I say to Mistress Percy. "We can hide in the mill."

After all this, I do not want her found by any member of the Airl's household. Not until I know what is what and who is who.

Mistress Percy nods, redoubling her efforts to hobble beside me. But no matter how quickly we try to move, the pounding hooves draw closer and closer, the rider clearly having no concern for the health of his horse or his own neck, given the speed with which he is hurtling across the shifting ground.

In the shadow of the mill's sails, I stop, urging Mistress Percy to make her way around to the back door, urging her to stay hidden, no matter what. She is the key to Sir Brannon's code and, for us to remain safe, he must not get his hands on her.

I turn to face the lone rider, my breath catching in my throat as he pulls the snorting, sweating destrier up hard, meters from where I stand, and I realize it is Sir Brannon himself.

I pray that Mistress Percy will stay inside the mill, even as my eyes scan the surroundings for a way out — or a weapon. Neither presents itself.

"What are you doing so far from the castle, girl?" he demands, drawing his sword and holding it lazily in one hand. "Or do I need to ask? You think no one sees you, but I do. Always skulking about, asking too many questions. You and that strutting boy."

I say nothing, though the "skulking" stings and I know Reeve would feel the same about the "strutting."

"Where is she?" Sir Brannon continues, and now the sword is raised and his horse is taking almost imperceptible steps forward at the threatening tone, as it has no doubt been trained to do. "I saw two of you."

I take a deep breath, trying to stand my ground, aware of the looming steed and the long, sharp sword, aware of the sails spinning at my back, aware that I am the only thing between Mistress Percy and this man. Mistress Percy, who is his link to the King's spy network. If he can take her away with him, Sir Brannon can simply go to another loyalist household for sanctuary and start all over again.

No thought of what that might do to the woman. Never any thought of that.

"I have no idea what you're talking about," I say, pleased that my voice sounds strong and clear, even as Sir Brannon's horse inches ever closer and the sword glints in the pale sunlight. "I came to pick meadowsweet for my Lady Cassandra, and my horse took itself back to the castle without me."

When telling a lie, stick as close to the truth as possible – even if you are talking about a different day.

"You are a liar and a traitor!" Sir Brannon shouts, raising his sword high, and I step back as the horse again moves toward me, teeth bared as it pulls against the bit. Now, I can feel my skirts move, blown by the wind from the closeness of the ever-spinning sails, and my legs start to shake.

"Tell me the truth or you will feel the touch of those sails," Sir Brannon says, and there is no mercy in his face as he thrusts the point of the sword toward me for emphasis. "Have you ever seen what a body looks like after it's been hit? Think of a peach thrown against a wall. What a terrible accident it will be . . ."

I try to swallow but my mouth is dry and I am struggling to think. The horse moves close enough for me to smell the sweat steaming from its gleaming coat and see the whites of its unhappy, rolling eyes. It snorts, and my feet inch back of their own volition.

The wind whispers through the grass around me as the sail creaks on monotonously, and, for a long moment, Sir Brannon and I are frozen and silent in this wild landscape, as though caught in one of Lady Adelina's tapestries.

I see a hare poke its head up and sniff the air.

"Well?" Sir Brannon drawls, and the hare drops back to the grass at the noise — but the sight of it has given me an idea. I cannot afford to take another step back — I must go forward. Toward the sword. I coil inside myself, bracing, gathering myself, knowing this is my last chance.

And then I move, rushing at the horse, my arms flailing pell-mell above my head.

"Yah!" I yell, my shout like a whipcrack in the air. "Yah! Yah! Yah!"

The horse rears back, its front hooves scrabbling in the air as Sir Brannon draws on all his expertise to stay seated. But he has only one hand with which to control the beast for the other holds his sword.

"Yah!" I shout again, darting into the long grass where I saw the hare. To my relief, it has the effect I'd hoped as the spooked hare scurries without thought toward Sir Brannon's destrier before shying at the last moment and bounding away into the grass.

The horse has had enough. With an almighty effort, it flings itself backward, barely noticing that its rider has tumbled to the ground. Wild with panic, it hurtles off in the direction of Glawn Castle.

As the destrier thuds away and the rushing sound in my head begins to slow, I walk over to Sir Brannon, who is lying motionless, facedown on the ground, perilously near the path of the sails. I prod his ankle with my toe, but he does not respond.

"Is he dead?" Mistress Percy's voice does not quaver as she approaches me, allowing me to find the strength in my own.

"I do not think so," I say, detecting a slight rise and fall of breath beneath the cloak. I get down low and grab the sword lying beside him, dragging it toward me, well out of reach of Sir Brannon should he wake up.

A moment later, the cook's cold hand finds mine and she squeezes my fingers, before drawing me away. Once we are safely clear of the sails, she turns to me.

"What do we do now?"

"We wait," I say, knowing the arrival of the destrier at Glawn Castle will raise the alarm more effectively than even setting fire to the mill could. The horse will lead a search party back here.

Quite how I will explain Sir Brannon's current situation is a bridge I will cross when I come to it.

"We wait," I repeat.

My attention is drawn by two horsemen on the horizon, making their way toward the mill. I push Mistress Percy behind me, holding the sword in two hands as I watch them approach.

They hurry, but they do not move with the breakneck desperation Sir Brannon displayed.

This tells me that they chase him, rather than racing

to meet him.

It seems Mistress Percy and I will not need to wait long at all.

CHAPTER EIGHTEEN

"I can't believe you went out there all by yourself, Maven." Cassandra's admiration is tempered with admonition.

"As I said, I didn't want to alert anyone within the castle walls, just in case," I say, for the umpteenth time. "Once I saw on the map how close the hides really were, I knew it was worth a look. After all, all I had was a hunch."

"Your hunches are formidable," Cassandra says, stretching her arms above her head as I help her into the linen under-tunic. "But you took a terrible risk. You were lucky that Sir Brannon's horse was startled by the windmill sails."

"Very," I say, leaving it at that. Gerard and Hugh,

chasing Sir Brannon and relieved to discover their pursuit was over, had accepted my story. Mistress Percy had also gone along with it and so the poor destrier, raised around mills and trained to remain calm at all times, had taken the blame for Sir Brannon's fall.

I plan to sneak out to the stables with an apple later to make up for the insult.

"I must say, though," Cassandra continues, "I'm glad this is our last night at Glawn Castle. After today, I'm not sure I want to stick around any longer."

I have to agree. While all ended well for Mistress Percy, the memory of watching Mistress Gyles and Evan being sent without mercy from Glawn Castle, the only home they'd ever known, with their few pathetic belongings and nowhere to go, was one that would stay with me for a long time.

"I know Mistress Gyles and Evan did the wrong thing," Cassandra says, almost as though reading my mind, "but strangely I think they saved us by doing so."

I nod, as I take the deep blueberry-colored woolen gown from the dressing room and bring it over to the bed. "If the Five had been able to get that message away, King Bren's men would be on their way even now. We were saved by the fact that the message had to be sent in code to be verifiable as authentically from them, and that only Mistress Percy would have been able to tell them which recipe to use . . ."

Cassandra stands so that I can help her don the gown. "She was so angry with Jonty for mixing her up in all this," Cassandra says, with a laugh. "I don't think I'd like to be a fly on the wall at their next family gathering."

"Yes, well, that won't be for a while," I say, beginning to work on the tiny buttons at the back of her dress. "Fortunately for Airl Riding, Mistress Percy is very loyal to him and not very impressed with the King at the moment, so she's agreed not to talk to her sisters about what's happened. Hopefully, that will give Airl Buckthorn and his allies time to decide what to do next."

I pause. "Ingenious, really, to use the five sisters like that. Every family has its special recipes, handed down step-by-step over generations, creating a living, breathing collection. They're not written anywhere because women are the custodians and women don't read or write. It's a clever man who's thought of exploiting that to create the most secret of codes."

"Sir Brannon?" Cassandra asks, smoothing her skirts around her as she sits back down on the bed.

"I don't think so," I say. "He's part of it, and he brought Jonty in here to make it easier for him to deal with Mistress Percy, but I don't think he's the mastermind. I think there's a 'Sir Brannon' in every one of the five households, and each of them has been given an identical list of the family recipes. There would be hundreds of recipes, and the list forms the key to the code. When messages are sent, the 'Sir Brannon' in the household simply goes down the list to the next recipe and the message is sent as the name of the recipe, then the numbers, as we saw. Each number represents a different word in the recipe and so the message is formed."

"But who's behind it all?" asks Cassandra.

I think of all we've learned today. To Airl Riding's surprise and without explanation, Sir Garrick had questioned Mistress Percy closely about the great houses in which her sisters were employed.

"I think," I say slowly, "the key lies in the fact that one of Mistress Percy's sisters cooks at Wigston Hall, home to Airl Broadfield's mother."

Cassandra's mouth opens in a silent *O*, and we are both remembering Lady Rhoswen's words of caution about Airl Broadfield.

It seems that as Airl Buckthorn seeks to rally those who feel the King needs a firmer hand, Airl Broadfield has a network in place of those who are happy with the status quo and a king who has little interest in the business of governing Cartreff.

One can't help but wonder why this might be so.

"But that means that Airl Broadfield has been gathering information and allies for years," Cassandra says. "Long before King Bren even came to the throne. What can it mean?"

I shrug. "I am not sure. But whoever it was that Sir Brannon was corresponding with, via Mistress Percy's recipes, will soon begin to wonder why no further messages come from Glawn Castle. We will need to move quickly to warn Airl Buckthorn."

The mention of Mistress Percy refocuses Cassandra's thoughts.

"Poor Mistress Percy has had a bad few days. First, the horror of discovering how she and her sisters had been used – and then the betrayal by Mistress Gyles on top of that."

Strange to think that had it not been for Mistress Gyles and her jealousy, we would never have stumbled across Airl Broadfield's network. Mistress Gyles had sworn that she and Evan had only planned to "hide Mistress Percy for a day or two."

"Until I proved my worth to everyone," Mistress Gyles had said, staring defiantly around the hall when questioned by Airl Riding. "To show you all that I was just as good."

But I can't see how they planned to return Mistress Percy to the castle kitchens without consequence. It wasn't like the cook would simply step back to her bowl in the kitchen as though nothing had happened.

The way Mistress Gyles told it, the whole thing had happened on impulse. She'd seen Mistress Percy talking to Jonty and then the next thing, another of the guardsmen – perhaps Hugh – walking out the door with the cook, without a backward glance.

Angry that Mistress Percy would leave them in the middle of the feast preparation, Mistress Gyles had sent Evan to fetch her back. But when Evan had seen the guardsman lock the cook in the bridle room, he hadn't known what to do and had returned to Mistress Gyles.

Mistress Gyles had realized this was her chance and decided that if the guard wanted Mistress Percy out of the way so badly, then Mistress Gyles and Evan would make it happen.

So, they'd bundled Mistress Percy into Evan's laundry cart, fixing down the wicker lid so that she couldn't escape, and then Evan had simply wheeled her away under the noses of the gatekeepers – all the way to the furthest bird hide on the moor. Mistress Gyles had gone back to the kitchen to "save the day."

When Mistress Gyles heard that a ransom note had arrived – one she hadn't sent – she and Evan had decided they'd stepped into something bigger than they'd imagined, and had decided to stay quiet.

Which, given Reeve's experiences at Glawn and Sir Brannon's attempt to engineer my own death, was probably for the best.

I feel we are all safer now that he and four of the Five are tucked up safely in the castle dungeons while Airl Riding decides what to do with them. Jonty remains free after Mistress Percy begged for his release, but he has been stripped of his guard status and must remain in the kitchens, scrubbing pots under her direct supervision.

The theft of the twenty silver pieces meant the Airl has enough reason to lock them all away for a very long time without ever having to whisper the word: betrayal.

I can't help thinking this is also probably for the best.

"Right," I say now to Cassandra, pushing all thoughts of politics from my mind for a moment to deal with my next challenge, "let's get that headdress on you and you'll be all set."

"All set to fly away," she grumbles, as I bring the butterfly-shaped confection over to her. Created from silk in deep pink and turquoise and sewn with thread of gold, it was a gift to Cassandra from her older sisters.

"It is the very latest fashion," I remind Cassandra now with a grin as I set the headdress in place. "Though I think it a good thing you're not going outside — the wind would take you all the way back to Rennart Castle."

"Strangely enough, I would not be sad about that," Cassandra says, standing and walking over to look at herself in the looking glass. "And who'd have thought I'd ever say those words?"

I peer over her shoulder, and our reflections share a smile.

"You look as pretty as a picture," I say.

"I suppose I might as well make a splash now that we're leaving Glawn," Cassandra says, with a sigh. "Though I'm bound to have a headache by the time I retire."

"Well, you're all ready," I say. "Is Anice walking down with you?"

It is Cassandra's turn to frown. "She requested a meeting with Sir Garrick before the feast. Heaven only knows what that's all about."

"Has there been news of Lady Rhoswen?" I ask, even though I have a fair idea of what it is that Anice wants to discuss with Sir Garrick.

"Yes," says Cassandra, with her first real smile of the day. "A note arrived while you were out gallivanting on the moor. She improves in tiny increments each day. Perhaps it is not as bad as she feared?"

"Perhaps," I murmur. "Does she wish Anice to return to Harding Manor?"

I try very hard to keep the hope from my voice, but Cassandra grimaces.

"Quite the opposite," she says. "She asks that we keep Anice with us for the next part of our journey."

"The next? Lady Rhoswen knows we are moving on?"

Cassandra sighs again, this time so heavily that the silk net adorning her headdress flutters from her face.

"She does," she says. "What's more, we know where. Sir Garrick has been given further instructions and

Airl Buckthorn requests that our honeymoon take us to Weldlon."

Our eyes meet and I can see how worried she is. I know little of Weldlon except that it is at the furthermost western point in the kingdom, and a place of rocky, barren coastline and ferocious seas. What there might be for Airl Buckthorn in such a place, I cannot imagine, particularly in light of all we have learned here at Glawn.

Speaking of Airl Buckthorn . . . "The Airl had no instruction for me?"

I cannot help but ask. I don't think there's any way that a note could have reached him by now, but who knows? Perhaps Anice simply stood on the top turret of the castle and the Wolf's Howl blew it all the way to Rennart.

"Why would he?" Cassandra says, with a laugh. "If you're lucky, my uncle will have forgotten you even travel with us."

I can only hope.

"Very well," I say. "I shall escort you to the feast."

"I won't miss all this gray," Cassandra murmurs to me, as we make our way to the Great Hall, "nor the wind. But I'm glad to have seen it all for myself."

Her words remind me how lucky I am to be able to journey across Cartreff, while girls like Ana and Ida stir tubs of hot water day in, day out. I cross my fingers that Anice has forgotten all about that message to her father.

Almost as though my thoughts have conjured her up, Anice's voice drifts out of the open door of a small parlor just outside the Great Hall.

"I expect that you will do the right thing," she says, imperiously, as she sashays into the hall, all but bumping into Cassandra. Anice looks stunning, as always, in a kirtle of deep moss green, her copper braid lying across her shoulder like a thick rope of contrasting color. Tiny red rosebuds are woven through the braid, and I think again of the Fire Star, which will one day adorn her ivory throat.

"Ah, cousin," Anice says, pushing me aside as she slides her arm around Cassandra's waist. "Just in time to make our entrance together."

Cassandra tosses me an apologetic look as Anice guides her forward, but I am happy to let them walk away, allowing me to linger outside the parlor and hopefully check on Reeve before he attends Sir Garrick at table.

"It seems that the Lady Anice wishes for Airl Buckthorn to recall Maven to Rennart Castle." Sir Garrick's deep voice was measured, but Reeve noted that his expression was carefully blank.

"I see," said Reeve, his thoughts racing, as he stood in front of the roaring fire in the cozy parlor. Though the room was decorated in the ubiquitous shades of gray, the solid wood chairs were covered in deep-red cushions — as though someone had decided to use up fabric left over from making the cloaks the guards wore.

Reeve wished he could sit on their padded comfort, but his bruises meant that standing was a better option for him today.

"And you have written the note for her?" Reeve asked Sir Garrick, wondering what to say to keep Maven with them without giving away *all* her secrets.

"I have," Sir Garrick confirmed, holding up a small sheet of parchment. "She wishes to spend more quality time with her cousin and therefore sees little need for Lady Cassandra's companion to journey with us."

Reeve winced, glad that Maven was not here to hear Anice's words, knowing they would both hurt Maven and rouse her fury. Reeve opened his mouth to speak again, but found he had nothing to say.

What reason could he possibly give to undermine the request of the Airl's daughter? Sir Garrick would send Maven away because Anice requested it, and Anice would do this to Maven just because she could.

Nothing Reeve said would change that.

"I think you know what to do with this, Reeve," Sir

Garrick said, holding out the parchment.

With a sigh, Reeve eased his way forward, every bruise and scrape adorning his battered body protesting at the movement, while his heart ached for Maven.

She would be devastated to be sent home and left to languish as a lowly castle maid while the mission continued without her. And Reeve knew that he, Sir Garrick and Lady Cassandra would miss her more than any of them could imagine.

To Reeve's surprise, though, Sir Garrick was not waving him toward the door to find a rider to send the missive on its way. Instead, and with a twinkle in his eyes, Sir Garrick nodded at the fire behind Reeve.

When Reeve hesitated, Sir Garrick nodded pointedly at the fire again.

"I, er, think I do indeed," Reeve said, feeling a surge of joyful surprise, unable to believe Sir Garrick's unspoken instructions.

"Before you do, though . . ." Sir Garrick suddenly rose from his seat and made for the door.

"Ah, Maven," said Sir Garrick, and Reeve could hear a thread of mischief in his voice. "Just the person I wanted to see. How fortuitous indeed that you should be right here."

Reeve suppressed a grin as Maven was ushered into the parlor to stand beside him, but sobered as he saw the sheen of tears in her eyes. Knowing Maven as he did, Reeve had no doubt she'd had her ear pressed to the outside of the parlor door, and he wondered how much she'd heard.

"How may I help you, sire?" Maven asked, with a curtsey.

"There's something I'd like you to see," Sir Garrick said, as he resumed his seat, relaxing back as though to watch a jester's performance. "Reeve."

"Indeed, sire," Reeve said, in the same serious tone, holding up the parchment. "I will treat it with all due respect."

Reeve turned to Maven with a big grin, before bowing and then tossing Anice's message into the hearth behind them. Red, gold and orange flames devoured it in seconds.

"Anice will want to know what happened to it," Maven blurted, and Reeve could see that she was half-bemused, half-horrified by what he'd done. "She will ask daily if you have received a response."

"It got lost," Sir Garrick answered, his dark eyebrows raised. "After all, we are on the move again tomorrow, leaving no forwarding address. Who's to say how long it might take for an answer from Airl Buckthorn to reach us?"

Maven shook her head and Reeve could see that, for once, she was at a loss for words. Sir Garrick seemed to recognize this, too, for his expression turned serious.

"I cannot imagine that I know all your secrets, Maven, and it is better for all of us that I do not, but I do know how useful you have proven yourself to be over these past few weeks. It is my preference that you stay with us, and as Knight Protector of Rennart Castle, I have the Airl's confidence in these matters. Do not fret."

Maven said nothing, but Reeve could only imagine her relief — and admit to himself that he felt the same. They'd been friends only a short time, but Reeve already knew he was better — in so many ways — when Maven was around.

"But now," Sir Garrick continued, "Reeve and I must attend the feast. Oh, wait, one more thing."

Standing again, Sir Garrick pulled two pieces of silver from a pocket in his tunic. "Airl Riding was most insistent that I take this generous gift for my role in unearthing the spy ring within his castle walls, and for returning his cook. But credit where credit is due."

He handed one silver piece to Reeve and one to Maven, before taking his leave.

Reeve stared at the silver in his hand for a long moment, thinking of the sword it would buy, before he sighed and turned to Maven, who was standing like a statue beside him.

"For Ana," he said, pressing his silver piece into Maven's palm. Reeve would never forget those dreadful hours when he was held captive, and he knew that he might still be lying there without the laundress's help.

Maven nodded, and Reeve noted that the tears were back. "Thank you."

"No," Reeve said. "Thank you, Maven."

Then, desperate to make her smile again, he bowed over her hand and dropped a faint peck upon it. "Thou art more persistent than a windmill in the Wolf's Howl."

Maven looked from her hand up into his face, a grin twitching at the corners of her mouth.

"Is that really your best attempt at a compliment?" she managed. "Anyway, I thought we agreed not to do this."

Reeve's laughter was almost a shout, so relieved was he to see this glimpse of the Maven he knew.

"Just testing," Reeve said, with a wink, sauntering toward the door, trying not to allow his stiff muscles to spoil the effect.

"Reeve, wait," Maven said, placing one hand on his arm. "I'm glad you're feeling better. Now that I, er, know about the tincture, I will be better able to help you in the future."

Reeve couldn't look at her, shocked that she'd mentioned his innermost secret out loud. But Maven's expression was so concerned, he forced himself to relax. This was Maven.

"We both have our secrets," Reeve said, placing his

hand over hers and giving it a tiny squeeze. "I know you'll keep mine as I keep yours."

Even as he spoke, he knew it was true. Not a threat, but a promise. And his trust was returned tenfold when she turned his hand over, and squeezed back.

As I make my way down to the laundry to find Ana, I am still smiling after my encounter with Reeve.

I know that the two pieces of silver in my hand would allow me to travel a long way across Cartreff. A long way away.

But I knew the moment that Reeve put his silver piece into my hand that I would give both of them to Ana, hoping it will be enough for the Beech Circle to help her up and away from the laundry and into the life she dreams of.

I push open the laundry door and Ana turns to me, backlit by the open laundry door.

"Here to cause more chaos?" she asks, with a smile. "I need to find a new cart man thanks to you."

I laugh. "Definitely not here to cause more chaos," I say, gesturing her away from Ida and toward me. Once she is close, I whisper: "But I think Glawn Castle will be looking for a new laundress, as well."

As I drop the silver into one palm, the other hand

flies up to cover her mouth.

"Take them to the Beech," I say, keeping my voice low. "Widow Morris will know what to do."

Ana's eyes glisten with tears as she slips the silver pieces into her apron. "Thank you," she whispers, clutching my hand. "Thank you. I know what these could mean for you."

Fighting my own emotions, I manage a smile. "It's your time," I say. "Mine will come."

And as I say the words, I know them to be true.

Not today, but one day.

"Go," I say, giving her a little push toward the door behind Ida, who is not even pretending not to stare at us. "Now is as good a time as any."

Ana nods, and then is gone, disappearing into the rectangle of dying sunlight as though into another world, removing her bonnet as she walks, her skirts and hair flying around her in the wind. I watch her go for a moment, smile at the open-mouthed Ida, and then take my leave, heading back to Cassandra's chamber.

I must pack now for we travel to Weldlon first thing in the morning.

Despite knowing that it also means spending more quality time with Anice, I feel my spirits rise at the thought of leaving the gloom of Glawn behind.

Yes, we face another step on Sir Garrick's perilous journey, and more danger as rebellion stirs around us, yet I am strangely happy.

For a girl with a "forgettable face and an untoward mouth" (thank you, Mother), I seem to have found a place. A place where, even if I must keep my "special talents and resourcefulness" (thank you, Cassandra) hidden from the wider world, they are valued.

It is all and nothing. Enough. For now.

ABOUT THE AUTHOR

Allison Tait (A. L. Tait) is the internationally published best-selling author of middle-grade adventure series *The Mapmaker Chronicles* and *The Ateban Cipher*. A multi-genre writer, teacher and speaker with many years' experience in magazines, newspapers and online publishing, Allison is the co-host of the top-rating So You Want To Be A Writer podcast. *The Fire Star: A Maven & Reeve Mystery* taps into her passion for historical fiction and adventure. Allison lives on the south coast of New South Wales with her family. Find out more about Allison at allisontait.com

DID YOU READ
BOOK ONE?

ALSO BY A. L. TAIT

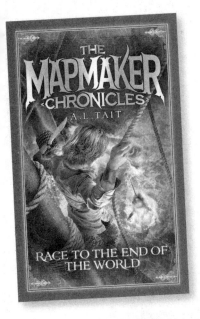

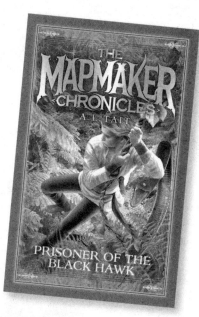

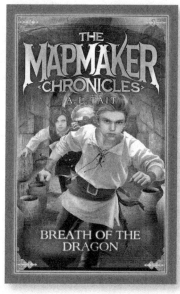

MORE BY A. L. TAIT

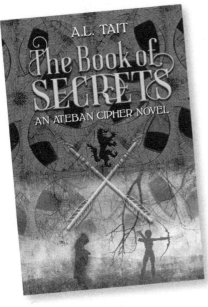

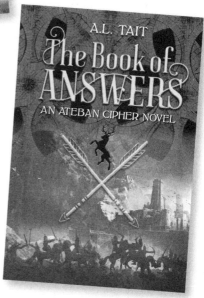